MW00608980

Until Next Sunday

Inspired by a True Story

Novel by Audry Fryer

Story by Linda Kotowicz, Susan Schobert
and Laurie Shanaman

Letters translated by Biagio Dorso

Copyright 2021 Linda Kotowicz, Susan Schobert and Laurie
Shanaman.
All rights reserved.
Published by Of Ink & Pearls Publishing Co.
Cover by JD Cover Designs.
Interior design by: Oprah Milan

ISBN: 9781951191078

This book is dedicated to Rosina and Gianni. Thank you for showing us that true love is worth fighting for.

TABLE OF CONTENTS

Letter to the Reader vi

Rosina's Gnocchi Recipe viii

From the Translator of the Love Letters x

Part I Prima Parte 1

Chapter One   Una Croce D'oror (A Golden Cross) 2

Chapter Two   Addio Torchiara (Goodbye Torchiara) 5

Chapter Three   Arrivando in America (Coming to America) 10

Chapter Four   La Festa (The Party) 15

Chapter Five   Il Primo Bacio (The First Kiss) 21

Chapter Six   Colpito Dalla Tristezza (Stricken with Sadness) 27

Chapter Seven   Un Calzolaio (A Shoemaker) 32

Chapter Eight   Una Miserable Signorina (A Miserable Young Lady) 37

Chapter Nine   I Disorsi Della Citta (The Talk of the Town) 40

Chapter Ten   ÈFinita! (It's Over!) 48

Chapter Eleven   Questa Casa è uno Zoo! (This House Is a Zoo!) 55

Chapter Twelve   Una Donna Forte (A Strong Woman) 62

Chapter Thirteen   Non Ho Scelta (I Have No Choice) 68

Part II Seconda Parte 71

Chapter Fourteen   Riunita (Reunited) 72

Chapter Fifteen   Vero Amore (True Love) 79

Chapter Sixteen   Non So Dove Mi Trovo (I Don't Know Where I Am) .. 92

Chapter Seventeen   L'infermiera (The Nurse) 106

Chapter Eighteen   Lettere dio Mio Padre (My Father's Letter) 113

Chapter Nineteen   Una Situazione Disperata (A Desperate Situation) ... 123

Chapter Twenty   Non Andame a Dormire (Don't Go to Sleep) 127

Chapter Twenty-One   Fino a Domenica Prossima (Until Next Sunday) 136

Chapter Twenty-Two   Il Dottore (The Doctor) 153

Chapter Twenty-Three   Caldo e Freddo (Hot and Cold) 163

Chapter Twenty-Four   Tutti I Santi (All Saint's Eve) 176

Chapter Twenty-Five   Addio Catherina (Goodbye Catherina) 187

Chapter Twenty-Six   Nato per Morrire (Born to Die) 198

Chapter Twenty-Seven   Lei Che Va Piano, Va Lontano (She Who Goes Slow, Goes Far) 214

Chapter Twenty-Eight   La Mia Vita è Incasinata! (My Life Is a Mess!) 221

Part III   Terza Parte **231**

Chapter Twenty-Nine   Se Tu Vai Via (If You Go Away) 232

Chapter Thirty   Auguri di Natale (Christmas Greetings) 235

Chapter Thirty-One   L'ultima Lettera (The Last Letter) 241

Chapter Thirty-Two   Cosa Stai Facendo Copodanno? (What Are You Doing New Year's Eve?) 243

Chapter Thirty-Three   Treni in Direzione Ovest (Westbound Trains) ... 247

Chapter Thirty-Four   Una Chiave (A Key) 252

Chapter Thirty-Five   Rose per Rosina (Roses for Rosina) 256

Epilogue   Da Allora in Poi (Ever After) **259**

About the Author **263**

Acknowledgements **264**

Book Club Discussion Questions **266**

LETTER TO THE READER

Dear Reader,

Several years after our grandmother passed away, an old cardboard box came into our possession. It had been passed around our family in much the same way steaming bowls of homemade gnocchi had once been handed around the table at our Sunday dinners. This box contained a variety of ordinary family heirlooms and one particularly curious find. This surprising item sparked our imagination so much, we couldn't live with the idea of packing it away again.

A binder, intended to store photographs between clear plastic sleeves, held a collection of over one hundred letters dated 1921, the year before our grandparents were married. We couldn't contain our enthusiasm to read what could very well be love letters. Once we opened the first envelope, we understood why no other family member had ever made a fuss: every single one had been written in Italian, and in a regional dialect not easily translated. Still, our minds spun with all the possibilities these letters could reveal. Admittedly, part of our excitement stemmed from missing our one-of-a-kind, larger-than-life grandmother.

To understand our grandmother, Rosina, you must know that at heart she was a true storyteller. It was no secret she loved drama. She thrived off of it in her everyday life. Her stories had entertained us with countless villains and touches of romance. As children, we'd gather on the front porch of our grandparents' home. With the heavenly scent of garlic, olive oil, and basil still drifting in the air from Sunday dinner, we'd wait in joyful anticipation for the next chapter of our grandmother's story. Before daytime soaps and prime-time television had mastered the art, our grandmother had the ability to keep our rapt attention from week to week. She always left us wanting more, waiting in suspense until next Sunday. It could even be said that our grandmother invented the cliffhanger.

For us, discovering these letters meant much more than uncovering part of our family's history. They were a chance to read one last tale from the greatest storyteller we'd ever known.

So it happened, by luck or perhaps by divine intervention, that we found a translator who happened to be planning a trip to the very same region of Southwestern Italy, in the hills beyond Naples, that our grandmother first called home. When he returned with a notebook full of handwritten translations, we finally had a glimpse into what must have been the most important year in our grandmother's life. Once again, we were transported to the treasured memories of finding our place at her feet for story time. And we learned that waiting "until next Sunday" began long before our days on Grandmom's porch.

The novel you're about to read is based on and includes the translations of some of the letters our grandmother lovingly archived. It is by no means an historical account, but rather a work of fiction, grounded by true events and inspired by our grandmother's talent to keep us all on the edges of our seats.

We invite you, the reader, to take a seat at our family table and indulge in the delicious details of one unforgettable year.

Rosina's granddaughters,
Linda, Susan, and Laurie

ROSINA'S GNOCCHI RECIPE

Gnocchi - Recipe from
+ Grandma

4 potatoes, Idaho or russet around
2 lbs. (medium)
1 - Tablespoon salt to taste
1½ to 2 cups all purpose flour

Wash potatoes and cook till they are
tender. When cool enough to handle,
peel the potatoes + put them thru a ricer
into a large bowl. Add the salt
and about 1½ cup of the flour.
Mix all together with your hands
until the dough begins to stick together.
Transfer the mixture to a wooden
board and knead lightly, gradually
adding the remaining flour. This
dough should not take no longer
than 4 or 5 minutes. The dough
is ready when it is soft and just
a bit stickery.
Cut the dough into pieces the size
of an orange. Flour your hands.
lightly and roll into 1-inch pieces
of dough with a light back and
forth motion and roll into 1-inch
the size of your thumb. Cut each

roll into 1 inch pieces.
Using your index fingers.
They can be cooked immediately or
kept in the refrigerator until ready
to cook uncovered —

Boil enough water, add the salt —
add the gnocchi until they rise
to the surface of the water about
1 to 2 minutes — do not over cook.

Drain well and add your sauce
& cheese,.

Hope you can read all this, my
hands sometime goes on me —

Love

FROM THE TRANSLATOR OF THE LOVE LETTERS

February 22, 2011

To Lillian's daughters, Linda, Laurie and Susan,

It has been a pleasure and an honor translating a so great love story. Through Gianni's and Rosina's letters, I have experienced and somewhat lived their lives's struggles. A period of time marked by uncertainties of life, tragedies, illnesses, deceptions, faith in the Lord, trust in one another and above all "love", the universe's strongest force.

Love, in Gianni's and Rosina's lives, has been the catalyst of their very beings. A constant strength that caused them to overcome their differences, their obstacles and the frailties of life itself. A seemingly spiritual force which ultimately unites two aching hearts into a monstruous, everlasting reciprocal affection that lasts their entire terrestrial life and behind.

It is my wish that many will read this memorable, beautiful, wonderful and exciting love story. And in some way, a splinter of Gianni's and Rosina's never dying love penetrates, as it did me, their very souls.

Thank You,

Biagio Dhs

PART I

PRIMA PARTE

CHAPTER ONE

UNA CROCE D'OROR
(A GOLDEN CROSS)

December 17, 1919
Torchiara, Italy

I knew by the ruffled feathers on my hen Piccolino that she wasn't happy with the packed bags I held in either hand. I set them down and stepped toward her, motioning to pick her up as I often did, ever since she'd been a fluffy chick. But Piccolino wouldn't have anything to do with me. My heart broke as she strutted in the opposite direction. The hazy morning sunlight gleamed off her russet speckled feathers. Though I called her name, she refused to turn.

"Oh no, not you, too," I said as Piccolino pecked the ground beside the crumbling stone wall lined with herbs and plants at the edge of our small yard. I took a deep breath of the sweet-scented, cool air. Piccolino, like so many others, wasn't reacting well to my decision to leave.

My cousin Filomena had cried large, round teardrops. She and I were especially close since her mother, my Aunt Teresa, had acted as my second mother. Though Filomena begged and pleaded for me to stay, she, like Aunt Teresa, understood why I was better off leaving.

My father, on the other hand, would never know the true reason I wanted to join my brother Tomasso in America. Tomasso, like so many in this time of desperation in Italy, had left three years ago to find prosperity in a country that promised so much. His last letter had offered a place for me in his home if I chose to make the long journey across the Atlantic.

My father hadn't wanted to show me the letter. I had made no secret of my deep desire to find a new life in America. Only because he had promised that when I turned twenty-one, I would be old enough to decide my own fate, did he begrudgingly share what my brother had written.

"I understand why you'd wish for a better life in America like your brother," my father had told me over the last Sunday dinner we shared together. Ripping the heel off a loaf of homemade bread, he'd swiped the last of the seasoned olive oil left on his plate. "I have saved enough money to pay for the ship's fare and a little extra. If you wish to leave, I will grant you my permission."

This morning, my father stood by the back door, waiting to say his last goodbye. When I walked toward him, he spoke with a heaviness in his voice. "Rosina, you must write to me often and let me know you are well. I will pray the rosary every day until I learn of your arrival." After wiping a stray tear from his cheek with the back of his hand, he reached into his vest pocket and pulled out a necklace. A small gold cross hung from its delicate chain. "This belonged to your mother. I had the Monsignor bless it to ensure your safe travel."

I placed the chain around my neck and hugged my father in a long, tight embrace, thanking him for his permission and the sacrifices he'd made to save enough money for my travels. Even as an older man, my father was strong and handsome, with thick, dark hair edged with only a bit of gray. The last thing I wanted was to deepen the worry lines on his gentle face. I made a promise to myself that moving to America would be worth all the pain and tears my leaving would cause.

As I bent to grasp the handles of my bags with one hand, my other hand reached for the cross at the nape of my neck. With a heavy heart, I took slow steps toward the wrought-iron gate.

Any other day, Piccolino would have dashed through the opening before I'd had a chance to clasp the latch. Most days she would follow me like a puppy down the stone-paved streets, accompanying me as I worked in the Uliveto, the olive grove of ancient trees on the hillside below my village. Though I wouldn't miss the backbreaking long hours of raking the plump, ripe olives from the twisted branches, I would miss the pure extra-virgin olive oil produced by the harvest.

Today, Piccolino went about her business of scratching and pecking as if I no longer existed.

I waved one last time to my father, then glanced toward my bedroom window. A shadowy figure of a woman moved out of sight.

I walked alone down my shady narrow lane. Only the *click-click* of my footsteps, like the ticking seconds of a clock, followed me to the edge of town and toward the horse-drawn carriage bound for the port in Naples. There in the harbor sat a passenger ship bound for America.

Chapter Two

Addio Torchiara
(Goodbye Torchiara)

December 17, 1919
Campania Region, Italy

Among the few faded memories I had of my mother, I could clearly picture her hands. She had long fingers that moved gracefully even while doing the most ordinary tasks, like kneading bread, folding our linens, collecting eggs, or smoothing the wild hair off my face. When I would sit on her lap in the evening, I'd place my small hand against her palm, and everything in the world would feel okay. She died a month before I turned five.

As I walked the streets of my village for the last time, I bought a single white rose from an elderly man selling bouquets in front of a cafe. Knowing I may not return for many years or perhaps ever again, I detoured to the cemetery where my mother was buried. There, I laid the rose upon my mother's grave. I placed a kiss into my right palm and pressed it flat against the cold stone bearing her name. A flock of doves took flight, startling me.

Picking up my two heavy bags, I walked as fast as I could, needing to keep moving forward. I broke into a run once I reached the outermost street overlooking the valley and the distant hills, partially obscured on this morning by sunlit mist.

Turning the corner, I spotted the horse-drawn carriage beginning to roll in the opposite direction. I called to the driver, an older gentleman, who pulled the reins upward. The stout brown workhorse expressed his dissatisfaction at stopping so abruptly, but the man was gracious as he helped me load my bags.

As we descended into the valley and away from everyone and everything I had ever known, I turned my attention to my own hands. Unlike the elegant softness of my mother's, mine had calluses and small scars from a life of hard work and little peace. Still, my father had often reminded me that I had grown to match the beauty of my mother. While I wasn't sure this was entirely true, I did like that it bothered my father's new wife, Seraphina, each time she heard him say these tender words.

Seraphina. If there were one word to explain why I had chosen to leave behind my loved ones and take the risk of traveling to America, it would be her name.

"She's an evil, dreadful woman," I told the young woman who'd boarded the carriage in Salerno. She, too, was on her way to Naples, also bound for America.

I was happy for the company on the long, bumpy ride toward the sea. Talking about the life I was leaving behind felt far better than listening to the persistent rhythm of the horse's hooves upon the road.

"My mother's body was still warm when Seraphina came knocking on our door," I explained to my new companion, who shook her head side to side. "I remember telling my father not to let her enter our house. But he reprimanded me for being rude and opened the door in spite of my protests. Seraphina walked right in and made herself at home. She even took a seat in my mother's chair." I paused, and then said in a hushed voice, "Eventually she slept in my mother's bed."

The young woman gasped.

"And I haven't even told you the worst of it," I continued.

"Please, do," she begged. But the carriage had rolled to a stop at the corner of one of the bustling main streets entering Naples.

Compared to Torchiara, a quiet village with narrow lanes, shady trees, and fragrant breezes, Naples was a large city with salty air and never-ending activity. Not far from the carriage, a woman poured a bowl of what looked like dishwater from her third-story window. It landed near a man pushing a vending cart of goods. A shouting match broke out between them. Meanwhile, people walked around the angry man as if it were any other day.

Two more passengers boarded, a middle-aged man and presumably his young son.

"Find me on the ship," I whispered to my travel companion, who nodded in agreement. But after this ride together, we never saw each other again. I would often wonder if she changed her mind and decided to remain in Naples.

As for Seraphina, less than a year after my mother's death, she and my father were married. Not two years later, I had a newborn brother, Cristiano.

Oh, how I adored my new baby brother! But still my heart ached. Not only had I lost my mother, but I'd had the misfortune of gaining a wicked stepmother. Gone were the carefree days of playing with my dolls and teaching Piccolino tricks as if she were a pet dog. Now I was put to work from sunup to sundown. I had to do all the cleaning, all the chores—it was a nightmare! I tried to complain to my father, but, loving as he was, he did little to help.

When I once refused to complete my endless chores, Seraphina banished every plaything and every comfort from my room. So I needed somewhere to hide, somewhere I could play with the only doll I had left. One day I found just such a place in the alleyway where a chunk of foundation had come loose. Not even Tomasso knew about it. Only Piccolino knew my hiding place, and she'd never tell.

"Rosina. Rosina!" Seraphina called one afternoon as I hid in my secret spot. "You come out here right now! These wet clothes have been sitting in this basket all morning. They need to be hung on the line right this minute!"

I didn't dare answer. Instead, I pressed my doll to my chest and made a quiet gesture to Piccolino with my pointer finger against my lips.

"Oh, this is the game you're going to play?" Seraphina said, changing her tone. "Well, it's one you're going to lose."

I shivered at the thought of what she might do, but still I refused to move. Later, my father's disappointed face told me all I needed to know about Seraphina's revenge. My father informed me that after my chores were done, I was to return to my bedroom, and that I would no longer have Sundays after mass as a day of rest. Still, I kept my hiding spot for as long as I could, until I outgrew it.

The years passed. My father had two more boys with Seraphina, which only meant more work for me. Fortunately, I had Aunt Teresa nearby. As I grew taller and stronger from all the backbreaking work, I would flee to her home as often as I could, even if it was against the rules. Aunt Teresa, my mother's older sister, loved me as her own daughter. And Filomena became more like my sister. Saying goodbye to the two of them had been every bit as difficult as leaving my father.

When the carriage finally reached its destination at the port, I considered for a moment taking the next carriage home. I pictured how happy Filomena would be. My last sight of her had been with pink, tear-stained cheeks—unlike my Aunt Teresa, who was a wiser, gentler soul.

"Rosina, look at me and listen," Aunt Teresa had said, taking my face into her hands. "You have a beautiful life waiting for you. Go! Live your dreams. It will be hard, but it will be worth it. You will find your place in America, and you will be happy." She patted my cheek and added, "I can see on your lovely face that this is true." Dropping her hands, Aunt Teresa grinned. "Maybe you'll meet a nice American boy? Ah, you never know." Becoming more serious, she said, "Don't worry about us. We will miss you, but we will go on. If you stay here, you may never know all the treasures of life that await you."

I gave her a long hug. It felt like I was holding onto my mother.

Standing on the dock, I hugged my own chest as if to hold Aunt Teresa's words close to my heart. I would need her strength to brave boarding the largest ship I had ever seen.

CHAPTER THREE

ARRIVANDO IN AMERICA
(COMING TO AMERICA)

December 24, 1919
New York Harbor
New York City, New York

Crossing the Atlantic Ocean felt like it took an eternity. For nearly a week, there was nothing to see out the round below-deck windows but water, waves, and sky. The Giuseppe Verdi Ocean Liner had come from America carrying supplies and goods to be unloaded in Naples. On the return voyage, the empty cargo area became the living quarters for those of us too poor to afford better accommodations. I would have lost my mind in the overcrowded conditions had I not struck up conversations with a few other young women. At first, we all suffered terribly from seasickness. Fortunately, it lessened with each passing day. As the week went on, we spent the long hours sharing the hardships from the lives we left behind and our hopes for our futures. No one could believe the misery my stepmother had put me through.

Finally, on the morning of the seventh day, there was a buzz of heightened energy. Hurried footsteps rushed toward the top deck. I followed the flow of people and pushed my way to the rail. There, in the harbor, stood the most magnificent sight! The Statue of Liberty in all her majestic glory glowed in the light of the morning sun. Her raised arm appeared as if she was waving us forward, welcoming us to her shores. I had dreamed of this moment.

I fell to my knees and wept with gratitude. My prayers had been answered! I was in America.

I wasn't prepared for what an ordeal Ellis Island would prove to be. Immediately, I was separated from the friends I had made on the ship, never to see them again. On my own, in a big hall filled with people having loud conversations, children running, and babies crying, I managed to find a place in a line that I hoped would grant me passage into the United States.

At a desk occupied by a tired, official-looking clerk, I explained that I was headed to Philadelphia. The clerk wrinkled his forehead up to his bald scalp and peered over his half-glasses, shaking his head at me. I realized I was speaking in Italian, and my cheeks flushed with embarrassment, making the already-stuffy, oppressively warm room even less tolerable. A river of sweat rolled down my back, but I didn't flinch in front of this man who held my fate on the end of his pointed finger. He gestured toward a hallway with yet another long line.

I wasn't worried about passing the medical exam until a young woman shoved past me with a look of terror on her face. She cried in Italian, "They're wrong! It can't be!" I wasn't sure what she meant until I noticed a white chalk X on her back. A young man followed her, carrying a small child and yelling, "We will not be separated. You cannot do this!"

From that point forward, I wasn't able to fully exhale until the medical examiner cleared me to continue.

Finally, after hours of waiting in a line that twisted back and forth so many times I feared it had no end, a new clerk—this time an older woman with several chins and tiny, pursed pink lips—reached for a stamp, slammed it on a document, and held out the paper to me. She pointed to a set of stairs while saying the few words in English I could fully understand, "Welcome to the United States of America."

I paused for a brief second in shock, then repeated "Grazie," several times before taking quick, light steps to the staircase. Outside, the afternoon sun hung low in the partly clouded sky. A short walk along a paved path led the lucky group of us who had survived processing to a ferry headed toward the rows upon rows of buildings lining the shores of Manhattan.

Upon exiting the ferry, I quickly learned that New York City was full of people wanting my attention, and I was certain no good would come of me giving them a second of my time. I gripped the cross pendant from my father, kept my eyes focused straight in front of me, and braved my way forward all the way to the train station.

Eventually, my travels ended at a two-story house on a quiet neighborhood block in Philadelphia. My feet ached. My shoulders were sore from carrying my bags. I felt worse than after a long day of chores followed by several hours raking olives at the peak of the harvest.

Double-checking the letter from my brother, I took tentative steps up the narrow cement walkway toward the door matching his address. All the windows appeared dark except for a low light glowing from the window above where I stopped. I knocked and waited. A dog barked from the neighbor's yard. The night air felt damp and chilly. My breath steamed with every exhale. It felt far colder than any winter evening in Torchiara.

After a while, I knocked again. This time, I heard a thumping sound followed by a snap of locks being undone. I anticipated the welcome upon my brother's face. The last time I saw him, he had been a handsome young man resembling my father.

The door opened not to my brother, but to a woman holding a baby that looked to be about six months old. Though I recognized the woman's features, three years had aged the once-youthful appearance of my brother's wife. My memory of her on their wedding day, glowing and beautiful, did not match the tired, sorrowful person glaring at me with confusion.

"Nicola, it's me. Rosina." How much had I changed in three years? Certainly, the long trip had done nothing to help my current appearance.

"I know," Nicola said, still standing with the door only partway open. "Why are you here?"

Now it was my turn to be confused. "Tomasso," I said as my stomach dropped to my knees. "He wrote." I held up the letter, which crumpled in my tight grip. "He said he had a place for me."

"Oh," Nicola said, looking at the letter in my hand. Taking a deep breath, she stepped back and opened the door fully. "Well, then come in. Come in. You must have had a long journey. Here, let me help you with one of your bags." The words were pleasant and welcoming, but the way she said them felt anything but.

"Tom," Nicola called in a loud voice. "Your sister is here all the way from Italy. Wake up and come see her!" The baby startled and began crying in loud wails. "Excuse me," Nicola said with a tight smile, stepping past me and carrying the crying child up the steps.

I dropped my bags and stood alone in the living room of my brother's house. Of all the ways I'd imagined arriving at his home, I never thought I'd feel as though I had made a mistake. It wasn't so much Tomasso's house, which could have used a thorough cleaning, as it was the sense that I wasn't wanted.

As I was figuring how the tiny amount of money I had left could get me passage on a ship or a train ticket to anywhere else but here, Tomasso descended the steps. "Rosie, you're here! And just in time for the Natale!"

The brave front that had lasted through my many days at sea, Ellis Island, and the chaos of New York City dissolved into tears at the warmth in my older brother's voice. Tomasso hugged me as I sobbed into his chest. He reassured me several times that he did indeed have a place for me in his small, cluttered house. "It's an attic room," he told me. "I hope you don't mind."

"I am thankful for whatever you can give me," I said, wiping the wetness from my cheeks as I followed him up the creaking staircase.

As I tried to fall asleep that night, holding the only doll to survive my childhood, I prayed I'd find a way to make my American dreams come true.

Chapter Four

La Festa
(The Party)

April 16, 1921
Germantown, Pennsylvania

I wrote to my father often to let him know that I was safe and well. I did not write to him that I was happy here in America. That would have been a lie.

Although I had lived for over a year now in the Germantown section of Philadelphia, learning many key phrases in English and adjusting to the much colder and snowier winters, my life hadn't undergone the amazing transformation I had expected. In fact, little had changed. Rather than doing chores for my father, I now took care of my brother's house. Rather than working in the olive grove, which was at least outside in the fresh air, I now worked in a shoe assembly factory in Norristown for eight hours a day, six days a week, with an hour-long commute on a trolley each way. My wages were handed to my brother in the same manner as I had given my father all my earnings.

Although Nicola had little in common with Seraphina, I had never met a more miserable, ill-tempered woman. It was as if pregnancy and raising babies had drained all the joy from the once-vibrant girl I had first met in Italy. And in much the same way I'd run to my Aunt Teresa's house for comfort, when I wanted to escape the oppressiveness of my brother's house, I'd visit my Aunt Isabella, my father's sister. However, Aunt Isabella had so many of my cousins living with her, I rarely found a peaceful moment there.

I hadn't become close with any of these cousins, but I did happen to make a new friend at the factory: Antoinetta. After long hours spent working and commuting together, Antoinetta became one of the few people I trusted to confide in about the disappointment my new life in this country had been so far.

"You should come with me tonight to the party at my Aunt Carmela's house," Antoinetta suggested as we sat side by side, heading home on the trolley one late Saturday afternoon. "They always get a band, and there's lots of people and plenty of wine. Besides, tomorrow is your birthday. You should be celebrating. What could you be doing tonight that's better than that?"

"Washing the dishes that Nicola left in the sink all day," I joked, even though it was the truth.

"So, it's settled," Antoinetta said. "I'll be by at eight o'clock. We'll walk there together. It's only a few blocks from your brother's."

I wanted to tell her that after yet another impossibly long week, I'd be ready for bed by eight. But the enthusiasm on her face won me over. I pictured the exact dress I'd wear. Flattering to my tall, curvy shape, the dress was a lively yellow, fitted at the waist, with cuffed sleeves and a flowing skirt ending perfectly at mid-calf. I felt a jolt of energy at the idea of fixing my hair and applying some lipstick to attend an actual party.

Antoinetta had barely had a chance to knock when I dashed out the door into the golden evening, leaving behind the sink full of dishes, untouched. It didn't matter. They would still be there waiting for me tomorrow morning. Tonight, however, I was going to enjoy myself, despite my nerves over not knowing a single soul at this party aside from my friend.

"You'll be fine," Antoinetta reassured me. "My Aunt Carmela loves having new guests."

As we approached the house, I could hear the band playing an up-tempo song. A few people occupied the front porch on this comfortable spring night, either standing or sitting on the railing, all of them with a drink in hand.

"Come on, Rosina," Antoinetta demanded, pulling on my arm.

After saying hello to those on the porch, I followed her inside to a living room full of more strangers, talking loudly with frequent bursts of laughter.

A young man with thick, dark hair and a medium build, wearing a white dress shirt unbuttoned at the neck, stood leaning on the arched doorway at the opposite side of the room. My eyes met his for a brief moment before I looked away.

"Come on," Antoinetta instructed. "First, we'll fill up our wine glasses, and then we'll go out back and listen to the band."

I nodded, allowing Antoinetta to take the lead through the narrow living room. From a few steps behind, I watched her greet people as she forged a path forward, her long, wavy dark hair flipping from side to side with each new person. She gave the young man standing in the doorway a hug. He walked close beside her as she entered the dining room and headed toward the kitchen. Perhaps he was Antoinetta's new boyfriend, although I couldn't recall her mentioning seeing anyone special.

Around me, people spoke to one another as if they knew each other well. Every now and then, someone would look at me and smile as if they were trying to place me, and I caught the eye of one or two young men. I suppressed a smile so as not to seem too thrilled that my yellow dress had the ability to turn a few heads.

In the kitchen, I met Antoinetta's Aunt Carmela, a petite woman with a personality large enough to fill the entire room. She embraced me as if she had known me my entire life and made me feel especially welcome with a hearty "Ciao, Bella."

Once Aunt Carmela released me, Antoinetta handed me a glass of cool white wine. She didn't give me a chance to thank her as she bounded toward the back door and held it open. A dewy breeze greeted me, carrying with it the sounds of a peppy melody.

In the small backyard enclosed by a low metal fence, three men played under the glow of streetlights. Couples moved and swayed to the quick beat. I finished half my wine, enjoying the tart, crisp flavor as I watched and listened to the lively group of partygoers dancing and singing the lyrics to a familiar tune.

When the band took a break, Antoinetta and I returned to the kitchen to top off our drinks. I spotted the same nice-looking dark-haired young man now sitting at the kitchen table talking with another man.

"Who is that?" I asked Antoinetta discreetly, gesturing his way. But she was distracted by an older woman telling an animated story about a stray cat in the neighborhood. I leaned against the counter and studied the pale straw color of the wine in my glass.

"I'd be careful if I were you," a man's voice said. I looked up to see the dark-haired young man. He was a bit shorter than me and had a grin that revealed the slightest dimple in each cheek.

He placed his hand beside his mouth as if telling me a secret and added, "There was a robbery in the backyard last night."

"Really?" I said, caught completely off guard that he was even talking to me.

"Well, it just so happened two clothespins held up a shirt," he said, holding up his hands like he was being robbed. He pinched the shoulders of his shirt as if they were hanging on a clothesline.

At first, I smiled with my mouth hanging open, trying to figure out how to reply. When I caught on that he was making a joke, I let out a small laugh.

"I've got a bunch more I could tell you," he said. The young man who'd seemed so calm and collected when I first saw him now appeared every bit as nervous as I felt.

Before he had a chance to tell another joke, Antoinetta approached us with a wide smile. "I see you met my cousin John," she said to me. "Isn't he handsome?" She jabbed her elbow into his side.

I smiled and nodded. "So, you're cousins?" I asked, relieved that he wasn't, in fact, her new boyfriend.

"Where are my manners? I'm Giovanni. Giovanni DiFerdinando. Um, but everyone calls me John or Gianni."

"Rosina Celano," I replied, placing my hand into his outstretched one. "You can call me Rosie if you like."

"Nice to meet you, Rosie."

"And you, too, Gianni." I removed my hand from his and took a sip of my wine to hide my burning face.

Outside, the band launched into another peppy melody. I turned toward the sound. Antoinetta reached for a tall, thin young man who was heading out the back door. "Come on, good-looking," she said, taking him by the hand. "Let's show this crowd how it's done."

I gaped at her bold nature, shaking my head.

Gianni laughed and shrugged. "How long have you been friends with Antoinetta?" he asked.

"A couple of months."

"Then you shouldn't be surprised."

I laughed and nodded in agreement.

Holding out his hands in a dancing posture, Gianni asked, "Care to dance? We can't let Antoinetta have all the fun."

"You're right." I set down my wine glass and raised my arms to match his.

He pulled me into a simple box step and then led me outside. We danced long into the night. I couldn't remember the last time I'd had more fun. When the party began breaking apart, well after midnight, Gianni asked if he could see me again.

The next morning, I awoke to the same sink full of dirty dishes and the same number of exhausting chores with the same long workweek looming ahead of me. Yet I went through the day feeling lighter, humming the songs I had heard the night before.

Nicola scowled at me and warned me not to wake the baby with my singing. I smiled and kept on humming. Besides, the baby seemed to like it.

CHAPTER FIVE

IL PRIMO BACIO
(THE FIRST KISS)

May 29, 1921
Willow Grove Amusement Park
Willow Grove, Pennsylvania

This past month, springtime had awakened the world with an abundance of color, leaving the dark, dreary days of winter a distant memory.

"I've never felt more alive and well," I'd told Antoinetta yesterday, after noticing how beautiful our commute to and from the factory had become. "I think it's the change of season."

"It's new love that has you feeling this way, and you know it."

"No, no, it's the flowers and the green leaves on the trees," I protested.

The look on her face showed she didn't believe a word I said. Ever since Gianni had suggested taking me to the amusement park, I'd been bothering Antoinetta with questions about what I should wear while counting the days and hours until Sunday.

Now, as he helped me off the trolley after a quick ride north out of the city, I could barely contain my enthusiasm. I clapped my hands and hopped in place at the sight of the grand entrance and a huge sign stating, "Welcome to the Willow Grove Amusement Park."

"Have you ever been to an amusement park before?" Gianni asked.

"No, never," I said with a shrug. I nearly admitted I never did anything that would be considered lighthearted and fun, but I didn't want him to get the wrong impression.

"Well, you're in for a treat," he said with a wide smile. "And I hear John Philip Sousa is supposed to be conducting today. I'd love to hear his band."

Despite not being familiar with the name, I nodded with enthusiasm and followed Gianni to the entrance, the crowd streaming into the park thick with people. Gianni reached out his hand so we wouldn't become separated. I liked how strong and reassuring his hand felt around mine.

The line for the ticket booth moved quickly. I spent the time watching groups of families and other couples. Some had brought picnic baskets, which seemed like a wonderful idea on this sunny, pleasantly warm day. The light breeze brought the smell of sweet and savory offerings from the food vendors inside the park.

"Where do you want to go first?" Gianni asked, holding up the fistful of tickets he'd purchased.

"I don't know." Though getting a bite to eat sounded good, the spinning movement and varied up-and-down motions of the different rides drew my interest. I turned toward the sound of happy screams overhead. "What's that ride?"

Gianni followed my gaze. "That's the roller coaster. I don't know if you're ready for that, since you've never been before."

"What are you saying?" I said, placing my hands on my hips. "You think I'm a scared little girl. Maybe you're afraid to ride it?"

Gianni's mouth dropped open. Then he grinned. "We'll see how brave you are when you're at the top looking down."

"I'm not worried," I said in the most confident voice I could muster.

I had to work hard to hide my nerves as we waited in line. The closer we got to the roller coaster, the more I noticed the speed and the height of it. Tall wooden scaffolding held up a track on which riders passed in a blur, their screams rising and falling. Gianni glanced at me several times, checking to see if I'd changed my mind. I shrugged as if it was a ride for a little child.

Soon it was our turn to board the steel carriage. We adjusted a strap to our waists, and then the attendant pressed a lever releasing our train of cars. As the ride clicked and clacked, higher and higher, I gripped Gianni's upper arm. The view was fantastic from this height. We were above the treetops and nearly into the bright-blue sky, among the puffy white clouds. For a moment the coaster slowed nearly to a stop. Perhaps it wouldn't be as bad as it had seemed from the ground.

As the ride plummeted downward, my own shriek joined the many screaming voices. Beside me, Gianni let out a whoop, although I could barely hear him over the whoosh of the wind.

The coaster climbed a smaller hill and dropped again, repeating this sequence of rising and falling several more times. I felt a flutter in my stomach at each gravity-defying crest. Finally, the coaster returned to the boarding platform, slowing down so swiftly that both of us jerked forward from the force.

Falling back, now at a complete stop, I began laughing. Gianni joined me as tears spilled from the corners of my eyes. My stomach ached from how hard I laughed. We were so ridiculous, acting as if we weren't scared when in fact, we both had screamed like frightened cats.

On the firm ground, several steps from the coaster, Gianni and I finally caught our breath as our laughter subsided.

"How about we try a ride that stays lower to the ground this time?" he suggested, and I agreed. We wandered around the shady grounds of the park, going on the merry-go-round and sharing a frozen dessert treat.

"Oh, look, a boat ride," I said, pointing toward an enclosure with a sign depicting a gondola and the name Venice.

"Let's go," Gianni said, counting the tickets for the fare. "We have just enough to get on."

Inside a large enclosed building, we boarded a rowboat, which bobbed past different scenes along a narrow canal at a relaxing, steady pace. It took a moment for my eyes to adjust to the dimness of the enclosure. None of it interested me as much as the nearness of Gianni. My heartbeat quickened. This was the first time I had ever been alone and this close to him.

Gianni adjusted his posture on the boat's wooden bench to face me. I smiled at him and then looked away at a painting of a bridge crossing a canal. I pinched the cross at my neck, trying to calm my breath and the heat rising on my cheeks.

"The cross you're wearing," he said, "I notice you always have it on. Is it special?"

I lifted the gold cross from my collarbone and gazed down at it. "My father gave it to me just before I left for America. He had it blessed. It once belonged to my mother." When Gianni nodded but didn't answer, I added, "She died when I was a young girl. I barely have any memories of her."

"Both of my parents died young," Gianni confided in a solemn voice. "It's not a loss you ever get over." I was about to tell him how sorry I was to learn he no longer had either of his parents when he asked in a soft voice, "Was it hard to leave Italy?"

"It was and it wasn't," I said with a sigh, releasing the cross. "Maybe if things were different, I would have stayed. But they were the way they were. My home hadn't felt like a home for many years, maybe most of my life." I lifted my eyes from the passing scenery and looked directly at Gianni. "And for you?"

He took a deep breath. "It's a long story, but yes, like you, I didn't have a place to call home anymore, so I came to America."

"Look at us. We're two of a kind. Aren't we?" I said, bumping Gianni with my shoulder.

He nodded and reached for my hand. He gazed at me with such compassion, I longed to be close to him, wished this ride with just the two of us would never end.

Slowly Gianni leaned toward me until he was a breath away. I inched forward, bridging the gap between us. As my lips softly pressed against his, the world around us seemed to disappear. Nothing else mattered but this very moment. We deepened the kiss, and it was new yet familiar, exhilarating yet comforting. I felt as if I was coming home after a long journey.

The next morning, as I boarded the trolley for my Monday morning commute, Antoinetta took one look at me and said, "Don't tell me that blushing glow you have all over your face is from springtime or I'll knock you right back out the door!"

I laughed so hard, I doubled over. Recovering, I took my seat next to her and teased, "What can I say? It's beautiful weather we're having."

"So are you going to kiss and tell, or what?" she asked, poking my shoulder with her finger.

I blushed and fell into another fit of laughter. Antoinetta's look of shocked recognition was priceless.

June 9, 1921
Ardmore, Pennsylvania

My Dear Rosa,

Since I left you Sunday evening, I can't stop thinking of you. Today I was waiting for your letter or phone call. I received neither. I would be very pleased if you would like to be with me.

My love, I hope you don't think I'm a pest if I ask to see you often. It's my affection for you that makes me ask such things. I hope you're kind enough to remember me and see me once a week. I have so many things to tell you, especially my admiration for you.

Sunday I will wait for you at Sixth and Market Street, between one-thirty and two p.m. Please call me if you can't be there. If you don't call, I will be there. I hope you'll come and be with your admirer who would do anything to see you happy. My only wish is that you are in perfect health. I end by sending you a warm greeting from the bottom of my heart.

Yours forever,
John

P.S. When I receive words from you, you can rest assured that I'll keep them in my heart for the rest of my life. Ciao!

Chapter Six

Colpito Dalla Tristezza
(Stricken with Sadness)

June 12, 1921
Germantown, Pennsylvania

"You're laughing now, but you'll be crying later," my Aunt Teresa used to warn me when I was acting too bold for my own good. I could have used her wisdom and her caring nature right now, when my head felt clamped in a vise, my stomach clenched with nausea, and my body ached in every joint.

Nicola pressed her cold hand against my forehead and proclaimed in an angry voice, "You have a fever." Then she stormed out of my attic room, yelling, "Tom!"

I squeezed my eyes shut and tried to will my body to feel better. Failing, I opened my eyes and rolled to my side, reaching for the letter on my nightstand. In a few hours, I was supposed to meet Gianni downtown in the city. I needed to let him know I wouldn't be able to make it. I pressed my arms behind my back and sat up. The room swirled for a moment but then righted itself. I swung my legs over the side of my bed and attempted to stand.

Heavy footsteps pounded up the stairs, and Tomasso entered my room. "Nicola says you're sick?"

I tried to gather all my strength to tell him she was exaggerating. The sweat beading on my brow must have given me away.

"Dear Lord, look at you!" Tomasso said. "We need to get you to a doctor."

"No." I pushed up to my feet. Again the room spun, but I fought against it. "I just need to rest and then..." I took a deep breath and straightened my posture. "And then I'll be fine. But first, I need to use the phone." I held out Gianni's letter and took a shaky step toward the stairs.

Tomasso dashed toward me as I swayed too far to one side. He caught me before I would have hit the floor. "Nicola said we should take you to the hospital," he said in a strained voice as he slid my dead weight back toward my bed.

"No, I'll be fine," I protested, pushing back up to a sitting position. "I just need to use the phone and then get some rest," I repeated.

"You're going to the hospital," Tomasso said authoritatively. "I don't know what you have, but I can't risk you infecting the children." He exhaled loudly. Then, in a quieter voice, he told me, "I'm sorry, Rosie. It's for your own good. Now, don't move. I'll be right back, and then we're going."

I dropped my head onto my pillow, small teardrops escaping the corners of my eyes. "Oh, Gianni," I said to my window as if he could hear me. "I hope you're not too upset when I'm not there to meet you."

I covered my eyes with my hands. I should have known my happiness wouldn't continue for long. Aunt Teresa was right: I was certainly crying now.

June 20, 1921
Ardmore, Pennsylvania

My Dear Rosie,

I'm so sad to hear you are hospitalized and suffer so much. But what can you do, but be of good cheer? When I first heard you were in the hospital, my heart was stricken with sadness. I have had two terrible weeks thinking of you suffering. Forgive me for not writing to you sooner. I did not have your right address. The only thing I want is to see you well. I hope you can leave that place as soon as possible. I want to take you places, and we can enjoy ourselves even more than before. Please have courage and try not to cry. Your recovery depends on you staying calm. Try not to think about your illness. Just think about getting better.

My dear, since you've been in the hospital, I cannot stop thinking of you. Every night, before going to bed, I pray to the Lord for your speedy recovery. I don't want you to think because you are sick, I am going to forget you. On the contrary, I love you more because of where you are. I will love you until I die.

My dear, when I heard only relatives were allowed to visit you, I began crying unceasingly. I am unable to go on without seeing you, at least once. See if you could do something. Perhaps I could come under the pretense of being one of your brothers or a cousin. I will try again to visit you next Sunday. I wish it could be sooner, but I am very busy. Please recover quickly.

I beg of you, write to me. If you don't feel up to it, ask one of the nurses. I understand English well. I am sending you a box of chocolates, writing papers, a pen, and some stamps. Please let me know if you received them. If not, I will send them all again. If you need anything else at all, please do not be ashamed to ask. I will do anything for you. In the meantime, from the bottom of my heart, I send you my dearest regards and a kiss on your most beautiful eyes.

Always Yours,
John

June 22, 1921
Rush Hospital for Consumption and Allied Diseases
Philadelphia, Pennsylvania

Dear Gianni,

Yesterday I received your bunch of flowers. Last night, at ten o'clock, as I was sleeping, my nurse came to me and said, "Look, Rosie. Who sends you this beautiful bouquet of flowers?" I was surprised. Immediately I took the attached note and read it. You cannot imagine how happy I was when I read your name, the joy I felt in that moment. I got out of bed and looked at the flowers as if I was looking at you.

Dear Giovanni, you have sent me my first flowers. If it is God's will, I will give you the first flowers of my life.

An hour later, I also received your letter. You want to see me, and I want to see you! It feels as if I haven't seen you for a thousand years. You can come see me anytime you wish and as many times as you can. Anyway, the doctor told me I'll be going home within a few days. I have nothing more to add. Receive a big kiss on your lips.

Your Very Affectionate,
Rosina

P.S. Please pardon my bad writing. I have written this letter in bed. Besides, my hand shakes.

CHAPTER SEVEN

UN CALZOLAIO
(A SHOEMAKER)

June 27, 1921
Rush Hospital for Consumption and Allied Diseases
Philadelphia, Pennsylvania

Because today would be the first time I would see Gianni since falling ill and being admitted to the hospital, I wanted to look attractive despite lying helpless in a hospital bed. The nurse, a friendly young woman with a kind smile, said she would try to find me a hairbrush or some beauty supplies. I didn't expect her to be back anytime soon. The nurses and doctors breezed in and out of here on their own schedule, only to return at the most inconvenient times, like when I had just fallen asleep. They never appeared when you actually needed them.

I slid out of the hospital bed and took slow, deliberate steps toward the bathroom. Once inside the small space, I shut the door and turned to assess myself in the mirror, tilting my face side to side. Since the nurse hadn't returned, I ran my fingers through my hair, breaking apart several knots until it lay softly upon my shoulders. The fever had added a natural flush to my cheeks and a brightness to my blue eyes. Perhaps Gianni would still find me desirable despite the unflattering hospital gown.

Weak from the exertion, I returned to my bed in the abysmal hospital room full of stale air and people in far worse condition than I was. Other than the grating sound of someone coughing or the occasional unsettling moan, the room remained deathly quiet. Exhausted from my short trip to the bathroom, I eased into my bed.

This relentless fever had enervated me more than I thought. Worst of all, the doctors couldn't diagnose the cause. Because I'd been working in a factory, they feared I might have contracted tuberculosis. Meanwhile, last week, they'd removed an infected molar, believing it might be the culprit. I'd been told my condition should improve as soon as they got the infection under control.

My only comfort came from the flowers Gianni had sent me. They sat on my bedside table, their cheerful colors reminding me of springtime, when my heart had felt light and carefree. As I waited for him, I closed my eyes and thought back to our day at the amusement park, the thrill of the roller coaster ride and the rush of emotions from our first kiss.

When I opened my eyes again, Gianni stood by my bedside, holding a small basket of strawberries and wearing a worried expression.

"Gianni, you came!" I said, sitting up as a burst of energy ran through me.

"I'm sorry. I didn't mean to wake you," he said with a shy smile. He placed the strawberries by the flowers and then grabbed a nearby chair, pulling it beside my bed.

"No, it's wonderful you're here!" I smiled at him. "All I do is lay in this bed and sleep. I could use a visitor." I brushed my hair off my face as he took a seat. He looked every bit as handsome as the first night we met. Gazing into his warm brown eyes, I couldn't hold back my joy at finally seeing him. "Oh, Gianni, I've missed you!"

He smiled and looked at me with such tenderness, it brought tears to my eyes. Leaning forward, he told me, "I wasn't expecting to see you so beautiful." Then, after a glance over his shoulder, he added, "I'm looking at everyone else here, and no one looks as beautiful as you. I can't believe you're sick. Tell me you're getting better. It's been such torture being apart for so long."

"I still have a fever," I admitted. I wished and prayed and begged God every day that this awful affliction would leave me. And yet, here I was, unable to tell Gianni good news.

"Please have courage," he said, picking up on the change in my mood. "As soon as the fever disappears, you'll be out of danger. I don't think you have a bad disease, because when someone has an incurable illness, it shows in the face and the way they speak."

"You think that's true?" Maybe Gianni knew something I didn't.

He clasped his hands together. "Well, I'm no doctor, but it's what I can see."

"Tell me, what did you bring me?" I didn't want to waste any more time discussing my illness.

"Strawberries. They're in season. Will you be able to eat them?"

"My mouth is a little sore, but I can try." The back of my jaw throbbed with pain, but I didn't want Gianni to think I was being ungrateful. "You're such a dear for bringing them. And I love my flowers. I think of you every time I look at them."

"Then I will send you a bunch every week you're in the hospital," he proclaimed. "I'll fill up this whole area with so many flowers, you'll think you're in a garden."

I laughed as I pictured a nurse or the doctor trying to get through a wall of flowers.

Gianni took a deep breath. "I wish you could come out with me today, but I know that's not possible. I know you have to get well. But I'll wait for you. I won't enjoy myself until you're better."

"Oh, Gianni!" I shook my head in disbelief. "What have you been doing while I've been trapped in this hospital bed?"

"Mostly I've been working," he said with a shrug.

"And what is it you do?" I asked, realizing I had no idea. It wasn't something we'd ever discussed.

Gianni sat up straight. "I'm an apprentice for a shoemaker. Someday I'd like to own my own shop. But right now, there's much to learn."

"Shoes. That reminds me of the factory," I said, rolling my eyes. Perhaps there was one benefit to being stuck in this hospital bed.

"It's an art and a skill. Nothing like working in a factory." Gianni paused for a moment. "Why? Don't you like that I'm going to be a shoemaker?"

"Oh, I didn't mean anything by it." Had I offended him? "I just wanted to know what you did. Besides, it's none of my business. Maybe I'm coming off wrong because I feel weak."

"Should I leave you to rest?" he asked, concern lining his face.

"I don't want you to leave, but maybe I shouldn't push myself." Feeling terrible that our visit was coming to an end, I asked, "When will you be back?"

"Next Sunday. And then, I hope, God willing, I'll find you in good health and take you away from here. I'll take you anywhere you want to go. I'll show you a great time. You'll see."

"Oh, Gianni, I want that, too."

Gianni placed his hand on my cheek and smoothed back my hair. "I want to kiss you and hold you tight." I would have welcomed his kiss, but he pulled back as a nurse entered the room.

"I'll get better. Then we can be alone again." I reached for Gianni's hand, grazing the top of his knuckles. The tension in his muscles eased beneath my touch. He turned his palm to face mine, and our fingers gently laced together, sending a ripple of electricity up my arm. "By next week," I promised myself as much as him, "I'm sure I'll be walking out of here with you."

Chapter Eight

Una Miserable Signorina
(A Miserable Young Lady)

July 3, 1921
Rush Hospital for Consumption and Allied Diseases
Philadelphia, Pennsylvania

When Gianni came to visit a week later, he was turned away. My fever had escalated to a life-threatening level. The only visitors I had throughout the day were a succession of nurses and one doctor. They spoke about me as if I wasn't lying right below their conversations.

Through my weakened condition, I heard snippets of phrases.

"Very serious."

"Need to bring the fever under control."

"A dose every four hours."

A few moments later, a nurse reappeared, holding a brown glass bottle and a spoon. Gently, she placed a pillow behind my back to prop me high enough to swallow whatever was in the bottle. She took extra care to fill the spoon to the edge with the syrupy tan medicine. I opened my mouth and immediately regretted it. The spoonful of bitter, pungent, acrid-tasting liquid made me gag. I would have spit it out, but I didn't want to get the awful concoction all over my chest. Instead, I forced myself to swallow, which prompted a fit of coughing.

After a few minutes of my choking and sputtering for air, the nurse removed the pillow and helped me lay flat. The room spun in circles like the merry-go-round at the amusement park. But instead of enjoying the sensation, I felt the uncontrollable need to vomit everything I had just swallowed. The nurse hadn't given me medicine at all! She and the doctor had conspired to poison me.

They'd determined I couldn't be saved, so they decided to take matters into their own hands and finish me off. Perhaps they needed my bed for someone else, a better patient, someone they could help to become well again.

I was a lost cause.

When the nurse returned with my next dose of poison, I had given up all hope for recovery. The fever and the intense nausea were withering me to an early death. And I would die alone. I surrendered to my fate and swallowed the foul liquid with barely a cough. Soon I would leave this Earth and be reunited in heaven with my long-lost mother.

I was awoken a short time later by a light burning through my eyelids. I opened my eyes, expecting a doctor inspecting me for signs of life. Instead, a woman stood at my bedside. At first, I figured she was a nurse, bringing me one last spoonful of poison to put an end to my suffering. But there was something different about this woman. She didn't talk, only smiled. A sense of peace unlike anything I had ever felt filled me.

Then, just as quickly as she appeared, the woman faded away. I said a prayer of gratitude and drifted into a peaceful sleep, knowing now that I would survive.

July 10, 1921
Rush Hospital for Consumption and Allied Diseases
Philadelphia, Pennsylvania

Dear Gianni,

I feel much worse than before. I am now bedridden. This accursed hospital will be the death of me. The doctors said my illness isn't what everybody thought it was. They gave me a very strong medicine that tastes like poison. It makes me vomit all the time. My stomach is weak.

You must think I don't want you here, but think about the state I'm in. I want you here every moment of the day so we can spend time together, for I am always alone. If you feel you cannot visit me, go ahead and curse at me. It makes no difference. I'm only a miserable young lady.

My brother wrote to me. He is visiting next Sunday. I have nothing else to tell you. I'm sending you a thousand hugs and warm kisses.

Yours Forever,
Rosina

Chapter Nine

I Disorsi Della Citta
(The Talk of the Town)

July 17, 1921
Rush Hospital for Consumption and Allied Diseases
Philadelphia, Pennsylvania

News that I had been near death must have spread throughout the neighborhood because the very next Sunday, my Aunt Isabella sat by my bedside in tears.

"I had a vision of the Virgin Mary," I told her. "At first, I mistook her for a nurse, but then I noticed she wasn't wearing the uniform. She had on long, flowing blue robes and a crown. And there was a golden light that gleamed from above her head. It had to be her."

Aunt Isabella swiftly made the sign of the cross. She finished by kissing her fingertips and throwing her hand upward, as if she were tossing the kiss to heaven. "Oh, my dear, I've been praying for your recovery. This morning after mass, I lit a candle at the base of the Virgin Mary statue for you." Placing her hand on mine, she added, "This is a sign. You're going to get better."

"I hope." I pressed myself up into a seated position.

"Have you written to your father?" she asked. "He needs to know you're hospitalized."

I took a deep breath. I only wanted to write good news to my father. I couldn't bear thinking of him worrying himself sick so far away. "I'll write him when I'm fully well again."

"You wouldn't want him to hear about all this from anyone else," Aunt Isabella warned.

I was about to ask if there was something I should know when I spotted Gianni walking toward us, carrying a small container.

Aunt Isabella turned to see where I was looking. "And who are you, visiting my Rosina? And you come with a gift?"

"Aunt Isabella!" I chastised, sitting up fully. "You be nice to him. This is Gianni. Remember, I told you about him. You know his Aunt Carmela."

Gianni shuffled the container between his elbow and his side to free his hand. Holding it out, he said, "Nice to meet you."

Aunt Isabella remained still, as if trying to determine whether she approved of him. "So, are you planning to eat all those yourself?" she asked, pointing to the container, which held strawberries and a variety of other fruits.

"Oh, no, please, have one," Gianni hurried to say. "Have them all. Or, well, save some for Rosina. I brought them for her."

I had never seen him so nervous. My heart softened as I suppressed a smile.

Aunt Isabella broke into a hearty laugh. "I like this one," she told me. "He treats you well. Brings you gifts. Wants to take care of you." She kept laughing as she looked Gianni up and down. "And he's handsome, too."

I couldn't hold back my amusement, covering my mouth as I giggled. Poor Gianni's cheeks flushed.

Before he had a chance to recover, Aunt Isabella asked, "Would you be so kind as to walk me out? Then you can have Rosina all to yourself."

"Of course." He set the fruit on the small table beside the bed. Aunt Isabella bent to give me a tender hug. Over her shoulder, Gianni shot me a desperate look, but there was no rescuing him now.

While they were gone, I leaned into my pillows. Aunt Isabella seemed like she wanted to warn me about someone. What was being said about me around the neighborhood? If I had one guess, it would be that Nicola wasn't crying over my hospitalization. She must have been quite satisfied that I might have become as miserable as her now. The good mood I'd been in since meeting Gianni had seemed to inflame her dislike for me. I could only imagine what she might be saying to people, including my brother.

Gianni returned briskly to my bedside and dropped into the chair vacated by Aunt Isabella.

"Welcome back," I told him with a broad smile.

He grinned at me. "Every time I see you, you look more beautiful."

My heartbeat sped with his words. Still, I argued, "You're too kind. I hardly look presentable in this hospital bed. Today is one of the first days that I haven't felt awful."

"How about eating something?" he asked gently.

"Maybe later," I said, looking at the fruit he brought. My stomach still throbbed with soreness from the poison.

"I know you're feeling terrible, but please try." Gianni reached for the basket. "You can't get better unless you eat more."

I sighed, reached into the container, and pinched a cool, plump strawberry between my fingertips.

He smiled briefly, but then turned serious. "There's something I need to tell you." My breath stilled with uneasy anticipation. Gianni dropped his gaze as he explained, "I can't stay long today, and I'm not sure if I can see you next Sunday. I belong to a club, and there may be some things I need to do."

I dropped the uneaten strawberry back into the basket. A fresh wave of nausea washed over my insides. I'd known it was only a matter of time before Gianni would tire of visiting me in this hospital bed, but I didn't want him to see how much it upset me. "I don't care," I said with a carefree shrug. "Come and go whenever you want."

Gianni looked as if he was about to say something, but he was interrupted by a young feminine voice calling out, "Oh, Rosie! You poor thing!"

"Antoinetta!" In my excitement, I sat fully upright and raised my arms to hug her. As we pulled apart, Gianni eyed me, probably confused by my newfound energy. He offered Antoinetta the single chair beside the bed.

She thanked him and perched on the edge. "Everyone's talking about how you have a terrible disease and that you're on your deathbed. I told them it can't be true. Tell me it isn't true!"

Once I convinced her I wasn't as sick as she feared, Antoinetta plunged into stories from home. "Rosie, you will not believe everything you missed at the factory. We got a new boss, and this one is worse than the last. Oh, and you'll never guess who called the house after another one of Aunt Carmela's parties last Saturday night." Antoinetta emphasized her words with wide hand motions.

Gianni took two steps to the side to give her room. He looked less than pleased. After tracking down a second chair for himself, he selected a strawberry from the basket and bit into it. Fortunately for him, Antoinetta didn't stay for very long. Once her stories had all run their course, she stood to leave, wishing me well.

"You seemed so happy to see her," Gianni commented sullenly.

"She's my friend. Of course, I was excited she came to visit," I replied, meeting his gaze.

"Do you even want me here?" Gianni crossed his arms over his chest. "Or am I a bother?"

"Oh, Gianni," I whispered. I dropped my eyes as my cheeks flushed with heat. How could he think that I didn't want him by my side? As much as I enjoyed talking with Antoinetta, Gianni should have known by now that I most looked forward to his visits.

I opened my mouth, searching for the right words to make him understand how important he had become to me. It was all there, sitting on the tip of the tongue. But the words, perhaps afraid of another rebuttal, remained unspoken.

"All I want is to see you healthy again," Gianni said, taking my hand. "I wish I could be here day and night, encouraging you, helping you, making you better."

Our hands fit so perfectly together that I didn't want to let go. I knew Gianni's visit was coming to an end, and I wanted to hold on for as long as I could. How I wished he could be here with me as he said, day and night!

"I want that, too," I admitted.

"But I have to go," Gianni said softly, releasing my hand. "You know I don't want to leave you, but I have other obligations."

I nodded as if I understood and stared at my hand, now empty of his. How long would it be before he held my hand again? How many days and hours would I sit here alone, missing him until we were together again?

The soft warmth of Gianni's lips on my cheek took my attention off my empty hand. I tried to smile, but it only reached the corners of my mouth. My eyes remained heavy with the sorrow of missing him before he even left.

With the heat of his kiss lingering on my cheek, Gianni stood and straightened his shirt. "Promise you'll write and take good care of yourself," he said.

"I'll try."

My eyes clung to him, memorizing every detail as he turned to leave. On his way out, Gianni pushed open the door to allow someone new to enter my room.

"That guy," Tomasso said, motioning toward the door after he had greeted me with a light hug. "You know him?"

I nodded, glancing toward the fruit basket.

"Where'd you get all this?" Tomasso asked. "From him?"

The heartache I had felt with Gianni's departure was replaced with frustration at my brother's perturbed tone. He seemed more interested in who was visiting me than my health. Despite my annoyance at his intrusive questions, I couldn't stop beaming as I spoke about Gianni. "His name is Giovanni, or, well, John. He's learning to be a shoemaker. We met at the party."

Tomasso took a seat. "And he's not afraid to visit you since you've become so sick?"

"I'm going to get better and leave here," I told him, sitting up and straightening my posture.

Tomasso shook his head as if he wasn't quite as sure, resting his elbows on his knees with his hands clenched together. He reminded me so much of our father, the way he held the weight of all his burdens on his shoulders. As much as I didn't want our father to know how sick I had been, I also longed for him to be here by my side.

"You realize you've had this fever for quite some time. And you're not eating properly." Tomasso stared at his hands. "Everyone is stopping me and asking about you. They're all worried. And for good reason." He paused and looked at me. "Your doctor is concerned that you may have tuberculosis."

I gasped. The doctor had mentioned tuberculosis but seemed more inclined to believe that I had an infected tooth. Tuberculosis, known as consumption because it consumed a person's body to its ultimate demise, wasn't a diagnosis to be delivered lightly. "The doctor isn't exactly sure what's wrong with me," I insisted.

"I don't know what to do. I want to offer you your room back once you're well enough, but I can't risk you infecting us."

"How can you say such a thing?" My stomach betrayed me, tightening to the point that I might have vomited. It was that medicine. I was still certain they were trying to kill me with it. And now, here was my own brother accepting my inevitable demise as truth.

"It's your symptoms. And, well, you were working with a lot of people in close proximity at the factory. It just seems possible."

"Just because it seems possible doesn't make it true," I said, my voice rising higher with each word.

He tossed his hands in the air and shook his head. "I don't want to upset you."

"Well, that's exactly what you're doing," I said with more force than I'd thought I had in me. My head swam with dizziness. I squeezed my eyes shut and pressed my palm against my forehead, willing it to go away. I wanted everything to go away, especially this illness.

Whatever it was, it wasn't tuberculosis. It couldn't be. When I'd been so sick that I could barely function, I hadn't been plagued by coughing or chest congestion. Wasn't that one of the main symptoms of tuberculosis, a nagging cough? I wished I knew more about the disease, other than that it killed too many innocent people. Maybe I really was next. My brother certainly seemed to believe that.

"Please, Rosina," Tomasso said in a soft voice. "The doctor called on the telephone. Nicola spoke to him. She's concerned about you, too." I wanted to tell him the only thing Nicola was concerned about was keeping me out of her house, but Tomasso continued, "On the phone, he explained what could be wrong with you, what could be causing you to have this fever. He said your condition is serious. And he did mention tuber—" Tomasso cut himself off, perhaps thinking better of mentioning it again.

I lifted my hand off my forehead and punched it into the mattress, glaring at my brother. "Fine. Believe what you want."

"Maybe I shouldn't have come."

I dropped my gaze to the floor on the opposite side of the bed.

"I'll be on my way and let you rest," he said.

I slid my right hand up to grasp the cross dangling from my neck as Tomasso's heavy footsteps strode out of the room. As infuriating as the conversation had been, I dreaded the sense of loneliness that would follow his departure.

The door closed with a bang. I imagined Nicola slamming her own front door in my face.

My safety and security in this new country depended on Tomasso's willingness to open his home to me. My illness had given Nicola every reason to deny my return. Much like my father, my brother was entirely unwilling to stand up to his wife on my behalf. It felt all too familiar, that pain of being cast aside, the shame of feeling abandoned. Although my day had been full of visitors, I had never felt more alone.

CHAPTER TEN

ÈFINITA!
(IT'S OVER!)

July 31, 1921
Rush Hospital for Consumption and Allied Diseases
Philadelphia, Pennsylvania

Dear Gianni,

I would like to know the reason you haven't come to see me anymore. I, thank the Lord, feel much better. I need you no more. God will give me strength and health. I don't need anybody. Maybe you thought you were going to catch the disease, and that's the reason you didn't come. So, listen to me, dear, if you think I will not forget you, you are wrong! I have already forgotten you. I understand everything now. One day you'll regret it. You think I am going to die. No way! I hope to live a few days yet to spite all those who hate me.

So, my dear Gianni, do not think I write you out of anger. As God is my witness, I only write to you for the promises you made me. Somehow, I knew those words were all lies. As for the one bouquet of flowers you once sent me, I'll send them to you when you get married.

I also want you to know I was bedridden for eight days. But, thank God, I feel much better. As soon as I regain my strength, I will go for sea bathing. The doctor wanted to send me now, but I am too weak.

So, I will stop now. My hand is unsteady, and I am making too many mistakes. I have written this letter to you like a child, only to let you know how I feel. I don't want an answer from you. I will not accept your letter. I will send it back to you. I've had enough of your bad deeds. If you didn't want to come, you could have at least sent me a letter, which I am waiting for, just like I am waiting for my recovery.

I do not want to bother you any longer. I send you my last greeting.

Rosina

P.S. It's over!

July 31, 1921
Ardmore, Pennsylvania

My Dear Rosie,

    I was not able to come and see you today because of the heavy rain. You can imagine how disappointed I was. I was about to leave when it began to rain cats and dogs. Maybe it was a sign for me to stay home. I hope you're not angry with me. Did anyone see you today?

    My love, I hope you're getting better. My heart is broken knowing you are suffering. If I could, I would be with you day and night, always encouraging you. But this cannot be, for where I work, I have no vacation time like people have in factories.

    All my life, I never had so much faith in God and never prayed so heartily as I do now for him to perform a miracle and heal you. I will be the happiest man in the world when you come out of the hospital. Even if you do not love me, I would be happy just seeing you happy and in good health.

    Antoinetta sends her regards. And from me, receive my dearest regards from the bottom of my heart, an embrace, and a thousand fervent kisses.

I Am Yours Forever
John

P.S. When you receive this letter, please kiss it, as I have done a few times.

August 7, 1921
Rush Hospital for Consumption and Allied Diseases
Philadelphia, Pennsylvania

Last Sunday, I waited the entire day for a visitor, and not
one person walked through the hospital doors, not even my
Gianni. Two days later, a nurse handed me his sorry letter, but it
was too late. By then he had certainly received my own letter.
Hopefully, he regretted blaming a little rain for not visiting me.
And if he thought he could see me today, he'd be in for a shock.
He wouldn't find me in the hospital.

"You're being moved to a different room. I think you'll
like it better," Dr. Masterson had told me this morning. "Since
your fever has not returned for over a week, I changed your status
to 'good condition.'"

All the frustration of being trapped in this hospital
pounded like a drum in my head. I both needed to know and feared
the answer to the only question that truly mattered. "What about
my diagnosis?"

Dr. Masterson studied the chart in his large hand. The top
of his shiny bald head pointed toward me. I held my breath as I
waited for his answer. Shifting his considerable weight forward in
the chair beside my bed, he said, "It does appear you're recovering
well. Your chest x-ray looked clear. However, we can't rule out
tuberculosis because of your history of factory work and of
attending multiple crowded parties." He looked at me over his
glasses. "Which I confirmed when I telephoned your brother's
house."

I wrinkled my nose, imagining Nicola answering the call.
I had gone only to that one party. Was this what she was spreading
around the neighborhood? I considered correcting the doctor, but
I doubted he would believe me. He might think I was desperately

making excuses for my past behavior. I had no way to prove I was telling the truth. And even if he did believe me, there was little chance it would change anything.

"I would like you to remain here a few more days so we can monitor you. It's still a real possibility that you could have a setback." Removing his glasses and rubbing his eyes, he added, "There's something else I need to discuss with you."

I didn't like the gravity in his voice. I was sure he was going to tell me I had only days to live. Although, that wouldn't make sense since I was indeed nearly fully recovered.

"When I spoke to your brother," Dr. Masterson continued, replacing his glasses and sliding them up the bridge of his nose, "he told me that he had young children and that he feared you could be contagious. I told him you have no outward symptoms and that the possibility of you being infectious was low. Unfortunately, I couldn't assure him that it was impossible." Dr. Masterson paused and looked directly at me. "I highly doubt you'll be welcome where you were living."

I gasped. How could my brother turn his back on me? Despite our last conversation, I didn't want to believe he'd actually have it in his heart. And yet, it seemed my brother couldn't care less that I was about to be cast homeless onto the streets.

"So," Dr. Masterson said in a commanding voice, refocusing my attention on him. "I have two options for you." Holding up his pointer finger, he said, "Either find a new place to live on your own, where you would have little to no interaction with others, or"—he flipped up his second finger—"we have a facility in the country, a sanitorium, where we send patients diagnosed with tuberculosis. It would not be my preferred recommendation. However, you would qualify to be admitted there, if you so choose."

"The country?" I dropped my gaze and smoothed my palms, now damp with sweat, along the tops of my thighs. The country would be far from everything and, more importantly, everyone I knew. I'd be far from Gianni. I hadn't really meant that it was over between us. But the extra distance might become the obstacle that truly tore us apart.

"Is there any other family member you can discuss this with?" Dr. Masterson asked kindly.

"Well, there's my aunt, but I don't think she's visiting me today. And she doesn't own a telephone." I had to find a way to see Aunt Isabella. I imagined my aunt coming home from mass, changing into more comfortable clothes, and getting to work in her tight kitchen to prepare a large Sunday dinner. If I could see her and explain my circumstances, maybe she would figure out a way to help. Maybe one of my cousins had recently moved out, leaving behind an empty room. It was only a short distance from my hospital room to her doorstep. If I could persuade the doctor to let me see her, maybe I wouldn't have to be sent away to yet another hospital. "My aunt lives within walking distance of here. It's only a couple blocks away. Just up Broad Street."

Dr. Masterson leaned back in his chair and steepled his fingers. "I could arrange for you to be released for a few hours this afternoon. You'll need to keep your distance and limit your interactions with other people. Meet only with your aunt and return immediately. Like I said, your infection risk is low, but it's not out of the question. I wouldn't normally allow this, but your living situation needs to be sorted." He nodded decisively. "Yes. Visit your aunt and discuss your options. Very good."

After making a note on my chart, Dr. Masterson handed the clipboard to a nurse. She looked me over, then said, "Looks like you're on the move. It's a hot day out there. Dress light."

All I had to leave the hospital in was the one dress I had worn when I arrived here back in June. The thin cotton was light, as the nurse had advised, but what I had to discuss with my aunt felt heavy as a winter coat.

CHAPTER ELEVEN

QUESTA CASA È UNO ZOO!
(THIS HOUSE IS A ZOO!)

August 7, 1921
Broad Street
Philadelphia, Pennsylvania

I couldn't even begin to describe how invigorating it was to leave the hospital under my own power. As I walked along the sidewalk toward Broad Street, it felt as if I was breaking out of prison. On the short walk north, I became a member of society again. The other people walking past me didn't act like I was a malicious carrier of a contagious disease, which I certainly was not. They had no idea I had ever been hospitalized. No one gave me a second glance, but the invisibility was a comfort.

About twenty minutes later, I stood on the familiar street corner near my aunt's house. I nearly cried. The last time I'd been here, the leaves had barely appeared on the trees lining her block. Now it was a hot, humid summer day, with big green leaves providing much-needed shade from the oppressive sun.

I wiped the sweat off my brow as someone called my name.

"Rosina! Rosina, is that really you?"

I turned to see one of my cousins, Gina, running toward me. "It is you!" She clasped her hands to her mouth. "I thought you were on your death bed. How is it that they let you out of the hospital? Aren't you still contagious?"

"I'm fine," I said, holding out my hands with my palms facing outward as if to show her I wasn't marked by a horrible disease. "I need to speak with Aunt Isabella. Is she home?"

"She's probably in the kitchen. Wait here. I'll go get her." Gina dashed up the steps and disappeared into the house.

I stayed in place on the sidewalk, not entirely welcome in my own aunt's house. A light breeze brought some relief from the oppressive heat. It carried the savory aroma of the meal Aunt Isabella must have been preparing. I peered at the house, searching for signs of my aunt. In one of the second-floor windows, shadowy figures watched me. When I waved, the figures receded, replaced by a swinging curtain. My cousin's question from moments ago echoed in my mind. *Aren't you still contagious?*

Aunt Isabella came out to her porch. She wiped her hands on a dishtowel as she greeted me. "Rosina, it is you. I didn't believe Gina when she said you were here. But look at you. You're dressed and walking around. It's a miracle!" She dabbed her eyes with the dishcloth as she wept in relief.

After she had collected herself, Aunt Isabella took a moment to study my face. Her beaming smile faded. "What's wrong? Something is wrong. I can see it. Come inside, so we can talk."

"Thank you," I said, glad to leave the spotlight of the hot sun.

Aunt Isabella held open her front door, which led directly into her living room. I walked inside a few steps and stopped. The small room appeared cluttered. A rancid odor mingled unharmoniously with the fragrant scents of Aunt Isabella's cooking.

Removing a blanket from the couch, she patted the cushion and demanded, "Here. Sit. Talk to me."

I followed her orders, moving a pillow out of the way before I took a seat.

"Stay here. I'll get us a couple of glasses of ice-cold lemonade and then we'll talk." Aunt Isabella gathered up the pillow and blanket while yelling to one of my younger male cousins to come put them away. The distant hope of room for me in this house quickly faded with the realization that the couch where I now sat had been someone's bed last night.

I leaned into the cushions in dismay, and something jabbed into my back. Turning to inspect what it was, I discovered a dog bone. Aunt Isabella had three small dogs, who at the moment were all in the backyard creating a ruckus, barking and yipping. I tossed the bone to the floor among the other clutter of discarded mail, old newspapers, and mismatched shoes.

When Aunt Isabella returned with two glasses dripping with condensation, she stepped over the mess on the floor, commenting, "This house is a zoo, and zoo animals live here!" Taking a seat in an armchair beside the couch, she handed me my drink. "So, talk to me. How is it that you're out of the hospital? You should be thrilled, but I can tell something is troubling you, dear."

"The doctor only allowed me to leave for this afternoon so I can see you. I have a difficult decision to make, but I'm afraid it's already been made for me." I stared at the ice cubes floating in my lemonade, trying to find the words to explain that my own brother had abandoned me.

"Nicola's not going to let you back in her house," Aunt Isabella concluded. "Is she?"

I could only nod.

"Mm-hmm, I heard her running her mouth about you last week at the market. She's going around telling people you were always out at parties, drinking too much. That you were an ungrateful house guest who never lifted a finger to help with the chores or the expenses. And," Aunt Isabella said in a low voice, "she said it was your own doing that got you so sick. And now she doesn't want that awful disease coming into her house."

No wonder Gina had acted afraid of me and none of my other cousins had come to greet me. I pressed my palm to the top of my head, so angry I felt like it could explode. "You know those are all lies."

"So, what now?" Aunt Isabella asked, letting out a long sigh. "You can't stay at that hospital forever. I wish I had an open bed to offer you here. But you're certainly welcome to stay if you have no other options. At least you would have a roof over your head."

"I know. Thank you. But I'm afraid that you have too many people living here." I rubbed my temple, trying to ease the overwhelming tension.

"That's true." Aunt Isabella shifted in her seat, glancing toward the staircase in the far corner of the room. In a hushed voice, she informed me, "Your cousin, Gina, just found out she's expecting. Perhaps it may not be a good idea for you to stay here in case you may be a bit contagious."

The insinuation that I could be a danger to others constricted every muscle in my body. I wanted to protest and make a case for my renewed health. But I didn't know for certain if I was fully free of infection. Instead, I plowed forward, explaining my situation with the hope that Aunt Isabella would come up with a viable solution. "The doctor made it clear that either I must live on my own or there's a sanitorium in the country where I could go. They house people diagnosed with tuberculosis there. The doctor said it's an option for me."

"You don't want to go there!" Aunt Isabella slid forward in her seat, leaning toward me. "Really sick people go to those places. What if you catch what they have and get sick all over again? You can't do that!"

"But where else can I go? That's why I came here today. I need your help." I pictured myself homeless, wandering the streets of Philadelphia, or boarding a ship back to Italy. Tears welled in my eyes. I would be leaving all my hopes and dreams behind. Worst of all, I would be leaving Gianni. My chest tightened as if a hand gripped my heart, desperately trying to hold the broken pieces of it together.

Aunt Isabella placed her hand on her mouth as she thought. "What about that nice fella who brought you all those gifts the day I came to visit? He certainly seemed serious about you. Maybe wedding bells are in your future. That would solve everything."

"Oh." I bit my lower lip. "You mean Gianni?" My cheeks burned with heat at the revelation that she had noticed Gianni's affection for me. "He hasn't come to visit me for a few weeks." Regret and shame weighed heavily on my shoulders. "I got angry and wrote that it was over between us."

Aunt Isabella pointed at me. "Well, you write him back and tell him you were mistaken."

"I don't know," I said quietly. How could I explain the conflict in my heart? What had started out as a beautiful love story had grown sick with my own illness. How I wished I could go back to that day at the amusement park. I would give anything to be able to relive the excitement and the rush of attraction from that day. Had I never fallen ill, Gianni and I could have made memories this summer that were fun and lighthearted. Now all we had was a brief love affair that felt like a distant daydream followed by a nightmare. No wonder Gianni was finding excuses not to see me. If I were in his position—a young, desirable, hardworking man—would I want to spend my free time sitting next to a hospital bed?

"I don't care what it takes," Aunt Isabella said, shaking her finger at me. "I liked that young man. He had a real steady head on his shoulders."

"We never discussed marriage." Maybe if I had been healthy all this time, our relationship would have progressed to discussing the future. And if Gianni had proposed to me? Would I have told him yes?

"I can tell you have strong feelings for him," Aunt Isabella commented, emphasizing the word *strong* as a warm and knowing smile spread across her face. The heat of the room, or most likely the intensity of my deepest desires about a future with Gianni, made my head spin. I took a long sip then placed the cold glass against my forehead.

"We need to get you back to the hospital," Aunt Isabella said quietly. "That's enough worrying for one day. Trust in the Lord. It'll all work out."

I wanted to tell her all the prayers in the world hadn't helped so far, but I felt guilty even thinking it. Instead, I thanked her for the lemonade, and she gave me fare for the trolley so I wouldn't have to walk.

Outside her doorway, the heat of the day pressed against my skin, blanketing me with defeat. What had I expected from my aunt? Did I honestly believe she could change my brother's mind? Was I foolishly dreaming Aunt Isabella would produce a living space for me out of thin air, one which my doctor would approve?

Her only suggestion was to marry Gianni. If only it was that simple. But my feelings for Gianni and the present state of our relationship were tied up in a complicated knot of emotions that I didn't have the strength to untangle at the moment. Especially now that all the misguided hope I'd had for this visit was gone.

"I wish I could do more for you, dear," Aunt Isabella called to me as I waved to her from the sidewalk.

The genuineness of her words did little to stem my growing disappointment. While my escape into the outside world had been reinvigorating, it only made me dread my return to the hospital that much more. I had no viable solution to offer my doctor. My stomach twisted with unease. Where would I go once I was released? Was I truly out of options other than a sanitorium far off in the country?

And still, in the face of all that, I wondered: did I have any hope for a future with Gianni?

CHAPTER TWELVE

UNA DONNA FORTE
(A STRONG WOMAN)

August 7, 1921
Rush Hospital for Consumption and Allied Diseases
Philadelphia, Pennsylvania

In my new hospital bed, I kept going over my discussion with Aunt Isabella. My thoughts jumped from her revelations of the lies being spread about me to the implication that I might be contagious. And Gianni.

She had been right about one thing: I did have "strong" feelings for him. For the past several weeks, I hadn't allowed myself to admit it. But now I could clearly see that I loved Gianni from a place deep in my soul. If only I hadn't written that angry letter! I had wanted to scare him into not taking my affections for granted, and to protect myself from inevitable heartbreak. Now I doubted I'd ever get over my love for him.

I decided to write him again. Would he give me a second chance? If he did, the next time he visited I would explain how I was being sent far away.

Perhaps I could find out if his plans for the future included me. I hoped he'd be willing to discuss such serious matters, since it seemed far too soon in our relationship to bring up marriage. Gianni may feel pressured and pull away from me.

If only he were here now. Perhaps he would sit beside me, telling me not to worry, or even that he loved me as much as I loved him—that he'd find a way for us to be together. Why had I been so impulsive as to declare it was over between us?

A hand waving from the bed beside mine broke my concentration. I had been staring toward the opposite wall, so deep in thought, the room had gone out of focus. Now I blinked rapidly and zeroed in on the owner of the hand.

"You look like you have the weight of the world on your shoulders," the young woman commented.

I laughed wryly, shaking my head. "You have no idea."

"Care to unload your troubles? I'm stuck here, and I just might die of boredom. You'll be saving my life, and maybe in return I can help you." The woman turned to fully face me. "I'm Maria, by the way."

"Rosina, but everyone calls me Rosie."

"Nice to meet you, Rosie. So, what's so awful that you're staring a hole into that wall?" Maria asked, pointing across the room.

I laughed again and plunged into my whole sad story. I began with the tragic death of my mother, described the harsh reality of life with Seraphina, and ended with how my wimp of a brother and his vindictive wife had turned their back on me. Then I filled her in on the highs and lows of my love affair with Gianni.

"Well," Maria said, "first of all, I certainly got my money's worth. About your so-called boyfriend, I wouldn't put all my eggs in that basket."

"I don't know if he'll even respond to the letter I'm going to write," I said, falling onto my pillow and gazing at the ceiling.

"Well, it's definitely worth a shot." Maria let out a long sigh. "Maybe I'm the wrong person to ask. This heart of mine has been broken too many times to place all my hopes on a man. Sometimes a girl has to look out for her own best interest."

I nodded in agreement, hoping it wouldn't come to me finding my way in the hospital system all on my own. "I suppose you have a point."

"After that story, you seem like you'll be fine no matter what happens. I can tell you're a strong woman like me," Maria said with a proud grin. Then she shared her own story of heartache and triumph, followed by more sorrows. As she spoke, I felt a little less alone in my suffering and a bit less burdened. I couldn't have been more grateful.

Later that evening, when I set my pen to the writing paper Gianni had bought for me, I thought back to our first kiss. It had felt as if I could make a home inside his arms forever. The risk of losing Gianni was so much more than a broken heart. A beautiful life together was at stake as well. I could picture it all so clearly: the modest house, my own kitchen to prepare the loveliest of meals with ingredients from our plentiful garden, and the children—lots of round-faced, adorable babies to fill our house with love and joy. It felt so real in my dreams, yet still so far from my reality.

With the possibility that I may be sent away to the country, it was urgent that Gianni knew how I felt for him in my heart. I couldn't leave without him knowing the truth.

August 7, 1921
Rush Hospital for Consumption and Allied Diseases
Philadelphia, Pennsylvania

Dear Gianni,

At first, I did not want to accept your apology for not visiting me when it was raining, but my aunt convinced me to reconsider. I want you to know, dear, I had already forgotten about you. I was not thinking about you at all. When I heard my aunt's words, I was moved. You certainly don't deserve a second chance. However, this time, I forgive you. But I urge you not to fail me again. I have grown frail, and every little thing hurts me.

Hear me, Gianni, I love you more than life. It was your love that comforted me through my illness and made those days go by so fast I hardly noticed them. But when I had not heard a single line from you, I was shattered. Days seemed like years. But you never gave a thought about your poor Rosina, so sick and bedridden.

My love, I want you near me always. I need you to comfort me and spend time with me in this hospital. I am all alone. I have no one. Gianni, can you imagine how upset I was when I wrote you that letter? I promise never to do that again. You should promise me the same. I did not deserve what you did to me. Because I love you fervently, I would not be able to live if you abandoned me. That is what love does to me.

I send you my dearest regards and a fervent kiss from my lips.

From Your Most Affectionate Lover,
Rosina

August 14, 1921
Boardwalk & Mississippi Avenue
Atlantic City, New Jersey

My Dear Rosa,

    It made me so happy to know you have returned to me, to love me. I will do everything possible to never anger you again. I'll think of ways to make you happy. I did not realize how much love I had for you until I read your last letter. It hurt and worried me so much that I had no rest. I wanted to die. If I had a choice, I would choose death over losing you. I cannot explain how I have come to have this great love for you. Believe me when I tell you I am sure I love you. You cannot imagine how happy I am that you are feeling better. I beg you not to overdo it. You must be careful. When I return from Atlantic City, I wish to see you well and always very happy.

    Have you ever been to Atlantic City? I am here for one week. I have to tell you, whatever a person wants, he can find it here. There is everything. They have the best entertainment anyone can desire. But I can't have any of it. When I think of the dearest person I have on this Earth lying ill in the hospital, it upsets me so much, I can't do anything. I know you won't believe me. The only pleasures I allow myself are swimming during the day and the theater in the evening. I used to love being young and having fun. With you sick and not by my side, I no longer find happiness in anything. If the Lord is willing, when you are well, you and I will come to Atlantic City. Even if you do not want to come, I will tie you up and drag you with me, whether we are married or not. You have no idea how I wish you were here.

    My love, try to be of good cheer. The day shall come for both of us to end our suffering and make up for all our lost time together. May the Lord give you the strength and courage to overcome your illness. My love, without you I cannot live happily in this life. Have no doubts, I will never abandon you. You must know you are not alone. I never allow myself to think that way, even when my life was in danger. When I fought in France, I always imagined I had a friend beside me. This wasn't just a person; it was the Lord. He protected me and guided me on the right path. And after a long time, I was granted the great joy of my life, to return home. You always have the good Lord who saved you from death. And please remember, you have me to protect you and make you happy in this life.

I wish you a speedy recovery and perfect health for thousands of days. Receive from me a thousand affectionate kisses.

Yours For Always,
John

Chapter Thirteen

Non Ho Scelta
(I Have No Choice)

August 21, 1921
Rush Hospital for Consumption and Allied Diseases
Philadelphia, Pennsylvania

Dear Gianni,

I received your loving and affectionate letter. I'm very happy to hear your long-awaited good news. You should know the doctor said my health has improved. He asked if I wanted to go home or to Malvern. I told the doctor I had no other option but to go to the country. Since there's no room yet, I'll be staying here a little while longer. I am comfortable as I can be for now and really don't care.

So, my dear Gianni, I cannot wait for next Sunday, to see you and speak to you face to face. Almost every night I dream of you. Then I wake up and realize it was only a dream, and I am left very sad. I cannot put on paper what I would like to tell you in person. In the meantime, I send you my most affectionate regards and a loving kiss.

From Your Loving
Rosina

August 21, 1921
Rush Hospital for Consumption and Allied Diseases
Philadelphia, Pennsylvania

Now that I knew what Nicola had been going around saying about me, I needed to face the fact that I would never return to my brother's house, no matter how much it pained me to accept this. My brother's loyalties remained committed to his wife. From the first day I set foot at their front door, Nicola hadn't wanted me to live with them. And now, I had given her the perfect excuse to expel me from her house.

Unfortunately, Nicola's disdain for me had spread like a virus, infecting other family members and friends who may, under different circumstances, have been willing to offer me a helping hand. The fear that I was contagious tainted every response to the desperate letters I sent nearly everyone I was either related to or had met in my brief time here in America.

My last hope lay with Antonietta coming through for me. I allowed myself to imagine the two of us sharing a room and spending each night staying up far too late talking. The setup would be perfect, especially since I'd be able to see Gianni often. Now that Gianni had written back to me with such love, our relationship could pick up where it left off in June.

When a nurse handed me Antonietta's letter, my heart raced with anticipation. I ripped it open with such enthusiasm that I tore off a corner. As I held the two pieces together, one in each hand, my eyes skimmed over her pleasantries as I searched for her answer.

When I found the phrase, "I'm very sorry," I dropped my hands and fell back onto my pillow. My vision blurred with my streaming tears. I let out jagged exhales. No one wanted me now that I had become ill. It was as if my sickness had become my identity.

Maria tried to console me, but the best she could offer was, "I wish I could help you out, but I've got my own problems."

When I had calmed enough to make out Antonietta's handwriting, I read her flimsy excuses for why I couldn't live with her. It all sounded familiar to the few other letters I had received in response to my pleas. Antonietta wrote that she would keep asking around, but I doubted she would find anyone willing to offer their home when she herself wasn't.

I met with Dr. Masterson and explained to him that I had failed to find a place to stay.

"That's most unfortunate," he replied in a somber tone. He explained that he would plan for my transfer to the sanitorium.

My breath hitched. What had seemed like an unlikely possibility was quickly about to become my reality. I had the sensation of falling despite being seated firmly in my hospital bed. My hands gripped onto a fistful of my sheets to keep me tethered as Dr. Masterson made notes on my chart.

When the doctor left, I wrote Gianni to let him know. My mind spun in circles. What would my life be like at the sanitorium? Perhaps I would enjoy the country setting. Or would I feel lonely and abandoned, so far from the city? Would Gianni be able to visit?

Would the distance cause him to forget about me?

My breath grew more rapid with each question. To steady myself, I focused on the window across the room. Outside, the warm, golden tones of the setting sun illuminated the buildings on the other side of the street. I reminded myself that for the moment I wasn't going anywhere. The transfer would take time.

I longed to see Gianni. I pictured him in Atlantic City, imagining that I had been by his side, walking along the sea. My arms ached to hold him. Instead, I pulled my knees up to my chest and hugged my shins, praying the days would pass quickly until we could be together again.

PART II

SECONDA PARTE

CHAPTER FOURTEEN

RIUNITA
(REUNITED)

August 28, 1921
Rush Hospital for Consumption and Allied Diseases
Philadelphia, Pennsylvania

It had been over a month since I last saw Gianni. In that time, I'd gone through a full cycle of emotions from hurt to anger to forgiveness and now, finally, to excited anticipation that we would be reunited.

"I've missed you," I said now, wrapping my arms around Gianni. He hadn't made it two steps into the room before I pounced on him. His body felt rigid in response. I'm sure he wasn't expecting me to be upright and dressed, especially considering how terrible I'd felt the last time he visited.

In the past month, my health had circled around for the better. No longer did I suffer from the persistent fever and the endless exhaustion that had accompanied it. My strength and energy had improved with each passing day, and I began to feel more and more like the young woman I had been before the infection had brought me to the brink of death. Although I'd become a bit thinner from the ravages of that awful medicine, it didn't show on my face, and my dress still flattered my shape despite being roomier around the waist.

It only took Gianni a few short seconds to recover from his shock. Wrapping his arms around me, he said, "I've missed you more than you'll ever know."

I inhaled his fresh scent and gripped his lean, muscular body. Closing my eyes, I indulged in the warm sensation of feeling at home in his arms. Here, I was safe and secure. For a moment, my uncertainties and worries ceased to exist. The two of us, finally together, was all that mattered. I didn't ever want to let go.

Finally stepping back, I noticed Gianni's face looked tanned from his week in the sun. Meanwhile, my own complexion must have paled from days spent trapped inside.

Together, we walked to a waiting room with upholstered chairs and carpeting that looked more like a living room than part of a hospital. I spotted a formal love seat against the wall and pulled Gianni's hand, leading him toward it. We each took a seat with our bodies twisted to face one another.

"You're so beautiful," Gianni said, smiling at me. Then, remembering what was in his hand, he held out a small white box. "These were my favorite when I was in Atlantic City." Opening the lid, he showed me a collection of cylindrical, pastel-colored candies. Like little gifts, they were each wrapped in wax paper with both ends twisted closed. I delighted at the sweet aroma. "They're saltwater taffy."

"Are they made with salt water?" I asked, pulling one out and rolling it between my fingers. The firm sweet smelled minty rather than salty.

"Maybe," Gianni said with a small laugh. "They scoop it right out of the ocean," he teased.

I frowned, thinking about Gianni enjoying himself outside in the fresh sea air while I laid in the stifling heat of my hospital room. "I don't like to eat too many sweets," I told him as my stomach soured with disappointment.

"Try it. You'll like it." He closed the box and set it aside, then took my hand. "I wish you could have come along with me."

I looked at our hands and nearly broke down in tears. I mourned the special moments we could have had together. I swallowed my sadness and whispered, "Me, too."

"I feel bad that I was away from you for so long. It wasn't my idea. My brother, Pat, insisted Aunt Carmela would be heartbroken if I didn't join the whole family. So I felt obligated. But I missed you the entire time."

Raising my eyes to his, I nodded. "Then make it up to me," I suggested in an upbeat tone. "Tell me everything you did. I want to feel like I was right there with you instead of stuck here, staring at the walls."

"Well, there's a wide, sandy beach. And the ocean has waves that aren't too big, which makes it perfect for going for a swim."

As I listened to Gianni, I unwrapped the taffy and took a bite of the chewy confection.

"I wish you were there the morning I woke up to watch the sunrise," he said. "It came right up over the water like a pink-and-orange fireball." He gestured to imitate the rising sun. I pictured the beautiful scene as the minty vanilla of the taffy dissolved in my mouth.

"Now, Atlantic City," Gianni said, "isn't like any place I've ever been. There are grand buildings lining the beach. And along the sand dunes, there's a wooden walkway called The Boardwalk. It's quite a place, with all the men dressed in expensive suits and the women in elegant dresses. I wanted so badly to be one of the couples walking arm-in-arm, with the ocean on one side and the entertainments on the other. You wouldn't have known which way to look!"

I laughed, imagining being right there with him. But a part of me couldn't forget where I had been. While Gianni had been gazing at the sunrise over the ocean, I was stuck in a hospital room, staring at the long crack in the ceiling above my bed. And hospital gowns were the only thing I got to see others wearing. I popped the last of the taffy into my mouth, hoping it would sweeten my mood.

Gianni continued his story, unaware of my envy. "I wasn't joking when I wrote that whatever people want, they could find it there. Prohibition may be the reality here in Philadelphia, but there, the law was more of a suggestion. And there were all these signs advertising something called a 'beauty contest' coming in September. I thought of you. If only you were well, I bet you could win it."

"And yet, here I was, stuck in this hospital room while you were off drinking and chasing beauty contestants." I didn't want to hear much more.

Gianni shook his head and laughed as if I had such a wonderful sense of humor. "Actually, I was more interested in the General Motors exhibit at the Steel Pier. They had so many new models of automobiles, you wouldn't believe it. A few were open for people to take a seat behind the wheel. I got in the Chevrolet 490 Touring, and it was incredible. Someday I'm going to save up enough to buy my own automobile. Then I'll put you in the passenger seat and drive you all the way to Atlantic City." He held out his hands as if he were grasping an imaginary steering wheel. "I'll drive you anywhere you want to go. No more waiting on the train or the trolley to arrive. It would be pure freedom." Dropping his hands, Gianni said in a softer voice, "You may have been far from me, but you were always right there with me in my thoughts."

"Oh, Gianni, it sounds wonderful," I said, not bothering to hide the sadness in my voice. "Right now, I'm not going anywhere." I paused, remembering my predicament. "Well, except maybe to that hospital in Malvern."

"I don't understand. You said in your letter that the doctor thought you were better." Gianni ran his hand over his chin, lost in his own thoughts.

"I can't stay in this hospital much longer, and my brother's house isn't the proper place for me to recover." I intentionally left out the part where Tomasso thought I was a contagious threat to his family. I didn't want Gianni to get the same idea about me. "If I had a quiet place with someone to take care of me, I'm sure I could go there." I pronounced each phrase slowly and clearly, hoping Gianni would get the hint.

Instead, he kept rubbing his chin and lifted his eyes toward his forehead. "I guess your Aunt Isabella's house isn't suitable either."

I sighed. "No. I went to visit her two weeks ago. She told me her house was a zoo, and she wasn't kidding. The doctor will never agree to me living there." Again, I left out that Aunt Isabella had feared I might pose a risk. If Gianni came to the same conclusion, he might want to keep his distance. My heart couldn't handle being far from him for too long.

"So," I continued, "I'm left with going all the way out to the country. It's going to be a much longer train ride to see me. You might forget all about me."

"Oh, no," Gianni said, taking both of my hands. "I'd never forget you, Rosie. I'll visit you. And I'll write you every day during the week. Is there anything you need? I'll bring it with me next time."

I shook my head. There was so much I wanted to say, so many questions I needed to ask, but I couldn't bring myself to do it. If I pressed Gianni to consider marriage, I might push him away.

"Please, Rosie, if you don't tell me, how will I know what you need?"

The very things I needed and wanted weren't actual things at all. After all we'd discussed today, he should have known that. He could change everything with a simple proposal. Then I wouldn't have to be sent away, and we wouldn't have to survive the distance between us. My heart ached at the thought of how little we'd see of each other.

"Please, Rosie. Let me take care of you. I just want to make you happy."

I sighed but refused to answer. I bit my tongue to prevent myself from saying, *I need you to take me out of here and marry me now.*

Gianni leaned into the armrest of the love seat and said in quiet, sullen voice, "Well, then, write to me. Write to me every day and make sure you tell me what you need."

"You're all I need, Gianni," I said, a wave of longing washing over me. "And even if I don't write you every day, you're always on my mind. I think of you constantly."

"Really?" Giovanni placed his hands into his pockets.

"You don't believe a word I say, do you?"

"Well, it's difficult when I ask you what I can get for you and you refuse to answer. There must be something I can do. I just want to make you happy, the way you make me happy. Why won't you let me do that for you? If you really have feelings for me, you should let me buy you anything you need."

"Fine. I'm almost out of writing papers." I smoothed my hair off my forehead and looked at the approaching nurse. Visiting hours were coming to an end. My heart raced. We were out of time. I wanted us to plan for a future together, but all Gianni could focus on was writing letters and promising to visit.

After he left, I prayed Gianni would realize he didn't want me to be transferred to Malvern. We'd lost so much time together already this summer. My heart wouldn't be able to bear the strain of more weeks apart.

CHAPTER FIFTEEN

VERO AMORE
(TRUE LOVE)

August 31, 1921
Ardmore, Pennsylvania

My Dear Rosie,

Please know, I had a great time with you. You looked so beautiful when I saw you, I didn't think you were sick at all. I missed you the moment I left and thought about coming back to you that same night.

On Sunday, you seemed truly like an angel descended from heaven. You appeared different than any other time I previously saw you. I don't know if my eyes deceived me or if the beauty I saw in you is true.

You have to promise me you will never forget me, and your lips will always be ready to give me a sweet kiss. It displeases me that when I come to see you, you don't kiss me. It's the first thing I think about when I come to see you. But you don't think about it at all. I would like to kiss you more than once and squeeze you tight to my chest. But I cannot, for there are many eyes that see me. Seeing you so close and not being able to touch you pains me.

My love, on the train while I was coming home, I saw young couples enjoying themselves. I began to cry, thinking my love was in the hospital. It hurts me to see you there when you could be with me having a good time, especially on Sundays. Instead, I have to deprive myself, alone like a dog. I know it's not your fault. I will be patient until you get better. The day will come when the Lord will allow us to enjoy ourselves and go anywhere we wish. I will take you anywhere you want to go. I will wait forever.

My love, since the first time I spoke to you, I believe you don't understand all the love I feel for you. I have not yet had the opportunity to express how much my heart yearns for you. I hope the Lord will heal you forthright, for you know that your wellbeing means my happiness. If you love me, all you need to do is write to me often and tell me all you think of me.

I hope when you reply, your letter will be so beautiful that I will treasure it in my heart forever. Meanwhile, I send you my dearest regards and a thousand soft kisses on your sparkling eyes.

Yours Forever,
John

September 1, 1921
Rush Hospital for Consumption and Allied Diseases
Philadelphia, Pennsylvania

Gianni,

This morning I received your very welcome letter. I felt such pleasure reading your words that I wasn't satisfied reading the letter only once. I read it three times before putting it down. Besides, the eloquence of your words is captivating. I love the way you express your thoughts.

My dear, I am going to tell you the whole truth. It's been three months that we have been madly in love. And I, being so sick, did not show it to you because I always thought I was going to die. But now that the good Lord has allowed me to recover, I want to tell you, I love you more than my very eyes. You are always on my mind, even at night, right here near me. You may not believe it, but this is the truth!

My love, to me, you are the most handsome man in the world. I believe there is no one like you on the face of the Earth. I have to confess, when I was sick, I did not see you that way. The illness took over my thoughts. But now, my love for you helps me see all that I was missing.

My love, you say when you visited me, I did not kiss you. Remember, I thought you did not want to kiss because I was sick. Believe me, I am very happy to kiss you. Do you remember when you took me to Willow Grove and when we went on the roller coaster, how scared I was? And when we took the boat ride and you kissed me for the first time? I remember everything. We were so happy. That first kiss touched my heart. Who would have imagined we would have to go through these hard days and be so far from each other? When you visit me, the hour flies. It seems like a moment. It feels as if we have been condemned for something. However, I believe that one day all this will be behind us and we will be together. If you marry me, rest assured you will have a good life with a good companion who will love you as long as you live. I will never betray you. I swear!

Thank you for the delicious candies you brought me. I'm sorry I can't return the favor. I am a prisoner of this place and trapped by my illness. But as soon as the Lord gives me freedom, my life will be yours. You can take me anywhere, and we can experience the burning, fervent love our hearts feel for each other.

My love, please come visit me on Sunday. I will get through these next days thinking of the hour we will spend together. I know I will cry when you leave. You are the person I hold most dear in my life. I can't even rely on my brother. He no longer thinks of me. Now I value your judgment and no one else's.

Receive from my heart a thousand fervent kisses from my lips to yours.

From Me, Who Loves You Forever,
Rosina

P.S. When your heart throbs, it's me!

September 4, 1921
Rush Hospital for Consumption and Allied Diseases
Philadelphia, Pennsylvania

"You have one hour," the nurse told me from behind Gianni, like I didn't know that after months in this place. She marked her clipboard and walked away with military-straight posture, as if her white uniform had been overly starched and her hair had been pulled too taut under her small cap.

In the bed next to mine, Maria performed a perfect impersonation of the nurse. I cupped my hand over my mouth to suppress a loud outburst of laughter. Maria's friendship had made everything about my impossible situation more bearable. I rolled my eyes at her and did my own impression of the nurse.

Gianni shook his head at our antics. "They're only looking out for your health. They don't want you to relapse."

"Please," I said, sitting up straight. "Look at me. Do I look like someone who's going to relapse?"

Gianni reached for my hand and said, "No, you look beautiful."

I smiled, even though I would have liked to have done more with my hair and perhaps added a swipe of lipstick. Still, his compliments were appreciated.

"And you look handsome," I said, taking in his hazel eyes, his warm smile, and his tanned skin. However, his cheeks didn't look as full, and his shirt seemed a size too big. "Gianni, you're getting too thin."

He shrugged. "I'm not much of a cook. Besides, I haven't been hungry lately."

"When I'm home with you, I'll cook for you and fatten you up," I told him, wishing that day would come sooner than later.

He smiled, but not as broadly as I'd expected.

"Gianni, what's wrong? Was it something I said?"

"No." His expression remained serious.

My chest tightened. Maybe he had changed his mind about me.

Casting his eyes downward, he explained, "I'm afraid my Aunt Carmela is very sick. I'm not sure what's wrong with her, just that she's been hospitalized. Not here. The one closer to her house."

At first, I felt relieved that his sullen mood wasn't about me at all. Then, a pang of sadness made my chest heavy as I remembered the night I first met Gianni and how genuinely warm and welcoming his aunt had been. "Oh, Gianni, I'm so sorry. I hope it's not as bad as it seems."

He nodded. "It's been difficult on the family, but there's a lot of people praying for her to pull through." With a smirk and a slight laugh, he added, "Everyone wants to see her being the life of the party again."

I nodded in agreement. I'd have liked to be at her next party.

"I don't want to make you sad," Gianni said, reaching into his jacket pocket. "So, close your eyes."

"Why?" I craned my neck to peer inside his jacket.

Gianni grinned, turning his shoulder away from me. "No peeking. I have something for you."

"What is it?" I asked before giving up. "Fine." Hesitantly, I placed my hands over my eyes.

"I usually bring you something to eat, but I didn't have time to stop, so I brought you this instead." I heard Gianni shift in his seat. "Okay, open your eyes."

I dropped my hands. He was holding up a photograph.

"I hope you like it. It was taken in the spring. I think I look different now," he said, flipping it to inspect it.

I took the photograph and held it up. In the black-and-white image, Gianni appeared strong and handsome. He had a slight, confident smile. "Oh, it's perfect!" I said, beaming at him. "Will you think I'm crazy if I tell you I'm planning to take it to bed with me and continuously kiss it?"

"Then I'm jealous of that photograph already," Gianni said with a wide grin, clearly pleased.

How long had it been since I'd actually kissed Gianni beyond a polite peck? Was he worried I might be contagious? "I guess kissing your photograph is safer anyway."

He leaned forward. A breath away, he brushed my hairline lightly with his fingers. In a deep and seductive voice, he said, "It would be well worth the risk."

I leaned closer. Just as my lips brushed his, a nurse cleared her throat. I startled and pulled back. He straightened in his seat. Why couldn't the nurse mind her own business?

Gianni sat with perfect posture like a well-behaved gentleman. With his back to the nurse, he smirked at me. "If we weren't here, I'd show you just how much I want to kiss you."

A rush of heat rose in my cheeks. "I feel the same way."

But a new thought crept into my mind. The nurse looming at the doorway meant the hour of visitation would soon disappear into thin air, and I still hadn't discussed an important matter with Gianni. "They have a room for me in Malvern," I told him.

I took a deep breath, trying to keep my composure. This hospital wasn't ideal, but at least Gianni was never that far. And I knew what to expect here. The new hospital would be much farther, with different rules. I had no idea how often I'd see Gianni or how our visits would be conducted. I studied his handsome features as if our impending separation might cause me to forget them, despite the photograph. "I'm leaving for the country in a day or two."

"Oh." Gianni's eyebrows shot up. "That's good, isn't it?"

"I'm not sure what's good anymore." I set the photograph inside my box of writing papers. I closed the lid firmly over it in case the nosy nurse decided I shouldn't have it. "It'll be different than sitting around here," I continued. "What other choice do I have? My brother won't let me return to his home." According to Aunt Isabella, Nicola hadn't stopped spreading rumors about me. Had any of her lies reached Gianni's family, who might pass them on to him?

His face grew serious again. Crossing his ankle over his knee, he told me, "I agree. Malvern is a better choice than your brother's house." With a shy smile, he added, "Of course, the best option would be to have you come home with me."

"Home with you?" I grinned, a flicker of hope rising within me.

"Well, I would," Gianni said with a shrug. "But I don't think my landlady would approve of me bringing home a girl. She might kick us both out into the street."

I dropped my gaze to my clasped hands as Gianni explained how, as an apprentice, he could barely afford the rent for a single room within walking distance of the Ardmore train station. Ultimately, it didn't matter if he could make more money. If we weren't married, living together wasn't going to happen. Not only would our families judge us, but I wasn't that type of woman.

"Someday I'll buy us a house where we both can live," Gianni said, straightening in his seat again. "It'll have to be small. I can't afford much. Would you be happy in a small house?"

"I'd be happy anywhere with you." I leaned against my pillow and closed my eyes, picturing a small house with a little front porch and a kitchen perfect for cooking my favorite meals.

"It makes me so happy just to imagine it," I said, reopening my eyes as newfound enthusiasm bubbled inside me. "I'll keep it clean and orderly, always. Oh, Gianni, a small house has been my life's dream. I promise it'll be as clean as a mirror."

Since this vision of the future existed only in my dreams, my smile faded. "I'm scared," I confessed, then paused, deliberating whether to continue. Admitting my fears would make me vulnerable. And yet, Gianni needed to face the fact that our situation would soon be drastically changing. "In a few days, I'll be in Malvern, all the way out in the country. It makes me nervous thinking that I'll be that much farther from you. Curse this illness and what it's done! What if I never return to the city?"

"Rosie, please stop," he said, grasping both my hands. "Maybe you'll like it."

I pulled my hands away. "Maybe you'll go off and find someone else who's more fun."

"Why would you say such a thing?" Gianni asked, his voice cracking a bit.

"I had a dream you were walking down Market Street with a girl," I told him, even though it wasn't a dream at all but an awful thought that kept me awake at night. I wanted to believe Gianni was dedicated to me, but how could I be sure when I had no way to know what he did after his visits with me? "Where did you go last Sunday after you left me? You said you were going to the theater. Which one did you go to?"

Gianni shook his head. "If I tell you, you won't believe me. As soon as I left you, I went home. I spent a few hours reading the newspaper and then went to bed thinking of you."

Part of me did believe him. But another part of me, the one so angry about my awful situation—with Nicola being like another Seraphina, my brother allowing my mistreatment just like my father had done, and Gianni acting sympathetic but offering no solutions—couldn't let it go. I crossed my arms. "Well, how can you explain my dream? When I come out of the hospital, you won't go out with those girls. Do you understand? When was the last time you got drunk? Listen, I don't like drunkards. If we get married, I don't want to be home alone. So, get rid of your bad habits now. Go to church instead and pray to the Lord for us."

"Now, you know I don't get drunk," Giovanni said, indignant. He shifted forward in his seat. "And after what happened in France during the war, I can't enjoy more than one drink a day."

"You've never been drunk? I don't believe you," I added, even though Gianni had never done anything to lose my trust. Well, not that I knew of, anyway, but he did have the freedom to come and go as he pleased. He could tell me all sorts of things, and I would never know any better.

"Once," Gianni answered. "Only one time, and it was for a bet to prove myself to my friends. It was right after I enlisted." His face perked up as he asked, "How about you, Rosie?" He pinched his chin between his thumb and fingers. He seemed to enjoy being able to turn the tables on me.

"I don't have time for drinking, cooped up in this awful place." The past three months, I might as well have been comatose. I wasn't living. I wasn't free to walk the streets hand in hand with Gianni, or attend a party, or do anything else.

Gianni held my stare with that boyish grin. Although I wanted to hang onto my mounting frustrations, his sweet expression made my heart melt. I didn't want to waste any more of our precious time indulging my sour mood. Guilt stabbed through me. I regretted implying I didn't trust him. He didn't have to spend his Sundays visiting me. I wanted so badly to grasp his cheeks in both of my hands and kiss him. Maybe I could go ahead and do it, strict nurse or not.

As if reading my mind, the nurse walked in our direction and tapped her clipboard with her pen. Gianni turned in her direction. When he turned back to me, his face had grown serious again.

"I'll write to you, and you do the same," he said, standing. "I'll miss you terribly. You have no idea how my heart aches when we're apart."

"Promise me you'll find a way to visit me in Malvern next Sunday," I pleaded. A bout of panic swept through me. What if he left me there, forgotten?

"I'll be there. I promise. I can never go long without seeing your beautiful face." Taking a step to leave, Gianni paused. "I hope my photograph keeps you company until then."

"I'll kiss it." I touched my fingers to my lips and blew the kiss toward Gianni.

Once he had stepped through the door and out of sight, a sob welled inside my chest. I pulled the covers over my head, covering myself entirely. I didn't want to be bothered even by the well-intentioned Maria.

Tucked inside a cocoon of sheets, with my knees pulled up to my chest, I released every bit of my misery. All the anger, all the sadness, and all the disappointment rose to the surface as if I were bringing it up and out of me like that poisonous medicine. I stayed like that until my eyes could no longer produce tears.

In three days, I would be far from here. The unease of not knowing what to expect rattled my insides. What would my life look like a week from now? How would Gianni and I survive the distance?

If I could have, I would have stopped time from moving forward. I'd have turned back the clock to spring. But all the wishing, praying, and hoping couldn't stop what had been put into motion. I recalled being on the roller coaster as it crested and paused ever so briefly before plummeting into the shadows below. The same anticipation gripped me now. At the amusement park, Gianni had remained by my side. Would he still be there when the tracks he'd have to ride would be far less thrilling?

September 6, 1921
Ardmore, Pennsylvania

My Dearest Rosie,

How many nice things I would like to tell you. Then I reflect. The time has not yet come. We will be reunited, and then we'll see the fruit of our suffering and the fruit of our love. I place my hope in the Lord and in you, my beloved. When we are finally home, alone in our beautiful little house, you will make me happy. I will be proud to have such a beautiful companion, and I will be full of love.

Monday, I had a terrible day. I was all alone. I desired many things, but I could not have them. I thought of you, my love, locked up in that hospital. It hurt so much. I wandered about aimlessly like a crazy man. I hated myself. I couldn't look at anybody's face. I got very angry.

I decided to go to a movie. There on the screen, I saw a couple who loved each other very much. After many trials, they got married. As I saw this, I began to cry like a baby. It seemed the tears were coming from my heart.

There is so much more I would like to tell you, but not on paper. I will wait for when the moment is right. I will visit you this Sunday in Malvern. In the meantime, I send you a thousand kisses.

Gracefully, I say,

Yours Forever,
John

CHAPTER SIXTEEN

NON SO DOVE MI TROVO
(I DON'T KNOW WHERE I AM)

September 8, 1921
Rush Hospital Country Branch
Malvern, Pennsylvania

My Dearest Gianni,
I am writing to let you know my health is well. Otherwise, I am very confused. I don't know where I am. I feel as if I'm in a cemetery. I have no one who loves me. I'm abandoned by everybody, and I do nothing but cry. It is useless that I am here, away from everyone. There are times I feel like poisoning myself. I don't know what to do. Here, I have to deal with so many wicked people. It's not like Philadelphia, where the workers were pleasant and easy to talk to. Here, I can't even ask a question. They are so haughty. The only thing I do is cry. My love, I urge you to visit me every week. If you abandon me, I will go crazy. I would have no one to comfort me and cheer me up. Please write to me as often as you can. Your beautiful words comfort and relax me.
My love, do not leave me. Think of me at least an hour a day as I do of you. I mean, you are in my thoughts every minute of the day. This is all I need. I believe your love has made me better. I have my health because I am so happy to be in love with

such a fine man. If anything happens between us, I would not want to live anymore. For today, my heart rests in yours, and I feel the beat of your heart.

My love, I find it useless to express myself on paper, for I get irate. These thoughts will make me sick again. I swear to you, I cannot write more. My tears just keep falling. Goodbye, my love! I send you a thousand ardent kisses.

Your Most Unfortunate,
Rosina

P.S. Please write to me immediately! When you write, use this address. Rush Hospital, Malvern. I can't wait for Sunday to spend all three of those hours with you. When you come, if you do not mind, I need two blouses.

September 11, 1921
Rush Hospital Country Branch
Malvern, Pennsylvania

The entrance to the hospital bustled with commotion. I scanned the foyer, searching among the many visitors for the one and only person who cared enough to travel such a distance to see me.

If only I could spot Gianni among the crowd! Maybe he had run into difficulty with the longer trip from the city. Malvern Station sat a few miles away. Gianni would need to secure a taxi to get here. More and more people flooded through the doors. They might have taken every taxi available. He could be stranded. Our hours of visitation would be lost. Or had Gianni changed his mind about visiting me at all?

A few days ago, the trip from Philadelphia had taken me well over an hour. The rush of being freed from my hospital room had lifted my mood. It had felt as if I were on an adventure.

Once we exited the city, an early morning fog shrouded my view of the passing scenery. When I arrived at the small, one-room station in Malvern, it seemed like another world. Rows of buildings and the constant rumble of automobiles were now replaced with the misty outline of trees and the repetitive call of crows. Even the scent in the air, a mixture of dew and decaying leaves, reminded me I was far from everything familiar.

The fog grew denser as my taxi traversed the curves of the country road. The stark stone construction of the sanitorium remained obscured until we were fully upon it. The grounds were dotted with large trees and neatly manicured shrubbery. As we climbed the concrete steps to the front door, the nurse accompanying me did not speak. The clacking of our shoes created jarring vibrations in the silence.

I shivered as I stepped inside the foyer of the sanitorium. The damp chill of the room cut through my light summer dress, so I wrapped my arms tightly across my chest. The nursing staff did not smile or make eye contact. A woman who I presumed to be a patient stared at me with a blank expression. I turned toward the heavy front doors, as if to leave with the same nurse who had brought me. Instead, the door slammed closed with a solid bang that shook the framed paintings of countryside scenes on the bleak gray walls.

Yet on this Sunday afternoon, this same space seemed transformed. Warm sunlight streamed in through the windows. Joy occupied the foyer now. I couldn't help but feel the same at spending three whole hours with Gianni. Around me, people were hugging and talking in excited voices. A young woman greeted an older one, calling, "Mother!" A pang of jealousy and longing gripped my heart. I looked away and back toward the door.

My heart skipped a beat. There stood Gianni! He craned his head back and forth, searching the room. He looked especially handsome in his best suit, the same one he must have worn to mass this morning. My heartbeat quickened at the sight.

Though I tried to maintain my composure, the tears began to flow as I ran to him. He must have had only a moment to recognize me before I threw my arms around him and held on for what seemed like endless minutes. My anxieties over being in this unknown, unwelcoming place overtook my reason. I wanted to cling to Gianni and never let go. I refused to release him until I could control what felt like an overwhelming flood of tears.

"Rosie, Rosie. It's okay. I'm here now," Gianni tried to soothe. "You've got to stop crying so I can give you what I brought for you. Please, Rosie, please."

With all the strength left in me, I eased my grip. Although my vision blurred with more tears begging to be shed, I attempted to smile at him.

"You see. There you are. My beautiful Rosina," Gianni said, producing a handkerchief and drying my cheeks. "Look. I brought you the blouses you asked for. Well, actually, I bought you four. I couldn't decide what you would like."

The sweet gesture made me laugh. "What would I do without you?" I didn't want to know the answer. My eyes clouded over as I resisted the urge to fall apart again. Instead I asked, "How was your trip out here? Was it difficult?"

"It was long. But on such a nice day, it was easy."

"I'm glad," I said, relieved it wasn't a terrible inconvenience to visit me.

"How about you show me around?" Gianni asked with a kind smile.

Together, we walked through the hallways to my room. I dropped off the blouses, but I didn't want to spend our visit stuck inside. Instead, I took Gianni down a staircase to a door that led to the outside and into the extraordinarily pleasant weather. It seemed as if summer had made plans to stick around for at least a little while longer.

Outside, I felt less like a prisoner and more like a young woman out for a walk with her love. With the sunshine, the blue skies, and Gianni by my side, I started to relax, grateful for his presence. As we walked, he took my hand and smiled at me. I leaned my head onto his shoulder and inhaled the fresh country air.

At a bench beneath a large tree providing much-needed shade, Gianni suggested, "How about we sit here? Maybe we can talk without so many people around us."

"It's much busier than I thought it would be," I said, taking a seat beside him. He had become so thin. It seemed as if he had lost more weight even since last Sunday.

"I haven't been feeling well," he admitted when I questioned him. "There's been a lot on my mind lately, that's all."

"Your Aunt Carmela? How's she doing?"

Gianni smiled at my remembering his aunt. "She's still in the hospital, and I'm not sure she's coming out anytime soon. She's well enough to receive visitors, but I haven't been over to see her yet." He shrugged. "Enough about me. How are you feeling? Are you still in good health?"

I sighed. "I feel terrible. All I do is sit around here missing you."

Gianni turned and placed his arm across the back of the bench. "Your mind is too focused on me. It's true, I do like that, and I can't help boasting about it. But," he said, taking a more serious tone, "you have to realize too much love right now can be harmful for you. You should be thinking only about your health and getting enough rest. And I don't want you crying anymore. Okay? Promise me you won't."

I narrowed my eyes at him. "You talk to me like I'm a child. You know I can't promise that I won't get upset anymore."

"Well, then, promise me no one will take your eyes," he said, shifting to face me. My expression softened as he continued, "I keep dreaming of when we'll have our own home. I'll spend all day staring at your beautiful eyes and then fall asleep in your arms."

My blue eyes had often elicited compliments from others, but no one's words affected me like Gianni's.

He looked toward the hospital building. "There's more men here than I expected."

"And that worries you?"

He shrugged.

I let out a small laugh. "Well, I don't worry about all the girls you go around with during the week."

"I told you, I don't have time for such things," Gianni said, his voice rising, "but you never believe me."

"I believe you," I relented, resting my head on his shoulder as a light breeze danced over my skin. The tension in his arm softened, and I closed my eyes. I could sit like this forever.

"Tell me about your time in the war," I said. Ever since he had mentioned his time in France in one of his letters, I'd been curious about his experience fighting in the Great War.

"Oh, you don't want to hear about that," he said, kicking out his feet in front of him and crossing his ankles.

"I do. I want to know everything about you." I gave his arm a squeeze. "Besides, here I am, crying my eyes out at a hospital, when you had been off fighting for your life. Maybe one of your stories will give me strength."

"Well." Gianni paused, thinking. "Did I ever tell you the story of my mule?"

"I don't remember you ever mentioning a mule," I said with a slight laugh. "But you haven't told me any stories, so whatever you tell me is new to me."

"When I was in France, I was assigned to the mule train," Gianni began.

I closed my eyes and listened to his smooth voice, both lulled by the comfort of it and interested to learn more about this man who had stolen my heart.

"Since I understood shoemaking, the army figured I could use those skills for harness-making. Of course, working with a mule is a different story. It's not like I ever spent that much time around horses, let alone a mule." He chuckled. "The first time I ever went to place one of the harnesses I made around a mule's neck, it didn't go well. The mule, dark as night, stood taller than me by nearly a foot.

"So, I said to him, 'Okay, now. I'm not going to hurt you. And I hope you don't hurt me.' Then I inched closer and tossed the harness over his back, only to have him step aside and the harness hit the ground. One of the other soldiers was watching. He laughed at me and said, 'You're gonna be there all day.' I remember him slapping his leg like it was a big joke. So, I turned to the mule, and I said, 'You see that guy. He's a real piece of work. If you let me put this on you, I'll see if I can get a little extra something in your food sack. Maybe an apple. Deal?'"

"Did it work?" I asked, keeping my eyes closed, picturing the scene.

"That mule was several hundred pounds of muscle. He didn't have to listen me," Gianni said. "And that arrogant guy kept at me. 'Well, are ya or aren't ya?' he kept calling out. So, I lifted the harness once more, and this time, I'm not making this up, the mule stood completely still."

"Did he really?" I opened my eyes and looked over at Gianni.

He nodded his head. "He really did."

"And then what happened?" I asked, enjoying his story.

"Well, that stopped the other soldier from teasing. He walked away without another word. And later that afternoon, once I had fitted several more mules with harnesses, I returned to the first mule with the apple I had promised him. He seemed to remember me, and from that point forward, a friendship formed."

"Did you give the mule a name? I had a pet chicken I named Piccolino. I raised her from a chick. She used to follow me everywhere I went." Except America. I still missed her.

"Piccolino, that's a great name," Gianni said. "I guess I should have named that mule. But then again, I knew we were at war, and I didn't want to get too attached. Still, I made sure I took his reins and led him everywhere we went. And boy, did we travel long distances together! The mules were made to carry ammunition boxes up and down the steep, rocky mountains. It was long, hard work. But the mules never complained. They kept on walking. Even when gunshots broke out, they stayed calm. They were amazing animals."

"It sounds like it." I could nearly picture a young Gianni, scaling the mountains of France with his mule.

"I took good care of all the mules, but I especially gave extra treats to mine. And one day, that mule paid me back for my kindness."

"How?" I asked, sitting up.

"He saved my life," Gianni said fondly. "I was sleeping. We were all sleeping. Crossing mountains was exhausting. Anyway, it's pitch-black, middle of the night, and my mule gives me a nudge. At first, I was mad because I wanted to sleep. I told him, 'Leave me alone. Not now. I'll get you something to eat in the morning.' But that mule kept nudging me, again and again. Finally, I had enough. I jumped to my feet ready to yell at him when I noticed something was wrong. The air smelled terrible, like burnt garlic. My eyes started burning." Gianni paused before explaining in a low voice, "The enemy had released mustard gas."

My hand flew to my mouth. "Oh, Gianni, that's terrible! Are you all right? I never knew." A heaviness pulled at my heart. How frightening it must have been on that unknown mountainside in the dark. I had heard about mustard gas, but I never met anyone who had been exposed to it. This new detail about Gianni's service in the war made him seem more mature. Often, he appeared only interested in lighthearted matters and in enjoying his youth. But now, I saw a young man who had endured unthinkable, perilous moments. No wonder he tried to embrace the pleasures of life.

"I'm okay now," he said with a shrug. "But that night I had to find a way to get out of there before the poison could kill all of us, including all the mules. So I ran, screaming and kicking, trying to wake my fellow soldiers. Everyone was coughing and spitting and panicking. And then there were the mules, nudging us to get up and braying. I took hold of my mule's reins. I didn't know what else to do.

"And you know what that smart mule did? He started climbing right up the side of the mountain. Higher and higher. I couldn't see or breathe, but I knew we were heading uphill. The poison was burning my eyes and my throat, but somehow, I held on. The mules didn't stop until the air cleared. All of a sudden there was a cold breeze, and everyone could breathe again. We had gone far enough up the mountain that the poison couldn't reach us. That mule, my mule, he saved my life, and the lives of all the soldiers."

"Oh, Gianni, that's an amazing story," I said, hugging him. "I'm so glad you survived. And you helped save the lives of the other soldiers you were with. They should have given you an award for that."

"I did get a citation, but it was for another time, when the mule train came under fire. That's not as happy of a story." Gianni cast his eyes around the grounds of the hospital. Taking a deep breath, he looked back at me. "Remember when you were asking whether I get drunk all the time? And I told you I could only have one drink a day?"

I nodded, dropping my gaze toward my lap, where I clasped my hands. I had taken my frustrations out on Gianni last week. I had nearly forgotten about this part of our conversation.

But it seemed my comments had stayed with Gianni. Had he been holding it against me since we last spoke?

"Well," he continued, "one drink a day is what the doctor told me I'll have to do for the rest of my life since I was exposed to the gas."

"I'm sorry for yelling at you like that last week," I said, fresh tears filling my eyes.

"You didn't mean it. I know it's been difficult for you since you've been sick for so long. Remember what I said about taking care of yourself and trying to be happy." I nodded as he added, "I know I sound fatherly, but if we're going to be together, then you have to trust my advice."

Rather than make him a promise I wasn't sure I could keep, I took Gianni into my arms. Over his shoulder, I saw groups of people heading for the door. Our three hours had passed in a flash.

"I guess it's time to say our goodbyes," Gianni whispered into my ear.

"I can't bear to hear you say goodbye. It feels so final. As if I'll never see you again," I said breathlessly. I squeezed my arms around him even tighter.

"Okay, so it's not goodbye," he said, pulling back and looking at me with such tenderness, my heart could have broken in two and fallen right at his feet. "Then it's 'until next Sunday.'"

"You better be here," I tried to tease, standing as my mood lightened a bit. "Or else I'll find my own mule and have him drag you here."

Gianni laughed and took hold of my hand. I laughed as well, but only to stem the tears that spilled out the corners of my eyes. We walked to the front of the hospital, toward a fleet of taxis ready to whisk my Gianni away.

September 12, 1921
Ardmore, Pennsylvania

My Dear Rosie,

My love, you cannot imagine the joy I felt being with you for three hours yesterday. Yet, I'm not satisfied. I want to be with you every day. Do you feel the same way? I hope that you love me more than everyone you knew before me. I want to be near you and make you happy. I don't want to see you cry.

Please let me know what you need to make you happy, and I will bring it to you. Today, I will send more writing papers. Write me a long letter. Also, let me know if anyone has stolen those eyes I admire. Do not forget your dear John. He lives only to make you happy.

I send my dearest regards and a million kisses.

Your Lover Forever,
John

September 15, 1921
Rush Hospital Country Branch
Malvern, Pennsylvania

My Love, My Dear,

Today I received your letter. Reading it gave me great pleasure. As for me, you know how I feel in this faraway desert. You cannot imagine the pleasure I felt being with you on Sunday. But soon after you left, I felt such anxiety that continued through the night. I had disturbing thoughts that were so bad, if I'd had a revolver, I would have taken my own life. My time here is useless. Please tell me what to do. You are the only one who can put my thoughts to rest.

My love, I urge you to take good care of yourself. Diseases are quick to come but slow to leave. I pray for the Lord to heal me so I can take care of you. I think I am the one who has caused you to lose so much weight. Please do not suffer for my love. It grieves my heart and makes me think you will become fed up with me. You have to think about your health and your future. There is a proverb that says, "Time shall pass and time shall come." Maybe it is better to have suffered now than later.

My love, you are my comfort and my treasure. My hope for the future rests on you. My lips speak only your name. My thoughts are directed at you. You comfort my anguished soul. My heart throbs when you squeeze me tight. I love you so much that as a token of my life, I would leave you my eyes.

My love, I do not wish to bother you with all these thoughts that I forget when I see you. They are like the wind; now you feel them, and soon they vanish.

I urge you to reply immediately, for I wait for your lovely news every day. I send you so many sweet and dear kisses on your lips and a greeting that comes from my ardent heart.

Always Your Lover,
Rosina

P.S. Reply immediately!

Chapter Seventeen

L'Infermiera
(The Nurse)

September 15, 1921
Rush Hospital Country Branch
Malvern, Pennsylvania

Setting down my pen, I reached into my box of papers and pulled out Giovanni's photograph. Expressing my deepest emotions in writing had exhausted me. After adjusting my pillow and pulling up my covers, I found a comfortable position on my side so I could stare at Gianni's handsome face until my eyes could no longer stay open. It was how I had gone to sleep each night since arriving here in Malvern. I held a vision of my future in my mind until the hospital room melted away and I could almost fool myself that we were in the small house Gianni had described.

Unfortunately, I was awakened a little while later by a nurse entering to check on me, reminding me once more of my reality.

"What do you have there?" she asked, motioning toward the photograph still in my hand.

Too tired to speak, I tilted Giovanni's photograph in her direction.

"Oh." A hint of disapproval colored her voice as she added, "You must really love him." Before I could respond, the nurse took on an authoritarian tone, ordering, "You mustn't do that. You'll never get better. You aren't married, are you?"

"We will be someday," I said, propping myself onto my elbows to get a better look at the nurse. Her stern facial features were accentuated by her tightly pulled gray bun. A diminutive woman, she appeared even shorter due to her hunched posture. The name tag affixed on the crumpled white material of her uniform read Nurse Edna Hicks. Her simple name offered me little comfort. With a name like that, I doubted she understood one word of Italian.

"Going to marry him, huh? Are you now?" Nurse Edna mocked in singsong voice. "Well, you'd better forget about him while you're here. It's not good for your health to be in love." She moved within inches of my left ear and whispered, "It'll only cause you pain."

I recoiled as a prickly sensation ran down my side and a knot of anxiety balled in my stomach. I thought about asking if it had been half a century since the old bat had had a lover. If she'd ever had one in the first place. Fear of retaliation kept my mouth shut. I pressed my eyes closed and pretended to have drifted off to sleep.

After a few minutes, I peeked from the edge of my covers to make certain Nurse Edna wasn't returning. Then I hid the photograph at the very bottom of my box of writing papers. There was no way I'd allow her to tell me what was good for me and what wasn't, especially if my being in love with Gianni would be frowned upon here.

The next day, as I sat reading Gianni's last letter to me, a nurse who seemed to be close to my age entered the room. "Is that from your lover?" she asked, pointing toward the letter.

Why did she assume it was a love letter? Perhaps other patients often received similar letters. I nodded in response.

"So, what does this fellow look like?" she asked.

I regretted showing Nurse Edna Gianni's photograph, but maybe this soft-spoken, round-faced nurse would have a kinder reaction. "I have a photograph. Would you like to see it?"

The nurse stepped closer to get a good look at the picture I held out.

"Handsome," she said, smiling at me. "You make a beautiful couple."

"Thank you," I said, admiring Gianni's strong features.

"And you're in love with him?" the nurse asked.

I set the photograph along with the letter I had been reading into my box for safekeeping. "Oh, yes. I love him very much."

The nurse raised her eyebrows, as if my last statement surprised her. "And is he coming to visit you this Sunday?"

"I hope so. I miss him terribly."

"Oh, I'm sure you do," the nurse said, using a tone that sounded as if she were speaking to a child. "I bet you'd like him to stay overnight with you, if you love him so much."

I gasped at the shocking implication of her statement. My face flushed with heat. "We've barely kissed."

The nurse shook her head, laughing at my reaction.

"I'm telling you the truth!" I yelled as she left. But by late afternoon, other nurses and small groups of patients had started watching me. Occasionally, they pointed toward me. When I looked directly at them, they quickly turned away. A splitting pain slashed across my forehead. My blood thundered in my ears. I wanted to find a permanent place to hide.

On my way back to my room, I tried my hardest not to make eye contact with anyone. I had nearly made it, only two doors away, when a young man stepped in front of me and blocked my path. He waved at me as if we knew each other. I didn't recognize him, and, after the day I'd had, I didn't want anything to do with him. I attempted to brush past him, but he grabbed me in a tight grip with a hand on each of my shoulders. I tripped backward until my back pressed against the wall.

"Tell me," he demanded with an awful grin on his blemished face, "how many kisses do you give him?"

I didn't think. I only reacted with a swift upward knee, knocking the breath out of him. Released from his grip, I rushed down the hall and quickly shut my door. It had no lock, so I leaned my weight against it. Sliding to a seated position, I tried to settle the shivering that rattled my body.

Long minutes later, someone pushed against the door to enter. I stood, allowing it to open enough to admit the other patient who shared my room. I apologized for blocking it. The middle-aged woman looked at me as if I'd lost my mind but continued to her bed.

That evening, I laid on my side staring out the darkened window. I refused to move even when I heard the nursing staff entering and exiting.

"What's the matter with you?"

I glanced over my shoulder to see Nurse Edna with her arms crossed. I returned to my position on my side and pressed my lips together. Nothing good would come of talking to her.

"Is it your love affair that's making you crazy?"

"No, it's you and your big mouth," I said, too quietly for her to hear.

If I'd had a place to go or even enough money to pay for the taxi and a train ticket, I would have put on a comfortable dress, packed my bags, and walked right out the front door. I imagined showing up at Gianni's one-room apartment and demanding he marry me on the spot.

He would think I was as crazy as Nurse Edna did. Maybe I truly had lost my mind.

And if I had, this place was to blame.

September 16, 1921
Ardmore, Pennsylvania

My Dear Rosie,

I'm so pleased to hear your beautiful words of love. Tell me, my love, are you having a lot of fun? Do as I advise, because I love you and desire to see you in blooming health.

I promise you, if the Lord grants me good health, I will visit you every Sunday. When I visit, I will bring you everything you ask for. However, I cannot visit you this Sunday. So, please, do not think badly of me. My thoughts are always with you.

In the meantime, I send you my dearest regards and a thousand affectionate kisses.

Your Dear Forever,
John

September 17, 1921
Rush Hospital Country Branch
Malvern, Pennsylvania

My Dear Gianni,
Unable to rest, I decided to write to you. The way you expressed yourself in your letter, you seemed very indifferent toward me. You asked if I would think kindly of you if you stayed in Ardmore this Sunday. As far as I'm concerned, do anything you please! I will not prohibit you from doing anything. You ask me if I mind. I could tell you that I will be happy if you do come and happy if you don't come. I tell you the truth: I do not care about your business.
My love, you have no idea how painful it is for me to write to you, since I know that I will not be able to see you on Sunday. My heart is broken and tortured by your love. At times, I curse the day we met. I always ask the Lord to make these sad days go by quickly. You told me whatever I need, you will bring it to me. I want to thank you for everything you did for me. That's enough!
I end with a thousand kisses and my dearest regards.

Your Very Affectionate,
Rosina

P.S. Pardon my bad handwriting. I wrote this in the moonlight.

CHAPTER EIGHTEEN

LETTERE DIO MIO PADRE
(MY FATHER'S LETTER)

September 18, 1921
Rush Hospital Country Branch
Malvern, Pennsylvania

For a week now, I'd been hiding and keeping a low profile among the other patients and the nurses. When Gianni wrote to tell me he couldn't visit, the anger and the fear that he'd already given up on making the trip to visit me, along with the pain of missing him, made my entire body ache. But if he had come today, who knew how much more ugliness would have been stirred up and directed at me after he had gone?

As it was, I had to endure plenty of comments from the nurses asking me why I wasn't getting ready for visitation hours. "Trouble in paradise already?" one asked, laughing and shaking her head at me. She left without waiting for my response.

I sat in my bed and refused to allow my face to reveal how I was falling to pieces inside. Perhaps Gianni preferred spending his Sunday doing as he pleased. He might enjoy the company of the people he saw today rather than visiting me. It was only a matter of time before the distance would tear apart our relationship.

The older woman sharing my room commented from her bed, "At least I'm not the only one neglected." Then she flopped to her side and laid with her back to me.

In a rare moment of solitude, while the woman snored and everyone else was occupied during visitation hours, I decided to distract myself by writing a letter to my brother. Amazingly, he had written to wish me well here. I congratulated myself for having enough restraint not to spit on his words. He must have been happy now that I was out of his house and away from his nagging wife. How bad did his house look, now that his servant sister wasn't there to do all the chores? Though I wanted to include all the livid thoughts roiling through my mind, I decided to keep to my main purpose in writing to him. Considering every single person at this hospital knew of the seriousness of my love affair with Gianni and my hopes of marrying him, so, too, should my own brother.

When I finished my brief letter, Nurse Edna hovered in the doorway with a new letter in her hand. "Do you have another lover you're not telling us about?" she mocked, waving an envelope in the air. "Maybe that's why your boyfriend didn't want to see you today. Is he jealous?"

Her question held such malice, it took all I had in me not to scream. Following a steadying breath and a long exhale, my curiosity won over my rage. "What are you talking about? Let me see that," I demanded, striding across the room.

Nurse Edna read the postmark and taunted, "So, you have lovers all over the world, do you? Who's the boyfriend you left behind in Italy?"

I snatched the letter from Nurse Edna's gnarled grip and read the postmark for myself.

"It's from my father," I said, half in anger and half in shock. I hadn't heard from him in quite a while. And despite Aunt

Isabella's advice to write to him, I hadn't had any good news to share. How did my father know to write to this hospital address?

Purposely turning my back to the nurse still lurking in the doorway, I frantically searched for my letter opener. I walked to the farthest corner of the room before beginning to read. Nurse Edna busied herself on the other side of the room, although surely she kept one eye squinted in my direction.

A few lines in, I couldn't believe my eyes. I grasped my cross pendant, still secure around my neck, and trudged backward to my bed, desperate to sit down. My vision blurred and the room spun as I read again what my father had written. I released my cross pendant and placed my hand over my mouth to contain my gasp. I pictured my father writing this letter and the grief he must have been feeling. I was to blame, for not taking Aunt Isabella's advice and writing to him about my health sooner.

I folded my father's letter and slid it back into its envelope. A rush of angry energy overcame me. I held back the intense impulse to throw the letter across the room. Someone had taken it upon themselves to write about me to my father, writing horrifying lies.

As I wrote back, my blood thundered in my ears and my breathing increasingly became more shallow and rapid. Hardly finished, I reached for a fresh piece of paper, addressing it to the only person I could trust.

September 18, 1921
Rush Hospital Country Branch
Malvern, Pennsylvania

My Adored John,
Right now, I can report I am enjoying good health. But I have to tell you, my heart is always anxious. You know how I feel about this place.
But my love, today I received a letter from my dear father. He complained that I haven't told him the truth about my health, that he had to hear it from other people. He said in August he received a letter from somebody that said I was dead! My poor father fell to the floor like a dead man. The letter said I'd been in the hospital for a year with tuberculosis. He was told not to think about me anymore, for I was dead!
Think, my love, how could I be happy hearing all that my father went through? Since the day he heard the bad news, he has been in great mourning. He had been dreaming that I did not die by that terrible illness. After all, it's only been nineteen months since I left Italy. And, thank God, before I had, I never even knew what a headache was. So my father was not really convinced. He said to himself, it cannot be that my daughter is dead. So, he decided to write to my brother to find out the whole truth.
My love, just imagine how much pain I was in, learning all this. I immediately wrote to him, telling him I was healthy and well. Within a few days, I will send him some of my pictures. My love, who could have done something so awful? They must really hate me. I have never done anything evil to anybody. I always minded my own business. So when these hateful people could not get to me, they instead wrote to my unfortunate father that terrible lie. My love, I asked the Lord to strike down the person who wished my death and sent this false news to my father.

So, my love, tell me how I can be happy in this hospital after receiving such a letter. If you were here, you could comfort me. But you are not. I have no one. My love, you tell me to listen to your advice. I do, but my heart is full of melancholy. I can bear it no longer. I swear to you, my adored love, if I continue as I am, I will end up in a cemetery. I don't know why I cannot appease this heart of mine. I cannot find peace. These past days, I have lived to see you on Sunday. But when I read your letter, I could not stop crying. Each day seems like a century. I have to deal with people who annoy me. They say things to upset me. They tell me to leave you. But I would rather die than abandon you. They're all jealous of our love.

My love, this is enough. I have nothing else to tell you. Besides, my hand does not want to write. I send you many dear regards and a thousand dear kisses.

Always Yours,
Rosina

P.S. Please write to me immediately. Your letters comfort me. With a broken heart, I say goodbye. Pardon my bad handwriting.

September 19, 1921
Ardmore, Pennsylvania

My Dear Rosie,

I am so sorry you received such bad news from your father. My heart is broken for you. Who would write to your father that you were dead or even that you were sick? It is a grave sin and in God's hands now. I don't know the words to comfort you. I can only promise to love you more and more in the hopes that it will strengthen you.

I hope you pay no attention to those people bothering you. If they do not stop, they will have to deal with me when I visit you. They must be jealous and have no friends. I will give them a piece of my mind and then we'll see what they have to say. You have suffered enough in the past at the hands of evil people.

My Rosie, I think about our future and it seems so beautiful. We will live together like two doves and always be happy. I wish you were home, where I could comfort you and let you be who you want to be. But I know we must be patient. I also suffer, not being near you. I would like to be a bird so that I could fly and visit you every day. But this is only a fantasy. Since I can't fly to you, I will write to you every day. There won't be one night when your Gianni does not write his Rosina.

I also hope the Lord comforts your father. And I pray for your health. My love, there is so much more I would like to tell you. I would rather wait to see you than express all my heart's desires on paper. In the meantime, I send you my dearest regards and a thousand fervent kisses.

Your Dear,
John

September 20, 1921
Rush Hospital Country Branch
Malvern, Pennsylvania

My Adored John,

I just received your letter dated September 19th, and I was so happy to read it. I anxiously wait for your news each day. You have no idea how your heartfelt words helped me today. They nourish my wounded heart. Please know your Rosina appreciates your love. I have known many young men, but no one has struck my heart like you. For a time, I refused to open my heart and love you. Nothing went my way. But now I listen to what my heart is telling me. Even when I am angered or hurt, I think of you and feel better.

My love, today I also received a letter from my brother. Also in the envelope was another letter from my father. He says that his mind is at ease now since my brother has let him know my condition is curable. He sends me a thousand blessings. My love, I am so happy that you share my pain. I also know that you love my mother, whom the good Lord took away when I was a little girl. When I knew not what death meant, I did not understand why the Lord took her away from me and left me and my father, who loves me so much.

Today, I have three hearts that beat in my chest. My heart is tied to yours and my father's blessing to us. So, my father has been assured that I am well. I feel much better that he knows that I am not dead. My brother tells me in his letter that he is happy we love each other and wishes us well. So, my love, put your mind at ease. One day I will be all yours!

My love, I would like to send the picture you have given me to my father in Italy. In his letter, he asked me for one and I hope you won't mind. I don't want to send it without your permission. But I do hope you agree. It's not as if I am sending it to a stranger. One day my father will be your family, and I am sure he will keep it in a safe place.

My love, last night I had a dream that will make you laugh. In it, we were playing tricks on each other. You took me to meet your mother and see your house. Then I woke up and was sad that you were not with me. I hope you plan to visit me this Sunday. If you do, please bring me cream and soap for my face. When you see me next, you will notice I am looking much healthier with a better complexion.

My love, you will be relieved to know these past few days I am feeling stronger and my health is improving. I end by sending you a thousand kisses.

Yours Forever,
Rosina

P.S. Thank you for the stamps! Write immediately!

September 21, 1921
Ardmore, Pennsylvania

My Dear Rosie,

I was delighted to read your letter today. It is the best letter you have written since you arrived at Malvern. I'm happy you are in better health and that you received a letter from your father. My love, I am honored that you would like to send my photograph to your father, but I do not want to lose it. The photograph is too big to send by mail. I would be saddened if it were ruined because it is the best photograph I have ever taken in my life. If you wait, I will send you one the size of a postcard, which is a better size for the mail.

My love, when I read about your dream, I laughed. I thought about it all day. You must really love me to have such beautiful dreams. I wish my dream of you was as lovely. Last night I had a dream that you were dead. Imagine how devastated I was to see you lying in a coffin. I was crying and wanted to die also. I could not leave you. When I woke up and realized I was dreaming, I said, "Thank God!" This morning I asked my landlady, Mary, what she thought of the dream, and she assured me it was good news. She believes you are going to be all right. I told her that even in my dreams I can't live without you.

You will be happy to know I will visit you on Sunday and bring everything you need. I'm not sure what kind of cream or soap you use. Let me know because there are so many varieties. Also, they're changing the time and making the clocks run one hour behind. What time are visiting hours on Sunday? Remember, I have to follow the train schedule to see you.

My love, in keeping my promise to write to you every day, I do not have as much news. Please know you are always on my mind and missing you makes me anxious. I have to be patient a while longer. The time will come when I will be happy with you by my side. In the meantime, accept my dearest regards and a thousand kisses.

I Am Yours,
John

CHAPTER NINETEEN

UNA SITUAZIONE DISPERATA
(A DESPERATE SITUATION)

September 21, 1921
Rush Hospital Country Branch
Malvern, Pennsylvania

Nurse Edna announced that I was overdue for a physical, making it sound as if it was my fault that I had yet to be seen by a doctor here. She instructed me to immediately report downstairs to the wing where the doctors had their offices. I nearly gave in to the temptation to argue with her, but it was easier to do as I was told.

The doctor assigned to my case, Dr. Solomon, held up a bright light and told me to look into it as he shined it into each of my eyes, temporarily blinding me. When he removed the light, I squinted in response, rubbing my fingers over my eyelids. After a few seconds, I opened my eyes and was still partially blinded by a remnant spot, as if the light had stained my vision.

Dr. Solomon leaned against his desk. His pen made scratching sounds over the paper on his clipboard. I adjusted my weight on the exam table as my heartbeat raced. Although I felt strong and healthy, there could still be something wrong with me.

Was the tickle in my throat this morning a sign that whatever had caused my last illness was returning?

Dr. Solomon stopped writing and looked up from his clipboard, his right eyebrow raised as he assessed me. Compared to the other doctors I had seen over my long hospitalization, he appeared rather young, perhaps only fifteen years older than me. He had a tall, thin frame and wore his dark-brown hair slicked back, yet a piece of it fell forward. "Your weight, blood pressure, and lung capacity are all at healthy levels. Therefore, I'm listing you as ambulant."

"Is that good?" I asked, unfamiliar with the term.

"I'd say so." He set the clipboard on his desk but slid his pen behind his ear. The loose lock of hair remained dangling over his forehead. "We have three classes of patients here. Hospital, semi-ambulant, and ambulant. Of the three, *ambulant* describes our patients who are in the best condition." He rose to a full standing position and gave me a slight smile. "And you, my dear, meet that qualification."

"Oh, then, that is good." Would this new label benefit me?

"Yes, good news indeed," Dr. Solomon said, walking to the opposite side of the room. He had a slight limp, which seemed unusual for a man presumably in his thirties. Was he suffering from an injury? Had he served in the war?

At the window, he propped his forearm on the frame. With his back to me, he continued, "You will be moved to the wing with other patients in similar condition. As an ambulant patient, you are encouraged to spend as much time as possible outside in the sunshine and the fresh air."

The idea of being outside more gave me hope. I preferred the natural beauty of the grounds over the bleak, sanitized spaces found inside.

Dr. Solomon turned from the window and took slow steps back toward me, still slightly favoring one leg. He pulled the pen out from behind his ear and rolled it between his fingers. For several long seconds, he kept his attention on the motion of the pen. Despite the positive news about my health, a growing feeling of uncertainty made me anxious to end this appointment.

"Are you aware that this institution is privately run?" Dr. Solomon asked, still staring at the pen.

I didn't know what to say in response. I had no idea why he was asking or what it had to do with my health.

"No need to answer." He dropped the pen into the front pocket of his white jacket. "I'm sure you haven't been in America long enough to understand the ins and outs of how our hospital system works, so I'll make it simple for you. Staying at this facility requires a cost. That cost can be paid by you, a family member, or whomever you can find to foot the bill. Those that pay can stay." He paused and fixed his dark-brown eyes on me. "And those who cannot pay fall into a different category."

Clearly I fell into the "different category." Who would pay this bill? My brother? My aunt? Neither seemed likely. My breath came fast and shallow.

"I can see I've frightened you," Dr. Solomon said softly.

I wanted to scream, *You have no idea! Everyone has turned their backs on me. I have nowhere to go except on a ship back to Italy.*

Dr. Solomon grasped his hands behind his back and tilted his head to the side. "Such a pity that a beautiful young woman like yourself would be in such a desperate situation."

I crossed my arms over my chest, unease prickling over my spine. Where was this conversation headed? I wanted to return to the relative safety of my bed. Dr. Solomon broke into a smile and let out a small laugh. Was he enjoying my discomfort?

"There's no need to worry," he told me. "You aren't going anywhere." The way he said it reinforced how this so-called sanitorium doubled as a prison for me. "We have a program here at Rush," he continued, "where we offer ambulant patients the option to work in return for room, board, and care. There's a position open on the cleaning staff. You'll start on Monday."

Cleaning this place was among the last things I wanted to do. What if I refused the work? It might be worth the risk of being sent home. I had never wanted to be here in the first place.

But the attic room that I had once called home was no longer mine. If I pleaded with my brother, would he relent and take me in when he had so steadfastly refused?

"I'll see you in a week or two, and we'll discuss your situation more then," Dr. Solomon said, turning from me. It was clear our discussion was over. He opened the door and handed my chart to a nurse. I followed her into the hallway, relieved to be out of his office yet still wishing we could discuss my new "employment."

Before I had a chance to process it all, the nurse directed me to pack up my belongings to move to the new room that would go along with my new assignment. I felt like a child with no power over the decisions in my life.

When had I lost my freedom? Was it in Dr. Solomon's office just now, or the moment I set foot into this place?

CHAPTER TWENTY

NON ANDAME A DORMIRE
(DON'T GO TO SLEEP)

September 22, 1921
Rush Hospital Country Branch
Malvern, Pennsylvania

As an ambulant patient, I was encouraged to leave my bed. I planned to take advantage as often as I could. Instead of my meals being delivered to my room, I was instructed to visit the small cafeteria located in the front of the building. Sitting and staring at four walls for days on end had been maddening. The cafeteria, by contrast, had large windows that overlooked the long tree-lined driveway.

As I collected my dinner, I noticed that the kitchen staff was run by other ambulant patients. Soon I would be put to work as well. Should I be relieved that I had an option that kept me here, or anxious that I had agreed to further my stay? Maybe if Gianni came through for us, soon it would all be worth it. On the upside, the hours might pass more quickly if I was busy.

I found a seat at an empty table. My new roommate, Catherina, had said she would join me, but she hadn't entered the cafeteria yet. Since the food was warm, I picked up my fork. The roast chicken, mashed potatoes, and green beans all looked appealing.

As I checked if Catherina had arrived, I locked eyes with an angry young woman. She had a pale face with swollen dark eyes and mousy brown hair that desperately needed a comb or a brush run through it. I turned to my left and then to my right, trying to see if the woman was fixated on someone or something else behind me. When it became apparent I was her sole focus, I dropped my gaze to the plate in front of me, hoping she would lose interest. But if the past week was any indication, chances were high that wouldn't happen.

No matter how hard I tried to maintain a calm front, there remained a handful of people who taunted me with their unwanted opinions. "He's probably too busy with his other girlfriends," my last roommate repeatedly told me, ever since Gianni had missed visiting last Sunday.

A nurse who overheard her comment followed it up with, "He left you for good. Forget about him."

I had been tempted to argue with them until I was lightheaded and out of breath, but I knew better than to add any more fuel to their ridiculous fire. Now, days later, I thought most people would have lost interest, but this deranged-looking woman proved I would continue to have no peace.

Taking another bite of dinner, I felt her eyes on me, like when a cloud obscures the sun on a clear day. I resisted the impulse to raise my eyes for fear of encouraging her. I kept my head down until I heard a chair being dragged toward me. The crazed woman placed the chair directly across from me and took a seat. Instead of saying a word, she leaned forward and glared at me. Unsettled, I paused mid-chew, frozen in place. A sneer spread across her face.

"I don't like you," she finally said in a deep-throated voice.

I almost told her, "Join the crowd," but I thought better of it.

She pointed at me, stabbing her finger in the air with each word. "You think you're so special just because you have a boyfriend? Huh? You think that makes you better than me?"

I pushed my chair backward with such force, it made a loud, echoing, scratching sound. The entire cafeteria, which had been buzzing with multiple conversations, fell silent as heads snapped in my direction.

An older, broad-bodied nurse strode across the room. In a firm tone and a light Dutch accent, she pointed toward the woman and ordered, "Elizabetta, back to your seat."

The woman crossed her arms and tucked her chin into her chest.

"That's enough," the nurse said, reaching for her arm, but Elizabetta yanked her elbow out of the nurse's grasp.

"Don't touch me," she growled defiantly. Standing and regaining her composure, Elizabetta dragged her chair slowly and loudly back to her table, where she sat with her back to me.

I stared at my remaining food but had lost my appetite. I reached for my plate to return it when Elizabetta pivoted toward me. I didn't move, bracing myself for whatever this disturbed woman had in mind.

"Don't fall asleep," Elizabetta said, enunciating each word, repeating herself several more times before breaking into hysterical laughter as if it was the funniest thing she'd ever said.

Catherina finally appeared, holding her tray of food. Her raised eyebrows and loud exhale let me know that she had witnessed Elizabetta's outburst. Taking a seat across from me, she whispered, "I wouldn't pay any attention to her. Elizabetta's not right in the head. Ought to be moved to a psychiatric hospital, if you ask me."

When I first met Catherina yesterday, I nearly wept with relief. Not only did she have roots in the same region of Italy, but she was also the first person to speak to me in a friendly manner since I arrived at this joyless place. Now I confided, "I've had about all I can take from her and everyone else. I wish I knew how to make it stop."

"It will," Catherina assured me. "When I first got here and some of the other patients found out I was married, they told me my husband would find another lover and other terrible things. I cried every night. But after a while, they lost interest when someone new came along."

"You mean me?" I asked, slumping in my chair.

Catherina offered me a warm smile. "There'll be someone else soon enough. You'll see."

Her words did little to calm my rattled nerves. "I hope you're right. You think I can leave without creating more of a scene?" Once again, I gathered my plate and utensils.

"It's worth a try. I'll see you back at the room."

I moved quickly and resolutely, leaving the cafeteria unharmed, other than my stomach being twisted into an uncomfortable knot.

Back at my bed, I sought my box of letters to distract me from worrying about both the doctor and Elizabetta. My father's first letter from Italy still weighed heavily on my thoughts and my heart. That he'd believed I was dead continued to enrage me. I had promised him on the day I left Torchiara that I would be healthy and well as I made a happy life for myself in America. I still hoped the day would come when I could tell him I had done exactly that. In the meantime, I never wanted him to learn how near to death I had been, or the inexact diagnosis of my illness, which had caused me to be endlessly hospitalized. I would never say out loud to anyone—not even Gianni—who I thought had sent that hateful letter, but I would have bet all the money in the world that it could be traced to the same person spreading all those other lies about me. Had my brother come to the same conclusion? Even if he had, he'd look the other way and deny it to his grave.

Next I reread the last letter from Gianni, whose favorite photograph was well on its way across the Atlantic Ocean. Guilt twisted in my stomach. I hadn't given it much thought when I'd packaged it to be sent to my father. Now I'd have a difficult time retrieving it. Gianni would be upset when he learned the truth, but what could I do? Maybe he wouldn't bring it up when he visited on Sunday.

Setting aside Gianni's letter, I decided to take a hot bath and wash this miserable day off of me. Hopefully the warm water would ease my anxieties enough to get a good night's sleep for the first time since I'd arrived in Malvern. Most nights, sleep came in short spurts only for me to awaken on edge, unsure of my new surroundings and missing Gianni. The nursing staff hadn't helped matters. Last night, after falling asleep early out of exhaustion, I had been jolted awake by a cold hand pressed against my cheek. Nurse Edna had delighted in startling me with a throaty, gravelly laugh. Gianni's latest letter had arrived, and she'd wanted to deliver it herself. Along with another dose of mocking. Why couldn't she find someone else to harass?

After reading Gianni's kind and loving words, I had tossed and turned the remainder of the night, missing him even more than I'd thought possible. I had lain awake, counting the hours until next Sunday.

When I returned from taking my bath, Catherina was already asleep, so I didn't turn on the light to disturb her. As I climbed into my bed in the darkened room, I imagined Gianni right there beside me.

As I drifted off, my mind wandered to the angry woman from dinner. Her words of warning about not sleeping rang through my head as if she were right beside me, whispering them into my ear. *Don't fall asleep. Don't fall asleep.* Her face hovered beside mine with a malicious smile as she pointed at me, saying, *I don't like you.*

A jerking sensation and a loud scraping sound made my eyes shoot open. At first, I thought I had been dreaming, but then it happened again. I pushed upward into a seated position only to fall backward as my bed slid several inches forward along the floor.

"What's happening?" Catherina yelled into the darkness.

"My bed!" I yelled. "I don't know!"

My heart beat rapidly, and my breath came in ragged spurts. I grasped my sheets as my bed lurched toward the open door. High-pitched laughter filled the hallway. I lifted my head, straining to see through the blackness. Who was out there? In the darkened doorway, I could only make out a silhouette that receded as pounding footsteps retreated down the hallway.

Catherina turned on the light. "Rosie! There's a rope tied to the leg of your bed."

It seemed unbelievable until I crawled to the end of my bed and saw with my own eyes that she was telling the truth.

"Stunad!" Catherina yelled out the doorway, calling the person responsible for this act the Italian slang word for *stupid.*

A nurse appeared in the doorway. "What's all the ruckus?" She nearly tripped over the rope. She was joined by other nurses and what seemed like every patient from our wing, all wanting to see what had happened.

The nursing staff had a difficult time getting everyone settled down. "Whoever did this will be held responsible!" the head nurse, a small woman with a surprisingly large, commanding voice, announced. She removed the rope from my bed, taking it for evidence.

After my bed was put back into place and the door was secured shut, I dropped my head back to my pillow. For an institution dedicated to healing, this sanitorium was more toxic than anywhere else I had lived. Anything could happen to me in the middle of the night.

I barely slept for the remainder of the night. When, finally, the first hint of dawn offered enough light by which to see, I reached for my writing papers and whispered to the blank page, "Oh, Gianni, when will you take me away from here?"

September 23, 1921
Rush Hospital Country Branch
Malvern, Pennsylvania

Adored Gianni,

It is with great pleasure that I reply to your letter dated the 21st of the current month. You have no idea how your heartfelt words full of love affected me today. If you did, you would know with certainty how satisfying your love for me is! Your love made me understand that I am the only one in this world who could bring you happiness. And you, my love, are the most dear and most lovable of all men worldwide. When I read your letter, my heart burns and throbs like fish jumping out of the water. It feels your anxiety when you express your sincere love for me. It fully understands that our hearts cannot be apart, and that it's useless to fight this love.

My love, I was certain you would have agreed, so I already sent the photograph you have given me to my father in Italy. But the way you wrote makes me understand you are unhappy. Do not worry, for I sent the package myself with my own two hands in a box by registered mail. I have the receipt here with me, so rest assured that it will arrive safely. I was certain you would not mind. I am sure my father will keep the picture in a safe place; after all, you are family. I hope you are not too upset, for it has already left. I feel disheartened, especially when you wrote you had a dream that I was dead. I wish it were true! I would rather be dead than anger you in any way.

My love, I would like you to know another thing. Last evening, as I was taking a bath, one of these girls took a rope and tied it to my bed. I did not notice it when I went to bed. After I had fallen asleep, she pulled me and the bed down the steps. Thank God, I did not get hurt. She could have killed me.

So, when the nurses heard my screams and the loud noise of the falling bed, they all ran and lifted me up and placed me on another bed. They began to ask who could have done such a thing. When they find out who did this to me, she will be sent home. They warned all the other girls that if they do not leave me alone, they will all be sent home.

Just imagine me falling down the steps and the bed landing on top of me! When the nurses came to my rescue, they were screaming. They thought I was dead under the bed. But when they lifted the bed off me, I did not have a scratch on me. So, they were relieved. The Lord did not want me to die yet. My love, I was having such a beautiful dream of you when that happened.

So, my love, I have nothing else to tell you. I only count the hours until we are together.

Yours Forever,
Rosina

P.S. Let me know if you are upset with me about the photograph. Ciao!

CHAPTER TWENTY-ONE

FINO A DOMENICA PROSSIMA
(UNTIL NEXT SUNDAY)

September 25, 1921
Rush Hospital Country Branch
Malvern, Pennsylvania

Since Elizabetta's outburst in the cafeteria, all the talk had shifted, as Catherina had predicted, away from my love life and on to whether Elizabetta might be the one who tied the rope to my bed. Someone overheard a nurse saying that Elizabetta might be transferred out of Rush. That someone told someone else, until before long it was being discussed in rooms, in common areas, and around the cafeteria. Elizabetta hadn't made any friends during her stay at the hospital. In fact, there happened to be a long list of people she either offended or terrified. Comforting as it was that Elizabetta hadn't singled me out, I couldn't rest well until the rumors of her leaving became a reality.

Sunday, I wanted nothing to do with rumors milling about or, worse, another confrontation with Elizabetta. To be on the safe side, I waited for Gianni at the front of the building, watching every door of every taxi open to a different person until one finally held my love.

"Come on," I told him, pulling on his arm. "Let's go for a walk and get as far away from these people as we can."

As we walked in silence past the other patients receiving visitors, a few eyes took an interest in us. No one smiled or nodded as they might have if we were walking down the street in Philadelphia. Instead, they stared with either blank or agitated expressions. As unnerving as it was, I resisted the temptation to confront each one of them.

"I was stunned to read about what happened to you," Gianni said. He had turned his head hard to the left as he talked. I looked in the same direction. A young woman with messy brown hair glared at us. Elizabetta! Gianni turned toward me and asked, "Do you think it was a practical joke? When I was in the army, we used to do those sorts of things just to amuse ourselves. But this didn't sound like that. It sounds like she really tried to kill you. Are you sure you're okay?"

In my letter, I had added a few extra embellishments. Not only did it make for a more exciting story, but I had wanted the scene to seem as frightening as it had been to live through it. He needed to understand that I'd never felt safe here. Now I had even more reason to worry.

"It does seem like a miracle I wasn't hurt," I told Gianni, looking over my shoulder to check if Elizabetta had decided to follow us. She stood in the same place with a sneering smile and an unsettlingly steady focus on the two of us. She slowly raised her hand with her palm facing us, wiggling her fingers in a menacing wave.

I grabbed Gianni's hand and pulled him forward as I cast my eyes on the ground in front of us.

Following the same path we took the last time he'd visited, I changed the subject. "And how's my Gianni?" I asked, forcing cheerfulness into my voice.

"Much better now that I'm with you," he said with a smile.

"Oh, Gianni." I bumped my shoulder into his side in a loving gesture. "I'm so happy you're here!"

"I'm happy, too. I was afraid the time change would throw off our visit." He squeezed my hand. "I felt bad about missing last week, but I needed to help out at The Italian American Club. If I miss too many events, they might kick me out."

"You wouldn't want that to happen," I said, not bothering to hide my annoyance.

Gianni glanced at me with his mouth open, about to say something, but then he closed it and shook his head. Had my tone upset him? Well, he had upset me last Sunday.

"You want to hear something interesting my landlady told me?" he asked, clearly hoping to steer our conversation away from a fight.

Glad for the change of subject, I let him. "Tell me, I want to know." Maybe his story had something to do with me being able to live with him until he saved enough to purchase a house.

"Old Maid," Gianni said.

"Old maid?" I asked, confused. "Are you talking about your landlady or what they'll call me the longer I stay at this hospital?"

Gianni laughed. "Neither," he said, shaking his head. "There's a lot of stops on the Main Line between Ardmore and Malvern. It's not like when you were in the hospital in Philadelphia. I was telling Mary that I was nervous I'd get distracted and miss my stop. And she told me about Old Maid. The first letter in each word stands for a train station along the way. So, it goes, 'Old Maids Never Wed And Have Babies, Period.' It starts in Overbrook and ends in Paoli. And after Paoli, Malvern is next."

All I heard was how terribly long it took him to visit me here. The "old maid" might very well become my future. Lost in my thoughts, I hadn't noticed Gianni had ended his story.

He stopped walking and turned toward me, his face softening. "You must have taken my advice seriously. You wrote to me how much healthier you are, but seeing you now…" He paused, shaking his head. "I've never seen you look more beautiful."

"Is that so?" I faced Gianni with a grin. "That's what Dr. Solomon told me when I saw him. He asked me, 'What's a pretty young lady like you doing in a place like this?'" It, of course, wasn't exactly what Dr. Solomon had said. At the time, I hadn't been at all flattered by the doctor's comment. I much preferred my rendition, which I hoped would produce a rise out of Gianni.

"He did? That doctor of yours better not be coming on to you or he needs to watch out. He'll have me to contend with." Gianni balled his fists, trying to appear as if he was ready for a fight. It was the exact reaction I had wanted. Seeing him get a little jealous proved to me that he cared. He looked so sweet and comical that I couldn't help laughing.

"I tease you, my love," I said, and he relaxed out of the boxing posture. "Can you forgive me?"

"I can if you tell me what your doctor really told you."

"Well." I took a breath to steady my voice. "He told me that I'm in good health." Looking toward the building, I added, "They're putting me to work cleaning."

"Do you feel up to it?" he asked. "A patient shouldn't be asked to work. It could cause you more stress than you're already under. I don't think it's a good idea. You shouldn't be doing too much, or you'll relapse. I thought you were supposed to be resting?"

I opened my mouth to explain, but Gianni shook his head and continued, "I don't want you to risk it. Please. There are only two things in this world that make me happy. You and the Lord. Your health is my happiness. But your illness would be my death."

"I'll try not push myself too hard." I reached for his hand as I carefully considered my next words. "I have to work to offset the cost of staying here since I have no one who can pay for my care. And, as you well know, no one will take me in if I were released."

"Oh," Gianni said, pinching his eyebrows together. He rubbed his chin and looked out across the grounds, seemingly lost in thought. I knew he couldn't afford to pay for the cost of my stay any more than my brother or my aunt could. And Gianni wasn't ready to sweep me off my feet and take me home with him, no matter how hard I wished it to be true.

Since there was no use in discussing it further, I pulled on his hand and we continued walking. After a few minutes, we came to the same shady tree where we'd sat two weeks ago. "Sit with me."

I tugged on his arm, causing him to lose his balance just enough to gently tumble into a seated position, with me nearly falling onto his lap. His serious expression melted into a smile.

"I wish I could kiss you," he said as I adjusted to a seat beside him. He took a deep breath as he surveyed our surroundings. "But it doesn't feel right with all these people around."

"Be patient," I whispered, watching a group of people passing in front of us on the path. "When I'm finally home with you, I'll kiss you as much as you wish."

This man sitting beside me was the kindest, sweetest, most handsome man I had ever known. If only he had already found a home for the two of us.

"I feel so good being here with you," he said. I waited for him to proclaim his love for me, as he so often wrote in his letters. Instead, he dropped his gaze. "Every time I leave you, all of that vanishes and I'm sick again."

"Are you sick because I mailed your photograph?" I asked in a small voice. That photograph had been keeping me awake with more worry than even the threat of Elizabetta.

"Oh, that?" Gianni said as if he had all but forgotten. Hopefully, he was willing to let bygones be bygones. Besides, nothing could be done now. He smiled at me but remained silent.

The golden sunlight filtered through the eaves of the tree. Despite a light breeze adding a chill to the air, it was a perfect afternoon. "I wish I could take a picture of you right now under this tree," I said, never wanting this moment or our short time together to end.

"I have the perfect idea," Gianni said, grasping my hand. "I'll buy a camera and bring it next time. Wear your favorite dress, and I'll take your photograph."

"Oh, Gianni, that sounds wonderful! And I'll take one of you." Relief at such a fun solution to remedy the missing photograph eased my posture.

He twisted toward me and pretended to take my picture, mimicking an invisible camera in his hands. I practiced poses until we both fell into a fit of laughter.

Once we caught our breath, he said, "Tell me about your father. I wish I could meet him."

"You would like him, and I'm sure he would like you," I said, patting his hand.

"Are you sure about that? Fathers can be very protective."

"My father would understand. He once had a romantic side, or so the story goes." I reclined into the back of the bench and tilted my head upward to gaze at the tree branches.

Gianni wrapped his arm across the back of the bench. "Tell me the story. I entertained you last visit. Now it's your turn."

I laughed. "You did! And I liked it very much." Focusing on the leaves fluttering on the branches of the tree, I allowed my mind to travel to Italy. "My Aunt Teresa told me this story about when my father met my mother." My lighthearted feelings dissolved into contempt as I added, "And about the woman who became my stepmother."

I took a deep breath to calm the hatred for Seraphina that still ran strong despite the elapsed time. I imagined my father as a young man, walking along the narrow lanes of Torchiara. As I pictured my childhood village, my anger eased into nostalgia. "Salvatore, my father, has never been a rich man, by any means, but he more than makes up for it by being handsome, hardworking, and honest. One day, when he was young, about our age right now, he was walking through the village's piazza past all the vendors selling their goods of fruits and vegetables, rounds of cheeses, various cured meats and such. Well, as he walked past a flower vendor's cart, a single rose floated to the ground. Salvatore thought to return it to the old man selling the flowers because, as I told you, he was an honest man. But then a lovely young woman caught his eye. She was beautiful and delicate, as lovely as the rose he'd picked up off the ground. Walking with the flower, Salvatore excused himself as he passed a woman blocking his path and delivered the flower to the one who would become his wife and eventually my mother."

"I would do that for you," Gianni said. Then, thinking for a moment, he added, "And a rose. Is that why you're named Rosina?"

"It is," I answered, beaming that he had made the connection. My smile faded as I continued, "But there's more to the story, as you well know. There was one woman, known around the village as a real prima donna. You see, no one was better than this donna. Seraphina was her name. She had the most luxurious golden hair. Whenever she let it down, it hung like a heavenly veil to her waist. But she was more than just hair. No one in all of Italy could top her cooking. It was famous throughout the village and beyond. When she made a large meal, men, women, and children would line up for days, if only for a single taste. Of course, with such glorious hair and cooking skills that could turn a thin man fatter than a prized bull, Seraphina was considered the top choice for any man looking for a wife. Night and day men would serenade her in song, even if they were terrible singers—which most of them were, according to my Aunt Teresa, who lived next door and gained a reputation for throwing tomatoes off her balcony whenever one of them sounded like a dying cat."

Gianni laughed, and my heart filled with pride and happiness that he was enjoying my story.

"Anyway, the men got smarter and started bringing Seraphina overflowing bouquets of flowers, but that didn't work, either. After that, they set up competitions to win her hand in marriage. But even the victor, bruised and battered from his best effort to prove his worth, wasn't good enough for this prima donna. You see, Seraphina longed to marry the one man she couldn't have."

"Can I guess?" Gianni asked. When I nodded, he added, "Was it your father?"

"But do you know why?" I asked in return.

"I don't. Maybe because he was handsome, hardworking, and honest, just like me?"

I laughed. "Yes, just like you. But you're forgetting something. Remember the woman young Salvatore walked past when he handed my mother the rose? That woman my father carelessly ignored, without even a second glance, was the prima donna herself. What a slight! Seraphina was never so insulted. She never forgot it, and she never forgave Salvatore for walking right by her like she didn't exist. Didn't he know who she was? The most sought-after donna in all the village, if not all of Italy? That day, Seraphina set her sights on my father and vowed to make him hers no matter what it took."

As I spoke, the shadow from the tree stretched longer and longer along the lawn in front of us. Now groups of people were heading toward the entrance of the building. "Visiting hours must be drawing to an end," I said.

"I don't want to leave," Gianni said, helping me to my feet. "And I really want to hear the rest of your story."

"And I don't want you to go. Unless I could leave with you," I added in an attempt to joke, but Gianni must have noticed the sadness in my eyes.

"My heart all of a sudden feels ten times heavier," he said as we made our way to the entrance. "I don't know how I can leave you, even though I know I must."

I couldn't find the words as we inched toward the line of taxis.

"Promise me you'll write every day," Gianni said when I wrapped my arms around him for one last hug. He placed his hand on my cheek, and I leaned into it, placing a light kiss on his palm.

"Until next Sunday," I whispered, hoping he wouldn't miss another week.

Pulling his hand away and setting it on his heart, Gianni repeated, "Until next Sunday." Within a few minutes, he was gone.

September 28, 1921
Ardmore, Pennsylvania

My Dear Rosie,

I am writing to remind you the promise you made to write to me every day. Three days have gone by without a letter. I have been looking forward to hearing your news and your love toward me. If you knew what I go through when I don't hear from you, you would not forget me. Yesterday, I waited for your letter like a soul in Purgatory. Then the mail came, and again there was nothing from you. I couldn't sleep all night. If you treat me like this now, I don't want to know how you'll be toward me when you are home. Maybe you won't look me in the face. You used to write me beautiful letters with loving words of encouragement. Now I'm astonished by the sudden change.

Listen, my love, I will try to be more patient. Seeing you once a week is not enough for me. I want to know what you do each day and what those around you are saying about me. I can only imagine what those young guys are telling you. I'm sure it's nothing good. So much crosses my mind when I don't hear from you. Maybe you've forgotten me and love someone else. I wish you would always love me as I love you.

My love, when I visit you on Sunday, please fix your hair and wear your most beautiful dress. I will bring the camera and take your picture. I want you to know that I have cut off all of my hair. Sunday I will not take my hat off. I am ashamed. I look like a white honeydew!

Today, I sent you writing paper and stamps. Let me know when you receive them and if there is anything else you need. I feel so bad that I have nothing to bring for you on Sunday. I hope to receive a letter from you soon.

I send you a thousand affectionate kisses in the meantime and my dearest regards.

Yours Always,

John

September 30, 1921
Rush Hospital Country Branch
Malvern, Pennsylvania

My Dear Love,
This morning I received your letter dated the 28th. You
have no idea how happy I was hearing your lovely words. But I
was displeased to hear that you shaved your head. Please let me
know why you did that. Your hair was so nice! I think you're a bit
crazy. You don't know how I loved your beautiful hair, how you
combed it. When you come visit me, I will not speak to you. When
you told me in the past that you were going to cut your hair, I
thought you were kidding. You shouldn't disappoint me like this.
My love, you complain I am not writing to you as often.
Don't you remember when I told you I was going to be working?
I don't have as much time anymore. And you say I don't send you
amorous words. You know well how I suffer being so far from you.
I feel my words of love are useless. It's like I'm telling them to the
wind. I would rather speak to you in person, at least for a day.
Then you would know and understand how much I love you and
with what affection I call your name.
Gianni, I suffer being so far away from you. Last night,
this Italian lady named Catherina asked me why I was so worried.
I did not answer her, so she said, "I know what is bothering you.
You are thinking of Gianni, aren't you?" Then she proceeded to
tell me of her love and how she suffers not seeing her love at least
once a day. I couldn't sleep the whole night. You were constantly
on my mind.
My love, please stop your worrying. You should be crazy
with joy because I am madly in love with you. You must
understand how I think about you every moment of the day. At
times I worry that our future life together will never happen. But

I think the Lord will not allow this because we have suffered so much. My love, I have no more time. Please don't bring me anything on Sunday. I only want you! I send you my distinct greetings and a million kisses on your lips.

Yours Forever,
Rosina

October 3, 1921
Ardmore, Pennsylvania

My Dear Rosie,

Yesterday, I had three hours of pure pleasure with you. I wish that time would never go by because I never want to be away from you.

My love, when I arrived yesterday, you made me wait for over five minutes. At first, I was a little angry. But when I saw you, peace came to me and I felt much better. However, I detected a disturbance with you. I don't know the reason you were upset. My love, I hope you weren't disappointed that I did not bring a camera. I will buy one this week and bring it on next Sunday's visit. Perhaps you took it to heart that I thought to cut my hair. As you saw, I did not. If I did, it would have grown back more beautiful. But if it displeases you, I will not cut it. I only wrote that to you because I wanted to see how you would have felt if I had cut it.

My love, on the train ride home, I was thinking of you and our visit. If you were with me, you would have seen me smiling and laughing as I thought about us. However, I was upset to think about how you pulled a long face on Sunday. I did not like to see it. There's nothing in the world more beautiful than love. Please try to be more pleasant with me next time. Yesterday you told me you can't show all your love for me. Why are you talking like that? Do not be selfish. Tell me how much you love me. Do not keep the words locked up in your heart. When I write to you, I tell you what I feel. But when I am with you, I do not say things like that because of where you are.

My love, when you return home, I will show you what true love really is. I think about our future together, when we will be able to do all that we desire to do. We could see who is stronger.

Which one of us do you think is stronger? Ever since the first time we met, I longed to embrace you and to take you to bed. However, we are forced to wait. When I think of how you have to stay in that place, I become sickened. My stomach cramps and I can't eat. I suffer even more when I don't hear from you. Last week, I didn't receive a letter from you for four days. Remember, you promised to write twice a day. If you loved me, you would keep your promise.

Last night, you kept appearing before my eyes as I was trying to sleep. You were constantly in my dreams, looking so beautiful, so delightful, and so full of love. I will tell you more in my next letter. I hope to receive a letter from you tomorrow. In the meantime, I send you many greetings and the best kisses.

Your Darling,
John

P.S. Tell me, why are you thinking that our future together might not happen? Who would prevent it?

October 4, 1921
Rush Hospital Country Branch
Malvern, Pennsylvania

My Adored John,

I received your dear letter, and I did not hesitate to reply. I found pleasure in some of what you wrote. However, I am displeased that you continue to complain how you do not receive my news. I have not received the mail as quickly here either. Please stop writing to me the same sad story. And, how many times must I answer if I truly love you? Do you want to see me dead from trying to prove my feelings for you?

My love, you complain about my mood on Sunday. You tell me I was in a huff with you. Maybe if you listened to me when I speak, you would understand. My love, living here has caused me to be ultra-sensitive. Everything seems to annoy me. Even my heart aches. At times, I feel like poisoning myself. So please, try to understand that it is better to not upset me. You write in your letter how I don't tell you my love for you. You do not know me. I am not two-faced. When I have something to say, I say it. Instead, you are one way in person and another in your letters. But Gianni, I love you anyway. We should try to please each other. Instead, we are like two children. For me, the distance between us upsets me the most.

My love, the day will come when we will be able to please each other, and I can show my ardent love for you. I didn't want you to leave on Sunday. I would have liked to sleep in your arms. When I am no longer in this place and we are finally alone, I will show you how much I love you. You are the first and only person to whom I can express all that I feel, and I can truly open up. Please stop questioning my love for you. There are certain things I am too embarrassed to tell you. If you promise not to mistreat me any longer, slowly I will tell you things that will please your ears. I know how to love you!

Sunday, I went to bed at eight o'clock. I didn't want to be near anyone. They were all dancing and I had no interest in joining them. I couldn't fall asleep with you on my mind. I wished for you to be here with me. I wanted to tell you so many things. I wanted to embrace you and feel your warmth. However, I was alone in this room, surrounded by a deep cold and only my nervous thoughts to keep me company. When I did fall asleep, I dreamed you were in my arms. We clasped each other tight as we kissed and embraced. How can you say I do not love you?

Enough! I cannot continue under the light of this candle any longer. It makes me too tired to keep writing. My love, I was happy to read that you will buy the camera already. Leave it with me, and I will take a picture that will please you. I believe this letter will make you happy. I'm sending it from my heart. I send you a million kisses on your beautiful lips.

Always Yours,
Rosina

P.S. I hope you receive this letter soon! Reply with your news when you get it. Ciao!

CHAPTER TWENTY-TWO

IL DOTTORE
(THE DOCTOR)

October 14, 1921
Rush Hospital Country Branch
Malvern, Pennsylvania

My lower back ached from the nine-hour cleaning shifts. As I set a bucket full of soapy water on the floor of the women's restroom, it splashed over the edge and dampened my right foot. The shocking cold caused me to jump. How I wished I was cleaning my own home, one that I shared with Gianni, rather than this sanitorium. I needed to hang onto hope that the day was coming when I would walk out of here and never return.

By the time the restroom floor was clean and sparkling, I was eager to return to my room and change out of my damp stockings and into a clean dress. It would be wise to freshen up since I had to meet with Dr. Solomon today. I wasn't sure why, week after week, I needed a checkup, since he'd pronounced me in good health. Still, I pumped a spritz of my new fragrance onto the inside of my wrist to cover the fact that I didn't have time to bathe.

In the opposite wing of the hospital, Catherina was already waiting to see the doctor. "Hey, lady," she said as I took the empty seat beside her. She leaned toward me and asked, "Did you hear about the feast they're putting together for tonight? Should be a real fun time. Music. Dancing. Are you going to go?"

"I might," I told her with a smile. It would be nice to enjoy myself.

"So, I have to ask," she said quietly, "and excuse me for being nosy. But where were you off to so early yesterday? You were gone all morning."

"Promise not to gossip?" I said, equally quietly.

Catherina nodded and looked around to see if anyone was eavesdropping.

Since we were alone in this portion of the hallway, I admitted, "Dr. Solomon invited me to join him on an automobile ride into town."

"Alone?" Catherina asked, wide-eyed.

"No, there was a small group of us," I corrected. "But it was wonderful!"

It had been exactly what I needed. Yesterday morning, like most days, I couldn't sleep despite my exhaustion. Often, when the weather was pleasant, I would take a walk around the grounds to calm my nerves. As I approached the front drive, Dr. Solomon had been stepping out of his automobile. I couldn't help but stop and stare at the shiny metal and sleek curves. Gianni had marveled over similar models when he was in Atlantic City.

Dr. Solomon noticed my interest right away. Tipping back his hat, he beamed with pride. "She's a beauty, isn't she?" he asked, grinning at me. For a fleeting second, I wasn't sure if he was talking about me or the automobile. "Would you like to go for a ride?" he asked.

"Oh no, I couldn't." I shook my head for emphasis. How would it appear if I drove off alone with the doctor?

He must have had a similar thought. "Wait right here. I'll see if anyone else wants to join us."

When he reappeared, two young nurses and Antonio, a male patient, followed behind him. When the doctor opened the passenger door for me, I didn't hesitate to step into the cushy interior. I should have been getting ready to report to my cleaning job, but I figured the doctor would make sure I didn't suffer any consequences for my absence.

"We went to the train station and then to a fancy store on the main street," I told Catherina now. "The doctor said we could choose whatever we wanted, and he would purchase it for us. I picked up some soaps and this fragrance." I held out my wrist for Catherina to smell.

"That's lovely," Catherina said. "But what about Gianni? Won't he be jealous?"

I was about to say that it might help if Gianni did become a little jealous, but the door to the examination room opened with a jarring banging sound. A young female patient emerged, appearing pale and emotionally shaken.

"Must have gotten some pretty bad news," Catherina whispered to me.

The woman walked at a brisk pace down the hall, careful to avoid eye contact with anyone as she passed.

A nurse with a clipboard cradled in her arms first called Catherina into one room and then instructed me to go ahead into the room beside it. Inside, Dr. Solomon sat behind a large wooden desk. A certificate with his full name, Joel P. Solomon, hung on the stark white wall behind him. It was accompanied by intricate framed drawings of human anatomy.

"Have a seat on the table, and I'll be right with you," he told me without lifting his focus from the paper in front of him. Familiar with the routine, I climbed onto the metal table.

Dr. Solomon rose from his chair, still looking at his notes. When he spotted me sitting on the examination table, his face lit up. "Oh, Rosina, so good to see you again. You're looking well this afternoon."

"Thank you," I said, straightening my posture. "I am well. Do I still need an examination?"

Dr. Solomon laughed. "I could give you an exam if you really want one. But that's not why I called you here today."

"Oh?"

More seriously, he asked, "I'm wondering how the cleaning position here at the hospital is working out for you. It isn't too much, is it?"

"Oh, no. It's good to keep busy and moving." I clasped my hands in front of me. I wanted to admit it was awful, but I didn't want to appear ungrateful.

"Well, it's not easy work, but I'm glad you're managing," Dr. Solomon said, smiling warmly at me. "I want to ask you an important question, and I want you to seriously consider it." He paused. "How would you like to become a nurse?"

"A nurse?" I echoed.

He stepped closer. "I could teach you to read and write in proper English. Everything you need to know," he told me, as if he was offering the opportunity of a lifetime. "You could go from the manual labor you're doing now to a dignified career." He closed the space between us to a few inches. In a soft voice, he explained, "Think of the life you could have. You'd never want for anything again."

I leaned back, placing my hands behind me as I tried to form a response. "Dr. Solomon, I'm not—"

"Please. Call me Joel. We're friends now, aren't we? After yesterday morning? How did you like riding around town in style? We could do more of that."

"I did like that." I had come for a routine examination. But now, if I wasn't mistaken, I was being propositioned. "Doctor.

Um, Joel. I'm sorry, but I can't." I shook my head. "I can't become a nurse. I'm planning to get married. Become a wife and a mother. Take care of a home." Even if Gianni hadn't formally proposed marriage, I was certain it was where we were headed. Or, at least, it was what I wanted most. Perhaps I shouldn't have accepted the ride and little gifts from the doctor. I may have given him the wrong impression.

Dr. Solomon looked down as if I'd hurt his feelings. Returning his gaze to me, he said in a flat voice, "I should have known a lovely woman like you would already be taken." His expression brightened. "But you're not married yet. There's still time to reconsider. Think of all that I could do for you." Moving closer, he reached up and carefully shifted a strand of hair off my face. "I'd take care of you in ways you'd never have with that other fellow. Can't you see? I'm falling in love with you."

I inhaled sharply and started to decline his advances, but my words were blocked by Dr. Solomon's lips pressing against mine. His hands clasped my shoulders, pulling me closer into the embrace. My eyes widened as my hands braced against his chest, pushing him off of me. The doctor released me and took a step back.

"Please, I'm not interested! I told you, I'm involved."

Dr. Solomon stood in place, smoothing back his hair, which had fallen forward over his eyes. Straightening his white coat, he asked, "Your lover, where is he now? I see no reference to him in my documentation. No record of a formal inquiry into the status of your health or your impending release date. Why is that, do you suppose? If he truly cared about your wellbeing, if he had every intention of becoming your husband, this wouldn't be the first time I learned of him."

I didn't answer. I wanted to defend Gianni, but part of me was frustrated with him for leaving me week after week, with no progress made on our plans for the future.

Dr. Solomon nodded as if he knew he'd hit a nerve. "You'd be better off without him."

A sob was welling up from somewhere deep inside me. I needed to get away. "Are we finished?" I asked, keeping my voice strong and even so he wouldn't guess I was about to fall apart.

"For now," he said, stepping aside.

I hopped off the table and crossed the room, exiting as quickly as I could.

Behind me, Dr. Solomon called, "One day I'll take you away from here, and you'll be glad I did."

A few patients were waiting in the hallway. The same nurse cradled her clipboard, calling out names. Thankfully, Catherina was nowhere in sight. I didn't think I could have fooled her into believing I was fine. As much as I liked her, I didn't want her to know what just happened. I couldn't chance her judging me for the doctor's advances.

I lifted my chin and walked at a steady, reasonable pace. I knew better than to show emotion in front of these people who fed on pain like vultures. Hopefully, no one would notice the heat burning on my face. Even if they did, they'd probably assume I had a relapse. No one would guess what had actually occurred.

When I finally reached the front door of the lobby, I stepped outside, welcoming the cool breeze on my cheeks. Only a few people were scattered about the grounds, enjoying the sunshine and the falling leaves. Following the same path I often took when Gianni visited, I came to the bench beneath the broad oak tree whose leaves had begun to turn auburn. Collapsing onto it, I couldn't hold back the wave of emotion as sob after sob hiccupped through me. It wasn't the kiss so much as what the doctor had said about Gianni not making a serious effort to, at the very least, plan for my release. As much as I hated to admit it, I had posed these same questions to myself, only to push them to the back of my mind. But in the middle of the night or in the early morning hours, these awful thoughts returned.

Once I'd calmed down a bit, I decided to write Gianni. I couldn't face him the next time he visited if I didn't let him know what had happened.

I rose and walked toward the hospital entrance, swiping at my cheeks to hide the evidence that I had been crying. When I opened the lobby door, the buttery aroma of roasted turkey had replaced the usual stagnant air. I could hear the faint sound of music playing. I had forgotten about the feast.

After stopping at the bathroom to splash cold water on my face, I returned to my room to find Catherina getting ready. I wanted nothing to do with the festivities, only to write to Gianni and hide in my bed. But Catherina begged me to join her. Eventually she wore down my resistance and I agreed to go, if only to eat and leave early. But the entire night, my thoughts never strayed from Gianni.

October 14, 1921
Rush Hospital Country Branch
Malvern, Pennsylvania

My Dear Gianni,
 My love, it feels like a thousand years have passed since I last saw you! You don't know how much my heart aches and how it throbs being far away from you. Gianni, if you only knew how I feel when you write true words of love to me—as if I'm the luckiest girl in the world.
 Furthermore, my love, I want you to know I saw the doctor today. He asked if I wanted to become a nurse. He said he would teach me how to write in English. I answered I was in love and was not able to pursue a vocation. When he heard that, he embraced me and kissed me on the lips. He said he loves me too much. One day, he will kidnap me. I told him that I would never leave you. I began to cry from the shame. I felt like dying. That kiss did nothing for me. It did not move me. You're the only one I want to kiss. I only love you. My heart throbs only for you, no one else.
 When you visit, I will tell you everything you want to know about the doctor. Please, don't worry that I would ever leave you or allow anyone else to kiss me on the lips.
 My love, how long do you think of me before bed? I can't even pray. My thoughts are always of you. And when I fall asleep, I dream we are together. Sunday night, I dreamed you looked like an old man. You were skinny and pale. I was unhappy to see you like that, so I embraced you so hard that you couldn't breathe. Think, how could I leave you when you're in my dreams every night?
 My love, tell me about your dreams of me. Tell me everything, the whole truth, because I want to tell you everything,

too. When I see you on Sunday, I want to tell you so many beautiful things. How happy we will be to spend time together again! Tell me, my love, when I return home, what fun will we have? Where will we go when we're free to take trips? How will we lead our lives together? I want to plan for our future. When you build our lovely small house, I'll be so happy to spend all my days there with you. I will stay home, and you can go to work. I will clean the house. I will prepare the meals and wash your clothes. And then, I will smother you with kisses. I will prepare a beautiful bed, and you will go to sleep happy.

My love, tonight we had a feast to celebrate how many of us are cured. I wish you were here with me. We could have danced together. There was great music. Everyone was clapping their hands. I danced the waltz and did not make a fool of myself. You were on my mind the entire time. I couldn't go to bed without writing to you even though it was ten o'clock. Now it is midnight and I'm making too many mistakes. My friends keep bothering me to stop writing. They are pulling my hands, and now one of them dimmed the light. Look, look what they make me do! That's how I finish. I cannot write anything else. Meantime, I send you ardent kisses.

I'm Yours Forever,
Rosina

P.S. Look how they made me sign my name. Can you read it?

October 15, 1921
Ardmore, Pennsylvania

My Dear Rosie,

My love, my spirit was so high as I was reading your letter until I came to the part about how the doctor kissed you and you cried. At that moment, I will not lie, my blood boiled like a tempestuous sea. I considered going to visit him until I realized I don't know his name. I would like to speak to this doctor and ask his real intentions for asking you to become a nurse. I want to know if he really loves you or wants to use you. Is this the reason he requested to see you so often? If you see him again and he asks another question not related to your health, you tell him you have a boyfriend who may not be big in stature, but who is very capable of putting him in his place. My love, I hope something like this never happens again. I cannot allow anyone else to kiss your lips ever again except your dear John, and only if you permit him.

I have been a good and honest man, and we have gone through so many hardships and sacrifices. I know with all my heart you're the only one who can make me happy. In return, I want to make you the happiest woman in the world for as long as I live. With the help of God, I hope never to upset you. I know you're a dignified lady. With you by my side, I walk with my head held high. I only want you to know that I love you so much, I want you all for myself.

My love, write to me when you receive this letter. Your beautiful words give me such joy. I dream of you every night. You're beside me until I awaken, and then I discover I'm alone. It is torture. It's as if my dreams are against me. I hope you're healthy, and you are able to enjoy yourself. I send you a thousand kisses.

Always Yours,
John

Chapter Twenty-Three

Caldo e Freddo
(Hot and Cold)

October 16, 1921
Rush Hospital Country Branch
Malvern, Pennsylvania

In Torchiara, the air would become chilly for a few months out of the year, and the nightly low might approach freezing, but there was never a frost so thick that it looked as if it had snowed. The olive groves wouldn't have taken well to this kind of cold. Neither did I.

The cold had an effect on life at the hospital as well. Saturday night, the staff canceled the dancing, not that after a week of nine-hour cleaning shifts I had enough energy left to participate. Everyone had been ushered to their beds early and encouraged to find warmth beneath several extra blankets.

Of course, my two newest roommates, Betty and Margaret, weren't the least bit tired. Betty had been admitted on Monday. I hadn't gotten to know her much, other than that she, too, believed she had been misdiagnosed with tuberculosis and was sent to this sanitorium "for no good reason," as she put it. Margaret, who had arrived in the middle of September, had been newly transferred to the ambulant wing after a month of prescribed bedrest. Finally free to get up and move around, she hadn't taken too well the news that the dancing had been canceled.

"Ladies," Betty called out. "Anyone here stashing away cigarettes? I could really use one."

Margaret dove headfirst under her mattress, her curly blond hair spilling erratically, and emerged with a crumpled package of Lucky Strikes. "You didn't get these from me," she said, tossing the package to Betty. "Or else the whole hospital will be bugging me to share."

"You want one?" Betty asked me.

"I'd rather have wine." I sat forward, resting my chin on my palm.

"Suit yourself," she said, offering the package to Catherina.

"Oh no, I couldn't," she demurred.

Margaret used the matches she'd stowed to light her cigarette, then passed them to Betty.

"You wouldn't happen to have a bottle of Italy's finest shoved under there for Rosie, would ya?" Betty asked.

"Yeah, what else do you have under there?" Catherina asked through a laugh. She rolled onto her stomach to get a closer look at Margaret's bed.

"None of your business," Margaret said in light tone. She propped her cigarette between her lips and tucked the remaining supplies back into place. "Maybe I got a man hiding in here, for all you know."

"If you have a man wedged in there, then my hair is on fire," Betty replied. She took a long pull on her cigarette, releasing the smoke in a steady, rather elegant stream. With her short, dark, wavy hair and her tall, slender frame, Betty reminded me of the models on cigarette advertisements. "Tell me about your fellow," she said, turning toward me. "You two making the most of that bed when he visits?"

My mouth dropped open, but it was Catherina who exclaimed, "Betty!" Throwing a pillow, she added, "Leave her alone!"

"Yeah," Margaret said, before being reduced to laughter. "Maybe she would be happier if her John were here with her now. Did you ever think of that?"

I closed my mouth and scowled in her direction.

"Poor Rosie," Betty added, taking another long drag from her cigarette. After a smoky exhale, she flicked her ashes into a tray on her bedside table. "Here all alone like a poor soul. Never going home. Abandoned and forgotten like the rest of us."

I'd had about enough of this ridiculous conversation. I ducked my head under my covers, hoping that if they couldn't see me, they'd lose interest. My love life was none of their business.

I should have been used to this mockery by now, but the "abandoned and forgotten" remark particularly stung because it felt so true. I had spent most of my life trying to fill the void caused by the loss of my mother. When my father remarried, my home became no longer mine. Still, I thought I could take refuge with my brother until history repeated itself.

So, now I was indeed abandoned in this miserable place where people were sent when they weren't welcome in their homes anymore. The pretense that we were all ill and contagious was, for the most part, accurate. However, the underlying reality was that many of us were sent away for reasons that had nothing to do with our health. For all I knew, I might suffer this awful fate for a third time, forgotten here by Gianni. My heart would never recover.

Catherina tried to smooth things over. "Well, Rosie, it's not so bad. I guess you'll have to stay here forever and ever with us."

At that, I couldn't resist a comment. I popped my head out of my covers. "I'd die first!"

The room went silent for a few seconds before there was an eruption of laughter from everyone except me. I hadn't intended my remark to be funny—I'd hoped to shut them all up. Instead, it had encouraged the three of them to make even more rude references about the next time I would see Gianni. The optimism I'd had earlier that my new roommates, who were all about my age, would be enjoyable companions quickly dissipated.

"Are you going to hug him when he visits? Hug him right down onto the bed?" Margaret asked to more laughter.

Only after I'd bitten my lip so hard it nearly bled as I refused to respond did the conversation shift to other topics, including the other men at the hospital. Betty and Margaret didn't quiet down until well after midnight.

Sunday afternoon, I fought the exhaustion of a terrible few hours of sleep. Fortunately, the warm sunshine cut through the deep chill. I awaited the arrival of my Gianni, which had come to feel almost normal and predictable. It was as if this weekly routine had come to define my life, with no sign of it ever ending. Catherina's prediction that I'd be staying here "forever and ever" seemed more like fact than an exaggeration.

I sighed, pushing away these pessimistic thoughts. When Gianni appeared in the crowd carrying a case that must have contained his new camera, my mood brightened.

"Oh, you must be Gianni," Catherina said, once we entered my room. "I've heard so much about you. All good things, of course!" She giggled, then asked, "What do you have there? Is that a camera?"

"It is." Gianni held it up and tilted it side to side so we could get a good look at it. "It opens up like this," he explained, maneuvering the metal levers.

"I can't wait to use it!" I had never held a camera in my hands.

"Could I be photographed?" Catherina asked. "I'd love so much to send a picture back home to Italy."

"I'm going to leave the camera with Rosie," Gianni said. "Maybe the two of you can take some nice photographs." He smiled at me with a glimmer in his eye.

"Don't worry," I told him, "I'm sure you'll like the pictures."

"Oh, Rosie." Catherina laughed. "I'm glad Betty and Margaret aren't hearing this!" Patting me on my arm, she excused herself and left to find her husband among the visitors.

Gianni and I were left alone—well, for the moment. "I'm so happy when I'm with you," he told me. "You look so pretty today. You're the most beautiful woman here. No one else comes close."

I wanted so badly to take his face into my hands and kiss him, but I restrained myself. We'd never be truly alone at this hospital, with the nurses walking in and out freely without ever announcing themselves. I recoiled, imagining Nurse Edna appearing during a passionate exchange between the two of us.

Many of the other patients still hadn't given up their interest in me, either. As if to prove that point, Gianni said, "There's a man outside the door glaring at me."

I looked out and waved. "That's just Antonio," I explained, following Gianni to the opposite side of the room. "He likes to talk to me."

Gianni crossed his arms and leaned against the wall. "He's probably jealous. I'd give him the silent treatment if I were you."

"He thinks we're friends," I assured him. "I told him I'm taken, and I've tried to avoid him, but I don't want to be mean about it. I met him on the automobile ride I took into town."

"When did you do that?" Gianni asked.

"A couple of days ago. I was awake early, and some of the people who work here were accompanying my doctor on a trip into town. They asked me to come along, and I agreed. Oh, Gianni, it was the most beautiful morning. We left at exactly eight and didn't come back for four hours! We went to the train station. Then we went to a store, and I bought some soap." I didn't want Gianni to get the wrong impression from my letting Dr. Solomon buy me a gift. The day of the automobile ride, I hadn't realized the doctor's intentions, or I wouldn't have agreed.

"I could have brought you some soap," Gianni said, uncrossing his arms. "If you tell me which one, I'll bring it next time."

"You're so funny," I said, walking up to Gianni and giving him a hug. "You remind me of a baby. You think I know more about which soap or cream to buy than you do?" I released him and sat on my bed. "It doesn't matter."

Gianni's silence stretched out.

"What is it?" I asked.

"The doctor you went with in the automobile. Is that the same doctor who kissed you?"

"Gianni, I told you not to worry," I said quietly. "How could I leave you when you're always on my mind?"

"You have to understand," he said, running his hand through his thick hair, which he thankfully hadn't shaved off. "I'd give up my life if that's what it costs to have you all for myself."

He took a seat beside me on my bed. I took his hand into my mine, running my thumb across his rough nails that were too long. These hands must have put in a long week of making and repairing shoes. I grabbed my nail clippers out of the bedside table's drawer and told him, "Here. Turn toward me."

Gianni smiled and said, "You don't have to," but I took one hand at a time in mine and clipped his nails.

When I had finished, I felt Gianni looking at me intensely. I raised my eyes to his. "What?"

"Kiss me," he whispered.

The room remained empty. I would have leapt into his arms if not for the conversation with my roommates echoing through my mind. Their mocking laughter rang so loud in my head, I was surprised Gianni couldn't hear it.

"We shouldn't," I whispered. "What if someone walks in and sees us?"

"Let them look," he said, closing the space between us.

I dropped my gaze to my hands. Should I abandon all caution and indulge in what would be a satisfying, sensuous kiss? Would it be worth the ridicule if we got caught? As I turned to place the nail clippers back into the drawer, my eyes landed on the new camera. I decided to use it as a distraction.

"I'm so excited you bought this," I said in an upbeat voice, hoping to make him feel better that I had ignored his advances. I lifted the metal camera, which was heavier than it appeared. "You're going to love the photographs I take."

"How will you pose? Show me," Gianni asked, taking the camera from my hands.

I straightened, lifting my chin and pulling back my shoulders.

"Maybe you should unbutton there at your neckline," he suggested with a hopeful smile.

I paused, considering. I knew what he was insinuating. My heart rate sped up. I liked being the object of Gianni's desires. Slowly, I loosened a few buttons.

Heat rose in my face as Gianni glanced toward the door. Motioning to his own shirt, he whispered, "Open up. Let me see."

Under other circumstances, anyone making such a request of me would have regretted it immediately. But here, alone with my love, I was tempted to give him a peek at what he could have every night if he'd finally marry me and take me home with him.

"No one's around. Please. Real quick. It would mean so much to me," he added in a hushed voice, his eyes fixed on my loosened neckline.

I considered myself the kind of woman who was above such an act. But I couldn't deny the temptation to give Gianni a look, not only for the thrill of it, but also to drive him crazy. Without further thought, I pulled my neckline low enough to give him a full view of my breasts. Just as quickly, I scrunched the material closed and stood. As I buttoned my dress, striding to the opposite side of the room, my cheeks burned so hot, they threatened to catch on fire.

As I clasped the last button, Nurse Edna walked through the doorway with purposeful strides. I gasped at her appearance. She stopped in her tracks and darted her eyes from me, over to Gianni, and then back to me. Making a tutting sound, she asked, "Is somebody making the most of an empty room?" I was about to deny it, when she demanded, "Why don't you walk your boyfriend out to the lobby with everyone else?"

I nodded and held out my hand for Gianni. We practically ran out of the room.

"Your face is bright pink," he commented once we were on the stairs heading down. "Do you think she suspected anything?"

I shook my head. "Let's not discuss what just happened," I told him, both out of fear of someone overhearing and because I wasn't entirely sure how I felt about it. The thrill of it filled me with energy that was at the same time exhilarating and guilt-ridden. I wasn't raised to indulge in such acts before marriage. Did this make me a loose woman? Part of me wanted to find the nearest Catholic church and confess my sins. However, given a second chance, I'd do it all over again. I had never wanted to join a convent, and this sanitorium resembled one in many ways. It was so satisfying to enjoy this intimate moment with Gianni. And the risk of being caught only made me feel more alive than I had in months.

We found a pair of unoccupied chairs in the main lobby. I exhaled loudly, trying to catch my breath. Gianni dropped into the chair beside mine and looked around. We were both at a loss for words. My mind spun in rapid circles, replaying what had just happened in the room. Was Gianni picturing it, too? I needed to find something else for us to discuss, a new subject, something easy to talk about.

"I lost a half a pound," I told him.

"It's probably due to your job and the dancing," he said, leaning forward and placing his elbows on his knees. "You know both activities don't have my approval. And you shouldn't be dancing with the contagious people here."

Noticing my annoyance, he added, "Or you do what you think best. I don't want to upset you. God forbid!" He laughed nervously, as if he was teasing me.

I wanted to tease back, to tell him he'd never see me unbutton my dress again with remarks like that one. Instead, I remained silent, still fearful of being overheard.

Catherina and her husband approached us. Glad for the distraction, we spent the remainder of our visit speaking with the two of them. Before long, the growing crowd of people collecting at the front door indicated the end of visiting hours.

"How does it go by so fast?" I asked, standing.

Gianni also stood, taking my hand as we walked to the front entrance. At the steps facing the main driveway, he stopped and turned toward me. "I don't want to leave. I want to stay here with you."

"You know that's not possible," I answered in a hushed voice. My eyes dropped to the stone steps. Even if he could stay a few more hours, what difference would it make? Eventually, we'd have to separate, and I'd still be living here. When would Gianni finally take our future seriously and make real, concrete plans for us to be married?

"You're like an angel to me," he said, lifting my chin with the tips of his fingers.

"Hey, buddy! You comin' or not?" the driver of a taxi called.

Gianni lifted his head toward the sky and closed his eyes. His gaze back on me, he said, "I guess I have to go." My hand slipped out of his grasp as he took a few slow steps backward. With a small smile, he added, "Until next Sunday."

"Until next Sunday," I repeated as he climbed into the taxi. He gave me a wave through the closed window.

It didn't take long for a familiar pang of sadness to stab through me. I walked across the hospital lobby, carrying my dismay like an unwanted package. Unfortunately, Nurse Edna was still in my room, taking her sweet time changing the linens. I avoided eye contact, hoping the cranky old woman would get the hint to leave me alone.

"You two are like an old couple, holding hands," Nurse Edna told me in that rusted-hinge-sounding voice of hers.

I strode to my bed, which had been already made up, and fell onto it as if I'd dropped dead. The bed creaked from the force. Maybe now she'd get the idea I didn't want to be bothered.

"Why hasn't he kissed you?" she persisted. "If I could be young again, I'd never stop kissing," she added, shaking a pillow into its case. "You wouldn't believe it to look at me now, but I was quite a looker in my day. I had to beat the men away with a stick."

I rolled to my side and looked at Nurse Edna, trying to imagine the younger version. Instead, I imagined beating her with a stick.

Loading the dirty sheets into a cart, she kept talking. "Send your boyfriend my way next time he visits. Maybe he could benefit from a woman with mature experience." With that, she finally left the room, laughing. If only she and all of her ridiculous remarks had left for good, perhaps forever.

Lying down, I enjoyed the brief moment of quiet before my roommates would return. My entire body vibrated with a variety of emotions: sadness from saying goodbye, annoyance at Nurse Edna, and nervous excitement from my indiscretion this afternoon. My hand landed on the primly buttoned column of my dress. Was Gianni thinking of that moment, too?

October 16, 1921
Rush Hospital Country Branch
Malvern, Pennsylvania

My Dear Gianni,
This letter is truly out of place. But I won't be at ease unless I tell you something. My love, today, I was truly happy. Our time spent together was priceless. I can never get enough of you. However, today when you were asking for a kiss, I felt bad I could not give it to you. Then you compelled me to show my breasts. I swear to you on the soul of my poor mother, no one has ever dared to ask me something like that. I have always been a decent woman. Instead, you have conquered my heart. My love for you makes me do whatever you ask. You told me my face changed color. It's because I love you too much. When you visit, you're like a flower in my eyes. There is no one like you. When you left, sadness overtook me again. My time away from you is useless.

My love, I do not want to be here for another day! I am fed up with the people here. I can't bear to listen to them any longer. I feel like I'm losing my mind. I only want to be with you. Just the thought of you calms me. I would feel much better if I could talk with you every day. All I would need is one hour to hear your voice. I wish it were possible, even though I know it's not.

Dear Gianni, I have no one else in this world who cares about me. I have no other visitors. Hopefully tomorrow I will receive your news. It truly feels as if I am waiting for my salvation.

I send you my dearest greetings and a million ardent kisses.

Always Yours,
Rosina
P.S. Catherina sends her regards. Write immediately!

October 18, 1921
Ardmore, Pennsylvania

My Dear Rosie,

I want you to know how pleased I was at your kind thought toward me. I believe your love for me is strong. This is why I dared to ask you to show me your breasts on Sunday. I know that doing so is not suitable for a decent and honest young lady as you are. However, I want you to know how pleased I am for having seen a little of your physical attributes. I will never forget them. And if the good Lord allows me to lie down by your side one day and fulfill my inner feelings with you, my heart will no longer suffer as it does from your distance now.

My love, you tell me I have conquered your heart. If you only knew how I think about nothing else but our future together. I constantly dream of a long and happy life with you. I hope my dreams come true.

My love, yesterday I met a young lady named Maria who was with you at the Philadelphia hospital. We talked about you for a while, and it gave me great pleasure hearing what she had to say about you. I am proud to be in love with such a lovely young lady as you. You're always on my mind. I never forget you no matter where I go.

My love, I hope you took those pictures. When I visit, I'd like to take one home with me. I have enclosed a photograph of me. When you finish this letter, be sure to kiss it.

Please return my greetings to Catherina. I wish her well. And I send you my dearest greetings with a thousand affectionate kisses.

Yours Forever,
John

CHAPTER TWENTY-FOUR

TUTTI I SANTI
(ALL SAINT'S EVE)

October 31, 1921
Rush Hospital Country Branch
Malvern, Pennsylvania

While my roommates were all occupied with deciding what to wear for the Halloween party, I turned my back to them and reached into the top of my blouse, where I had secured a wallet-sized photograph between my breasts. Gianni's sweet, handsome face smiled in the black-and-white photo. I pressed the picture to my lips. Casting a look over my shoulder to make sure no one was watching, I pulled open my blouse just enough to tuck his photograph back into place. I smiled, knowing it would drive Gianni a little mad to know where I kept his picture, especially after his visit two weeks ago. But if he wanted more than his photograph close to his favorite physical attributes of mine, then he needed to find a way to bring me home. When I wrote that I'd had enough of this place, I wasn't exaggerating. Lately, I had been wondering if the day would ever come when I would be able to leave with my head held high.

With help from Catherina, who had generously offered to work the camera, I'd taken several photographs of myself. I wanted to show Gianni what he was missing, living alone in his one-room apartment. I had been so pleased with the resulting pictures, I couldn't wait to share them with Gianni.

"How am I so lucky, to win the love of such a beautiful woman?" he'd said yesterday as he admired all the photographs laid out across my bed.

"I had a dream we got married," I told him. "But when we crossed the threshold, I fell and broke my right foot and my tooth. You picked me up and carried me inside. I was crying in my dream." I made a sorrowful face, with my lower lip pouting. "I was also crying when I woke up. Do you think it's a bad omen?"

Gianni shook his head. "I think it's just a sign of love. Don't you agree?"

"I don't know. As much as I like to dream about you, I always wake up sad when you aren't with me."

He sighed. "I do the same thing."

Our visit had followed the same routine as so many of the other Sundays with, once again, too little time and too many people surrounding us, including Antonio, who seemed to follow wherever we went. When it came time for this visit to end, Gianni held my photographs to his chest. "I wish it was you I was bringing home with me."

My heart broke a little with longing as I whispered, "Me, too."

Tears threatened again at the memory of yesterday's goodbye. However, I wouldn't allow a single one to fall. My roommates, with the exception of Catherina, would be the exact opposite of sympathetic if they discovered how badly my heart ached. Fortunately, all three were preoccupied with pulling together costumes for Halloween.

"I never heard of dressing up like this," I said to them.

"I know," Catherina said, holding an eye mask adorned with feathers. "In Italy, we don't celebrate until tomorrow. All

Saints Day. Festa di Tutti I Santi." She smiled at the group. "We go to mass. We visit friends and family. We have a big meal. Sometimes we exchange gifts." Shrugging, she added, "Tonight would be All Saints Eve."

"Well, whatever you want to call it, you're stuck here with us, sugar," Betty said, twirling the end of a feathered boa, which she'd wrapped around her neck. "Might as well have some fun while you're at it and pick out something to wear."

"How do I look?" Margaret asked as she adjusted a man's black top hat on her head.

Betty tossed her pillow at her. "Like you should be making a speech about four score and seven years ago."

Margaret grabbed the pillow and threw it back. Pulling off her hat, she scowled in Betty's direction.

"Well, I'm not getting dressed up tonight," I told the group, sitting on my bed.

"Suit yourself," Betty said, stealing a cigarette from Margaret's stash.

"Hey!" Margaret protested.

"Well, you weren't using it." Betty shrugged, flicking a match to life.

"Oh, Rosie," Catherina said, walking over to my bed and sitting beside me. "Why not? It'll be fun, and you could use something to take your mind off everything."

"I'll think about it," I said in a depressed voice. I winked at Catherina.

"Oh, okay," she said in sing-song voice. "I guess there's no changing your mind."

"Your loss," Betty told me as she walked out of the room, swaying her hips side to side.

When they all left, I stepped into the hallway and motioned for Antonio to come over.

"Yes, my love. You call me?" Antonio leaned his elbow against the wall, his other hand on his hip.

"I need your clothes," I whispered to him.

"I thought you'd never ask," he said with a grin as he started unbuttoning his shirt. "I knew you couldn't resist me for much longer."

"No, no, no." I waved him off. "How many times do we have to have this conversation? No. Never. Not ever."

"Yes, yes, I've heard it all before." He straightened and placed both of his hands on his hips. "But then, why do you want my clothes?"

"Can you keep a secret?" I asked.

Antonio's face lit up with interest. An hour later, I entered the dining hall, marveling at how it had been transformed into a costume party. Every person wore a mask, making it impossible to locate anyone I knew. Through bursts of laughter, loud conversations, and festive music, I somehow recognized a familiar voice. Mask or no mask, Betty's tall stature and strong personality made her easy to pick out. Laughing to myself, I stepped beside her and joined the group who were all talking over each other. A woman to my left sneezed, lifting her mask. Margaret. The woman beside her kept her mask in place yet had lustrous, thick, dark hair. It had to be Catherina.

Betty paused mid-sentence and looked in my direction. Giggling to myself, I gave her a wave. She groaned in disgust and turned her back toward me. A jolt of excitement shot through me. She didn't recognize me.

Silently, I continued around the room, approaching different groups without anyone figuring out my identity, or even that I was a woman. Thankfully, Antonio kept his promise not to reveal that his clothing had helped pull off arguably the best costume at the party. He himself had quite a comical costume. I'd laughed until tears came out of my eyes when he'd tried on one of my dresses in exchange for his clothing.

The music paused and one of the nurses in charge of running the party made several attempts for everyone to quiet down. Eventually she succeeded, announcing that it was time for everyone to remove their masks. My heart pounded with anticipation.

"On the count of three," the nurse yelled, "everyone remove your masks all at once."

"Three, two, one!" we all shouted. As masks disappeared, the room erupted in outbursts of recognition. Catherina was the first person to come running up to me.

"Rosie! You fooled us all!" she shrieked. She turned and called Betty and Margaret over.

"Well, I'll be," Betty said as her eyes ran up and down, taking in my getup from head to toe. "I've got to hand it you. I never would've thought it was you in a million years."

I'd held in my laughter long enough. Now I couldn't stop as I took in their reactions, from awestruck to put out by the ruse.

"You said you weren't dressing up," Margaret accused, frowning and crossing her arms.

"Uh-oh. Here comes trouble," Betty said, looking over her left shoulder.

A woman with unkempt wavy brown hair approached us. She removed her eye mask and sucked in her cheeks. Staring at me with apparent disdain, Elizabetta pointed and said, "You think you're so clever, don't you? Well, you're not!"

"Beat it," Betty said. "Go back to the hole you crawled out of."

Elizabetta considered Betty, who loomed above her with her arms crossed. Making a growling sound toward me, she stormed off without another comment. I released the breath I hadn't realized I'd been holding and thanked Betty.

The nurses announced that anyone who felt well enough was allowed to dance for the remainder of the time. For the last several weeks, I'd refused to attend these dances. Fatigue, the weight of my emotions, and not wanting another confrontation like the one I'd just had with Elizabetta had prevented me from even considering it. Now, with my heart racing and my spirits high from pulling off such a fantastic prank, I enthusiastically followed my roommates onto the dance floor.

After a few songs, Antonio joined us. Wearing one of my older, rarely worn dresses, he told me with a pitiful look, "Everyone recognized me."

I shook my head and laughed. With his dark shadow of a beard, not to mention his hairy arms and legs, he made one unattractive woman.

Offering his hand, Antonio asked, "Sir, will you dance with this ugly lady before you?"

I wished it had been Gianni's hand instead. If only he could have been here to share in the fun. Stopping in the middle of the floor, I turned toward Antonio and raised my arms in a dancing position. "I'll dance with you. But remember, no funny business or you'll regret it."

He answered in a high-pitched voice, "What kind of woman do you think I am?"

I narrowed my gaze at him, trying not to laugh.

He rolled his eyes and answered in his regular voice, "Yes, of course. We're two friends dancing and nothing more. Come on. They're playing a tarantella."

Kicking up my heels, I couldn't remember the last time I'd had so much energy. We must have danced for hours.

When I finally took a break, Catherina called me over to the side of the dance floor where a camera stood on a tripod in front of a length of drapery. Taking our place in front of the camera, we replaced our masks and held still for the blinding flash. I couldn't wait to see how I looked once the photograph was developed.

I had planned to write to Gianni upon returning to my room, but the excitement of the evening left me too exhausted. I crawled into bed, hoping to have pleasant dreams of Gianni. Perhaps one in which we'd be dancing.

November 3, 1921
Ardmore, Pennsylvania

My Dear Rosie,

I am so pleased you are feeling well. I'm also happy you had a great time Monday night and that you danced a lot, as I know you're a good dancer. I imagine those young men there were all too pleased to be dancing with you and having a good time. But please remember not to exert yourself with so much dancing that you hurt your health. Still, I'm happy you were able to have fun, and I know you are saving your love for me.

Your letter said you weren't happy without me there with you. I feel the same way. Without you, my love, everything I once found enjoyable is no longer worth doing. You are always in the front of my mind. When I'm in the presence of other women, I find it difficult to speak. I don't go out with friends or dare to have the least bit of fun. Can you imagine how I am? It's as if I'm a dead man. Monday night I was home reading the newspaper, alone like a dog with no friends and no chance to go out and have a good time. You're the reason why. How can I have pleasure when you're so far away? If you think of me, gaze at my photograph and see the man I am. It will not take you long, perhaps only ten minutes, to discover you are loved.

My dear, if you only knew how many times I stared at the pictures you've given me, you would truly give me your heart. Even as I write, my glance goes to your photograph, the one in which you are only wearing a jersey. I wonder when I will see you in person looking like that. Tell me, do you ever think about our future together? My dream is to hold you close to my body as I do your picture. To smother your lips with kisses and squeeze your heart against mine as I listen closely to hear which one is beating faster.

My love, my patience has run out. The two of us have not had two hours of fun together. I have been waiting for so long and have yet to be happy. It's not your fault, but I am at the end of my rope. When you write to me, think about our future and write to me much more than the few lines in your last letter.

I hope to visit you on Sunday. I don't know if I can, but I will try my best. In the meantime, I send greetings and a million kisses.

Your Most Dear,
John

November 4, 1921
Rush Hospital Country Branch
Malvern, Pennsylvania

My Dear Gianni,

I feel great, and I hope you do too. Please let me know if you really did not dress up for Halloween. I find it hard to believe that you were home that night reading a newspaper and didn't go out with a girl to have a good time. You're telling me a big lie. But jealous as I am, I believe you. However, if we were to be married, it'll be better for you not to lie to me, or there will be trouble.

In the letter I received yesterday, you said you were not impressed with my words. Gianni, I am sick and tired of this. What can I say that you don't already know? You are bad. All that I do, you dislike. On the other hand, your letters never have anything to say. Please don't write to me that way. You offend me. But I have to make allowance for you, for I understand your suffering in my absence is overwhelming. Another winter is coming. I understand your pain, sleeping alone in a cold bed. Remember this winter will pass, and another will come. Then, if it is God's will, we will be together, and I will make all your wishes come true. Please understand, now I am in this place. I can't do what you wish. There are so many gossipers here. If they notice something out of the ordinary, they will label me. Please know I suffer as you do. I would like to squeeze you to my heart and kiss your ardent lips. But I cannot.

My love, the doctor wants me to stay here longer. He said I shouldn't plan to leave for at least another month. I don't want to be here. Tell me what to do. I'd also like to know how your aunt in the hospital is doing. If you come on Sunday, I need more writing paper. Until I see you, I send you a thousand kisses.

Affectionately Yours,

Rosa

CHAPTER TWENTY-FIVE

ADDIO CATHERINA
(GOODBYE CATHERINA)

November 7, 1921
Rush Hospital Country Branch
Malvern, Pennsylvania

My Adored Gianni,

Right now, I can't express what my heart feels for you. It feels grieved being away from you. Yesterday, it felt wonderful to be near you, my adored love. You are so sweet and good to me. I wish time would not separate us but bring us together. I want to squeeze you tight and not let go until my heart's content.

My love, at times you tell me that I do not love you. If you only knew how I feel about you, you would squeeze me to your heart. For me, you're the best young man in the world. No one has honey lips as you do. And when you kiss me, I taste that honey afterward.

My love, you can't imagine what time it is that I am writing this letter. It's two o'clock in the morning. And since I couldn't sleep, I got up and wrote down what I was thinking. As you know, I don't have the time to write to you during the day. You cannot believe how tired I am, but thoughts of you won't allow me to sleep unless I write to you first. I also know the mail is going to be picked up early.

Pardon me for my bad handwriting. You see, I am writing on a box inside the bathroom. Just to make you happy and not to hear that I do not write to you. Do you know any woman who gets out of bed to write to her love? So, my love, I rest my case. I only want to tell you from my heart, my dearest greetings and a thousand kisses.

Yours Always,
Rosa

P.S. Prompt response!

November 7, 1921
Ardmore, Pennsylvania

My Dear Rosie,

I cannot forget the time we spent together Sunday. When I left you, my heart became sad. I will never be happy as long as I'm away from you. My soul is always pushing me toward you. Truthfully, I never did think you loved me so very much. And when you asked me to kiss you yesterday, someone could have cut away my heart and I would have felt nothing. I could have given you a thousand kisses had it not been for those people near us.

My dear, there is not one woman in this world who could steal me from you. You are the most beautiful and lovable woman I have ever known. When I'm with you, I feel brand new. In all my life, I have never felt a more powerful love than the one I feel for you. For years, I searched to find someone like you. My heart was never satisfied. The day I met you, from the very first moment I saw you, I knew my search was over. When we're together, I feel like the luckiest man in the world. If you only knew how I adore your blue eyes; for me they are the world's treasure. And not to mention your beautiful and sweet lips and your angel's face. I never get tired of looking at you. Every time I look at you, you become more beautiful, because I see the true person you are. Your character is perfect. When I compare you with other people, you are the most beautiful rose in the garden. I will love you until the day I die. When you are in need, I would go hungry for you. I hope it's my destiny to spend life's happiness with you. I anxiously await your return and all the fun we will have.

My love, remember I told you that I plan to visit my aunt and uncle in Germantown? I would also like to see your brother.

Could you write to him and ask him to come to my uncle's house this Saturday evening at 7 p.m.? Tell him what you need from his house and ask him to bring it to me. I'm sure he will ask about your health. I will discuss your situation with him.

My love, I wait for Sunday, like a soul waits in Purgatory for God's grace, to come and visit you, to be near you. I would like to tell you so many things, however the pen is not able to express all that I feel about you. Greetings and my heartfelt kisses.

Yours Forever,
John

November 10, 1921
Rush Hospital Country Branch
Malvern, Pennsylvania

My Beloved Gianni,
I am writing these few lines to tell you what great pleasure your beautiful words of love bring me. I could read them over and over, especially where you wrote you have never met a woman like me. My love, I'm not really beautiful as you say I am, but the proverb says, what the heart likes is beautiful.
My love, I used to feel as if I had nobody in this world. I was a child who had lost her mother. Now I have you. But it feels like a thousand years since I last saw you. Three hours together is too little. I feel disheartened. I wish I knew when this distance between us will end. I cannot wait until we can be together and alone to do all things we can't do when you visit. We will be happy. You will see.
My love, if you go to Germantown, give my regards to Antoinetta if you see her. Tell her when I come home, we will both pay her a visit. Give my regards also to your aunt and uncle. I send you my dearest greeting and a million kisses.

Your Dear,
Rosina

November 13, 1921
Rush Hospital Country Branch
Malvern, Pennsylvania

Catherina repeatedly tucked and released the fabric of her skirt as we sat side by side in the lobby, waiting for visitation hours to begin.

"Are you all right?" I asked.

She shot me a forced smile. She opened her mouth as if she were about to speak but then seemingly thought better of it.

"You're going to rip a hole in your skirt if you're not careful," I said as she rubbed her palms across her lap in a soothing motion.

"There is something on my mind." Catherina offered me a look I could only describe as pitiful. "But I really can't say."

A gust of chilly wind accompanying the first visitors distracted me. Standing, Catherina said, "I'll tell you later."

I wanted to know what had her in such a state, but the lobby was overtaken with the weekly displays of loved ones being reunited. Gianni entered looking distinguished and handsome. I ran up to him and, despite my better judgment, wrapped my arms around his neck, pulling him into a passionate kiss.

When we broke apart, he said, "Wow! How did I get so lucky?"

I laughed. "That's all you get. Now behave yourself."

"I'll try. But I'll make no promises," he teased as we made our way to my room.

Margaret wasn't there, but we met Betty at the doorway. "Look who came back for more," she said as a greeting to Gianni. "Want to be our new roommate? A spot just opened up."

"What do you mean?" I asked. "Is Margaret leaving? Are you?"

"Nope," Betty said, darting her eyes into the room. Then she gave me a little wave and strode down the hallway.

Inside, Catherina stood next to her husband. An empty travel bag sat open on her bed.

"Catherina?" I said, my voice cracking.

"Oh, Rosie, I wanted to tell you, but I wasn't sure it was true." Dropping her gaze, she added, "And I wasn't sure how you'd react."

"You're going home?" I asked, stating the obvious.

Catherina nodded and walked toward me. "The doctor cleared me."

I swallowed, unsure if I could find the strength to speak. After taking a deep breath, I managed, "Oh Catherina, that's... that's wonderful news. I'm so happy for you."

She smiled despite her eyes filling with tears. I opened my arms and she stepped into them, giving me a hug. "I was so worried you'd be upset," she said once we parted, wiping her cheeks with the back of her hand. "I know it's your dream to go home, too."

I glanced over at Gianni, who watched us with a pale expression. "Don't worry about me. I'll miss you terribly, but I'll be fine."

She nodded and returned to her open bag. Gianni shook Catherina's husband's hand. I motioned for us to leave to give her time to collect her belongings. "Promise me you'll find me and say goodbye," I told her as we stepped into the hallway.

In the lobby, I took a seat on the sofa. Gianni sat down beside me, shifting to face me. I didn't speak. If I could have held a pillow in front of my face, I would have screamed my lungs out into it.

"When Catherina told you she was going home," Gianni said, propping his elbow on the back of the sofa, "you looked upset. Why?"

"Isn't it obvious? I don't want to be here any longer." The words came out louder than I had intended. Visitors filled the lobby with conversations and activity, yet no one seemed to notice my frustration. Crossing my arms over my chest, I added, "You will never see me happy as long as I am in this place."

"You must be patient," Gianni said, leaning forward.

"For what? Dr. Solomon could decide to release me tomorrow, and what good would it do me? Where am I going to go?" I asked, tossing up my hands. "I have nowhere."

"Did you write your brother?" Gianni asked.

"I did." The letter had been brief and to the point. I let him know that I remained in good health and that Gianni planned to visit with him.

"Hmm." Gianni's eyebrows knit together. "He failed to show up when I was in Germantown. I wanted to discuss bringing you home. Where you could stay." He glanced across the room in thought. "Perhaps you can write him again."

I shook my head. "I have nothing good to say to him beyond what I already wrote."

"This situation is very serious," Gianni said, fully turning to face me. I averted my gaze toward the windows. The bare trees shook in the wind against the dark, overcast sky. "I thought you'd be relieved I was making plans for your return home."

"You think I'm not worried where I'll go after I leave here?"

He inhaled sharply. "That's why I decided to discuss matters with your brother. You should write him again and let him know what you want."

I let out a small, bitter laugh. Even if I did write a second letter, Nicola would probably tear it up before he had a chance to see it.

"I can try again to speak with your brother the next time I go to Germantown." Once I'd refocused on him, he added, "I would like to prepare a home for you, for us, but I need time."

"How much more time?" I asked, gazing deep into Gianni's eyes, hoping for a definitive answer.

"I don't know," he said, reaching for my hands.

I pulled them away. Several eyes already watched our every move.

"I need to make sure I see Catherina before she leaves," I said, standing.

"Of course." Gianni rose beside me, trailing me back to the room.

Saying goodbye to Catherina was more difficult than I could have imagined. Besides the envy that had soured my mood, I would miss the only true friend I'd made at this awful place. Still, I was glad she could go and live her life happily.

"We're going to start a family," Catherina whispered as we hugged one last time.

I fell silent, too lost in my thoughts to speak. How could I get Gianni to understand how it felt to be left behind week after week with no idea when and if I'd ever have a place to call home? Catherina had the very things I most wanted and needed, a place to call home with a husband and the promise of a growing family. I could have those very same things, but all of it remained frustratingly out of reach.

Not long after she left, visiting hours came to an end. Gianni broke the silence between us. "I want you to know, while you're here, I'll have no peace. As soon as I leave, it's as if I'm hollowed out from the inside. Without you, I am nothing. You're everything to me."

"I find that hard to believe." I didn't bother to hide my annoyance.

"Why?" he asked, gripping his hat in his hands.

"This distance between us. It's difficult not to be discouraged. I imagine you going out with your friends, some of them women."

Gianni shook his head as if my comments were all wrong. "Even when I see my friends, it's no good without you."

"And yet, here I am, and here we are saying goodbye again." I motioned with both hands toward the front door.

Gianni glanced outside at his waiting taxi. Much like today, the man I first met at his aunt's party had seemed nervous and unsure of himself. He'd been sweet, and my heart had filled with hope at the prospect of a new romance. Standing here now, that hope was slipping away along with our dreams for the future.

"I'll speak to your brother," Gianni repeated. "I promise to find a home for you. Have patience, my dear. Take good care of yourself. Promise me."

When I didn't answer, he hugged me and whispered, "Until next Sunday."

I didn't echo the words. He paused as if he were waiting to hear them. Then, understanding that I wouldn't be responding, he replaced his hat onto his head and took slow steps toward the door. Holding the door open for a group of women leaving, Gianni waved one last time before leaving. A gust of wind entered the lobby with a bitterly cold bite.

I stood in place for several minutes, not wanting to return to my room and see Catherina's empty bed. One day, all the beds in my room, and even all the beds in this wretched sanitorium, would be empty. And I would still be standing here, alone in this barren lobby, until the day I died.

CHAPTER TWENTY-SIX

NATO PER MORRIRE
(BORN TO DIE)

November 15, 1921
Rush Hospital Country Branch
Malvern, Pennsylvania

My Dear Gianni,
    This letter is evidence of my good health. I hope you are well also. Dear Gianni, I want you to know that on the first of the month, my dear Aunt Teresa died. Her soul went to heaven. It has been a great shock to me. I don't have the strength to express my feelings. I feel truly out of myself. Monday morning, I received a letter from my father. It was full of sorrow. My heart ached. I feel devastated. I do nothing but cry. My younger brother also has been admitted at a hospital in Naples. He is stricken with pneumonia and bronchitis. He's my dearest brother. Just think, how can I comfort myself amid all my sorrows? I feel like the unluckiest woman in the world. It would be better for me if the good Lord would put an end to my life. I have a feeling, one day soon, I'll get news that my brother has died.
    Gianni, think of me no more. I will kill myself. I don't know what to think or do anymore. I have neither eaten nor slept for going on two days. I'm constantly crying. I am wretched. I am being punished by God, being made to stay such a long time in

this hospital. Couldn't God have sent me enjoyable days, too? Besides, you have not given me any pleasures lately as you used to do. You give me only regrets.

So, I end this letter because there isn't anything else to say. From my aching heart, I can only send you my dearest greetings and a thousand kisses.

Affectionately Yours,
Rosina

P.S. Reply immediately!

November 16, 1921
Ardmore, Pennsylvania

My Dear Rosie,

I was anxiously waiting for your good news. Instead, I was saddened to learn of the death of your dear aunt, as well as the grave state of your brother's health. But what can we do? Why are you so spiritually afflicted? You know what you have gone through with your own health. Listen to me, dear, we are all born to die. This is something we will all do. Life is nothing else than ups and downs. When the time comes, we all have to leave this world.

In the beginning, when I first came to America, I used to do the same thing as you. But then, I understood how the world was. And now, it does not affect me as it did before. Please, I beg of you, do not be disheartened. It won't be good for your health. You know how you suffered since you have come to America, and no one has given you a helping hand. I saw this with my own eyes. Even your own brother as well as your friends have turned their backs on you.

My love, I, too, feel terrible pains when I receive bad news. However, I never say I'm going to kill myself. I was stunned when I read this, and it has brought me much grief. Please do not hurt yourself. I think, my Rosina is so young and so beautiful, with her whole life ahead of her. How can she say such a thing? When you come home, you can be free to follow whatever your heart desires. You can choose to be married or to remain single. Either way, you will be a happy, happy young lady with so many opportunities. I would gladly trade places with you. As a beautiful woman, you have so many choices. Men will line up to marry you, but I hope you will pick me.

My dear, you must listen to me now. When you are well, I am strong. You said yourself how handsome I looked on Sunday. That is because of you! I wish you loved me. And if you did, I could be even more handsome. Two weeks ago, I went to the doctor. He told me I had to get married if I wanted to gain weight. Therefore, I really hope that you, Rosina, are the one who can make this wish come true.

Try to be of good cheer and to pay less attention to bad news. I hope when I receive your next letter, your mind will be at peace and your words will be uplifting. When I next see you, I will dearly kiss you.

Always Yours,
John

November 17, 1921
Ardmore, Pennsylvania

My Dear Rosie,

It is Thursday, and I haven't heard from you. I was sure I'd receive your news telling me how you're feeling. Now it's too late for today's mail. I thought you must still be so mired in grief that you couldn't find the strength to write to me.

My dear, please cheer up for the sake of your health. These bad thoughts will only harm you. I am here for you to vent your sorrow. Don't neglect your love towards me, but instead tell me everything so I may help you. It gives me pleasure to be able to give you whatever you need. Remember, I only wish to see you happy. We are so far apart from each other. You can't see how often I hold your picture against my heart, wishing it was you inside my arms. When I see you on Sundays, there are so many people surrounding us that I don't feel able to tell you and show you all my love.

For now, I see you in my dreams. Last night, I had a dream we were naked in bed together. You challenged me. You wanted to know which one of us could outlast the other. Of course, you won. I awoke and kissed your photograph. I would be the luckiest man in the world if that dream became a reality. Look at what I've gotten myself into! Look at this true love I have for you. I would pay anything to be able to express all the love I feel for you. So, please forget your misfortunes and remember you have someone who loves you very much and only wants to see you well.

Write to me soon with your good news. Please don't make me wait too long. In the meantime, I send you a thousand heartfelt kisses.

Forever Yours,
John

November 20, 1921
Rush Hospital Country Branch
Malvern, Pennsylvania

Aunt Teresa, my dear, precious aunt, my second mother, had been dead for weeks before I found out about it. And my sweet baby brother, though almost fully grown now, lay near death in Naples. For all I knew, the next letter might bring news of his demise.

"There's nothing worse than receiving terrible news when you're so far away," Nurse Edna told me in a matter-of-fact voice.

Her words, as usual, did little to comfort me. I buried my head under my pillow, tears streaming down my cheeks. I was, as she said, so very far away.

This was God's punishment for leaving my loving father behind in Italy. I must have brought all this suffering upon myself. After all, look where I'd ended up: in a hospital, alone and abandoned.

"No point wallowing in your bed all day and night. It's not like that's going to bring her back," Nurse Edna said.

In response, I pulled the sheets over my head.

"Suit yourself. Visiting hours start soon," she added.

From beneath the sheet, I listened to the sound of her feet shuffling away and the click of the door closing behind her. I peeked out, thankfully alone, so I got up and walked to the window. Wiping my eyes, I gazed at the distant hillside full of newly bare treetops, wishing I could see past the hills, past the city beyond them, and all the way across the Atlantic to my childhood home.

In my village, the air would be warm, and the surrounding hills would be green with only a touch of gold edging some leaves. Aunt Teresa would have been put to rest near my mother's grave.

I would never see my Aunt Teresa again. I would never have the chance to tell her how much I loved her. Losing her felt like losing the last piece of my mother. Filomena's grief would be worse. If only I could be there beside her, offering her support, a shoulder to cry on. But I was here, devoid of hope that I'd ever be free, ever begin the life I'd dreamed of when I left Torchiara.

Turning from the window, I walked to the small closet assigned to me and retrieved my travel bag. Unfastening a side pocket, I removed a threadbare cloth doll wearing a blue dress. Though it might have seemed childish to keep it, I hadn't wanted anything to happen to this treasured piece of my past. When I'd first fallen ill, I'd made sure I grabbed the doll off the bed in my brother's attic and placed her securely in my bag. Since then, she had followed me, silently keeping me company.

Hugging her now, I could hear the hallway becoming busy with visitors. I should have gone to greet Gianni at the door as was my routine. Instead, I slid to a seated position on the floor, leaning my back against the closet. He might be upset if he couldn't locate me, but I couldn't find the strength to stand.

Since my father's letter had arrived Monday morning, I hadn't had the motivation to do much more than "wallow in my bed," as Nurse Edna put it. The entire week, I simply had not reported to my cleaning position. The weight of my grief had crushed my spirit to the point that I didn't care about a single thing.

The door to my room opened, startling me from my thoughts. I leaned forward and peered around the closet door, steeling myself to see Betty or some of Margaret's family members invading the space with their obnoxious conversations. To my relief, Gianni stood in the doorway, searching the darkened room.

"Rosie, are you in here?" he asked, turning his head left and right.

"I'm here," I answered in a small voice.

Gianni craned his neck toward me. "What are you doing on the floor?" He rushed to my side, reaching out his hand to help me up. When it became apparent that I didn't intend to budge from my spot next to the closet, he lowered himself beside me. "I've been worried sick about you."

His voice sounded so tender that a levee broke inside my heart. I turned into Gianni's embrace and allowed sob after sob to hiccup through my body. He held me tight, every now and then whispering, "It's okay. I'm here now."

After I had recovered some of my composure, Gianni noticed the doll cradled in my arms.

"Aunt Teresa was a second mother to me," I told him, smoothing the hair on the doll. "She was my mother's older sister. If the light caught her just right, you would swear you were looking into the face of my mother." I paused to fight back another round of tears. "She lived only a few houses away. When my brother and I wanted to escape, we would run to her house."

"She sounds wonderful," Gianni said softly. "I'm so sorry."

"This doll means so much to me because of her," I said, looking at Gianni through my blurred vision. "When I was a young girl, I had so many chores. I was never allowed to play. One day, I had enough and refused to come home until well after dark. When Seraphina, my stepmother, found out I hadn't done anything she'd asked of me, she wanted to teach me a lesson I'd never forget. She took away what I prized most: my dolls." I took a deep breath as I placed the doll onto my lap.

Gianni remained in place next to me, listening closely.

"I was so upset, I ran all the way to Aunt Teresa's house," I continued. "I was out of breath when I got to her door. Aunt Teresa knew something was terribly wrong. I told her, 'She took all my dolls!' My cousin Filomena, who's about my age, heard my crying and carrying on. She ran and retrieved a tattered, old cloth doll and told me I could have it. Before I could reach for it, Aunt Teresa took the poor excuse for a doll, washed her clean, and sewed a pretty blue dress for her.

"A day or so later, Aunt Teresa handed me the doll. I couldn't believe it was the same one. I promised to take good care of her. Aunt Teresa cautioned me to be careful not to let Seraphina know I had it. So I took it to this secret hiding place I had carved out for myself in the foundation in the alleyway beside my home. Almost every day, I'd sneak to my hiding spot and hold that doll close and feel the love Aunt Teresa placed into every stitch." I held the doll out for Gianni to see and sighed at the memory.

"Did you ever get caught?" he asked.

"Well, there was one day. Seraphina happened to notice me holding something, but she didn't know what I had. She walked up to me, surprising me. My dear baby brother, the one in the hospital now, was standing in front of me. He froze in place as his mother approached me from behind. I had only a few seconds before she spun me around to see what I had in my hands." I stopped talking as the memory played out in my mind.

"What happened?" Gianni asked after a few seconds.

"I'll tell you later," I said, returning the doll to my travel bag. Finally rising to my feet, I told him, "My leg is falling asleep sitting on the floor for so long."

"Why don't we take a walk outside?" Gianni suggested. "You won't believe what a nice day it is. You won't even need a coat. And then you can finish your story."

I nodded, closing the closet door and taking his warm hand into mine. The day was bright despite the overcast skies, making me squint once we stepped outside.

"See," Gianni said, "I wasn't making it up. It's beautiful out. But not as beautiful as you, my dear."

"Oh, Gianni, stop. I haven't eaten or slept or stopped crying for days." I slipped my arms into the coat I had brought with me just in case. "It's not that warm. You should be wearing a coat, too," I said, looking at his thin dress shirt.

"I'm fine." He shrugged as he took my hand again. Giving it a gentle squeeze, he said in an upbeat voice, "So, tell me. How does your story end?"

"Well, do you really want to know?" I asked, enjoying his interest. I'd always loved telling stories.

"You tease me, my love." He shook his head. "Yes, I really want to know."

"Why don't you tell me a story? I'd like something else to think about other than my grief. I don't know anything about when you were a boy," I said, realizing I'd rarely asked Gianni about his past. There was so much I wanted to learn about him, things I would have already discovered if we could have been with each for longer than these meager hours.

"It's not a happy story. In your state, it may not help you feel better," Gianni said, his eyes focused on his footsteps.

"Tell me anyway." I gripped his forearm with my opposite hand. "I want to know everything about you."

He nodded. "My mother and father both died young. My father, Pasquale, came to America in order to make money to send back to us. We were so poor, I'm not sure how my mother fed us. In America, my father found work on the construction of the Brooklyn Bridge. Though he was able to provide for us, the job took years off his life."

"How so?" I asked, picturing the New York Harbor and the many bridges my passenger ship had passed on its way to Ellis Island.

"My father was a 'diver' or, as he called himself, a 'sandhog.' I remember him telling me stories of how he would travel down many flights of stairs into the bottom of this large wooden box structure that they sunk into the river called a caisson." Gianni let go of my hand to mime the shape of the box. "They pumped out the water and replaced it with compressed air from a boat on the surface to keep it dry so the men could dig. My father dug into the riverbed from morning to night in near total darkness. Being down there so long did something to his blood. He wasn't the same man when he came home. He lost his vision, his hearing, and then his life. My mother died a month later from an illness, but I think she couldn't go on without my father."

"That's so sad." I stopped to look across the manicured grounds of the hospital. Windswept leaves blew across the lawn. I knew the burden of the loss of one parent. Gianni had endured losing both of them, and in such a short period of time.

"I can stop. My story doesn't get any better," he said, stepping in front of me and taking both of my hands.

"No, I want to know."

Gianni hesitated, staring into my eyes for a long moment. "I've never told anyone in America this story. Only my family members know." He resumed walking, his focus returning to the path in front of us.

After walking several steps in silence, he said, "An awful tragedy was the reason I came to America at the age of sixteen."

I remained quiet.

"My younger sister and I were sent to live with my uncle in Teramo. All was fine for a short while." He took a deep breath.

I was about to tell Gianni that if it was too difficult, he didn't have to tell me today. But he continued, "I had been placed in charge of keeping watch over my sister, who was seven years old at the time. The house had been hot from the hearth and making dinner. I left my sister where she was playing so I could step outside for a breath of air. I was only across the street speaking with some friends. The next thing I knew, there was smoke billowing from my uncle's front door. I went to run inside, but some of the neighbors held me back. I told them my sister was in there, but it was too late. She had been playing too close to the hearth, and her dress caught on fire. She didn't survive."

"Oh, Gianni," I said. "That must have been terrible for you!"

"I couldn't live there anymore." Gianni shook his head. "Besides the grief, everyone blamed me for the tragedy. Aunt Carmela graciously offered for me to come live with her here in America."

I stopped, but it took Gianni a few steps to notice. I threw my arms around him. "Thank you for sharing that with me. I know it must have been hard for you."

As we pulled apart, he remained quiet, gazing toward the hillside. I could have started crying again, this time grieving for all Gianni had endured in his young life. But then I remembered I hadn't finished my story from earlier.

"Want to know if my stepmother caught me with the doll?" I asked now, breaking the silence.

It took a second for my question to register with Gianni, who seemed as if he were a thousand miles away in his thoughts. Glancing toward me, he smiled. "Yes, I want to know. Tell me."

"Well," I said, walking down the path toward the front of the hospital, "remember how my baby brother was standing in front of me as Seraphina approached me from behind?"

He nodded.

"I could tell she was coming from the scared look in his eyes. He always liked me better than his strict mother. So at the last second, I shoved the doll into his arms, and he ran into the house. Seraphina didn't pay any attention to him. She wanted to catch me and take away whatever I had in my hands. But the joke was on her, because when she spun me around, my hands were empty. Oh, she was so mad. I was banished to my room without dinner. But I didn't care. Besides, hiding beneath my bed was my baby brother with my doll. I hugged him so hard he couldn't breathe!"

Gianni laughed. "It sounds like you got lucky that time."

I nodded. "I did! Maybe the next letter I receive from my father will have good news."

"I hope so," Gianni said, turning away from me to sneeze.

"Salute!" I said as he sneezed for a second time.

At the front of the hospital, the taxis were lined up in their usual formation. Gianni looked toward the waiting automobiles and then back at my solemn face. "Before I leave you, I want you to know that I plan to visit with Tomasso to discuss you coming home. Have you written to him so he can expect me?"

The mention of Tomasso sent a wave of fury through me. It wasn't like he didn't know where I'd been all these months. "No." I crossed my arms over my chest. "I doubt he wants to hear from me."

"How can you say that? You're his sister. He must care what happens to you. If you don't want to stay in this place any longer, he should do right by you and bring you home."

Gianni sneezed again. Reaching for his handkerchief, he wiped his nose and looked at me expectantly. Instead, I stood scowling at him, wondering when he'd figure out my brother no longer wanted me in his home. If Tomasso had cared, he would have offered me my attic room several weeks ago.

"It's time for me to go." Gianni wrapped his arms around my rigid frame. "Until next Sunday?" he whispered as if he was asking a question.

I turned my head to the side as another round of tears rippled up from my gut through my chest and into my eyes. "Until next Sunday."

November 20, 1921
Rush Hospital Country Branch
Malvern, Pennsylvania

My Adored Gianni,
     This evening has been terrible. You know the state you left me in. I cried incessantly. I don't know how I am going to get better. It was my heart that cried. Besides, I have not touched any food. My stomach is sick. It would have been better to take a spoon of arsenic and end it all. Gianni, you will not see me happy again if I am left in this place. Everyone here looks at us. They have told me this place has never had a resident who had either a boyfriend or a girlfriend. Even the nurse told me this is not a place to make love and has warned me not to do so. You see! How can I be happy in this place?
     I want to leave. Please help me. Or else I might do something unpleasant to myself. Enough! I do not want to take up your time. I send you a thousand regards and a million kisses.

Yours Forever,
Rosina

November 20, 1921
Ardmore, Pennsylvania

My Dear Rosie,

Today I was deeply moved seeing you crying. Your sorrow pierced my soul. I didn't want to leave you, and now that I'm home, my heart is so heavy, I cannot sleep unless I write to you. I don't know what I said to anger you so much, but I beg your forgiveness. I never want to upset you. I hope I never see you crying again.

My love, until today, I did not take our relationship seriously enough. I didn't believe all the things you have been telling me. Now I understand the truth. Please understand that you are my only hope for happiness.

My love, I am sorry to have caused you pain. Send me a quick reply or I will carry this burden all week. I feel awful, and believe me, I will continue to feel this way until I see you again. I would like to come visit you. However, it's up to you if you want me to come or not. Also, I can bring whatever you need. I send you my dearest greetings and a million kisses.

Forever Yours,
John

CHAPTER TWENTY-SEVEN

LEI CHE VA PIANO, VA LONTANO
(SHE WHO GOES SLOW, GOES FAR)

November 24, 1921
Ardmore, Pennsylvania

My Dear Rosie,
I would like to thank you for sending me those postcards to wish me holiday greetings and lots of fun. My love, I never have fun when I am without you. I'm sorry I couldn't be with you today. However, when I see you again, I hope to find you beautiful and a bit fatter.
My love, today I went to visit your brother concerning your coming home. He assured me he will provide a home for you to come to immediately. He also promised to come with me when I next visit. Please, don't worry about your future. Be patient. Like the proverb says, "He who goes slow, goes far." I know you're tired of being there. You discourage me. That enraged state is harmful to your health. Please don't act as you did when you heard Catherina was going home.
My love, I might not be able to visit you on Sunday because I have a bad cold. I don't have a cough, but my nose runs and my throat hurts. Since I must continue to go to work, I would rather stay home and rest this Sunday. I hope you will not be upset. Someday, when we are together, you can take care of me.
My love, I had the most beautiful dream that we made love. I awoke on cloud nine. When you write to me, tell me about your

dreams. Your letters are all I have until I can see you again. Please let me know if my staying home on Sunday is okay with you. Also, if you need anything, tell me and I can ship it to you. I look forward to the next time I see you. Then, you will be more beautiful and full of love.

Please do not make me worry about you. I only wish to receive good news about your health and wellbeing. In the meantime, receive my dearest regards and a thousand kisses.

Your Most Dear,
John

December 1, 1921
Rush Hospital Country Branch
Malvern, Pennsylvania

The rain lashed the window, leaving so many droplets it was impossible to see through them. There wasn't much to see anyway. The world beyond had taken on a lifeless hue of gray clouds and muddy puddles the size of lakes. Though I never preferred dark, stormy weather, it did fit my mood this Thursday morning.

I had been missing Gianni terribly, especially because he hadn't come this past Sunday. Instead, I spent the entire day in the security of my bed, wishing he would have taken better care of himself. If only he hadn't been so stubborn and had dressed in warmer clothing, he wouldn't have gotten sick. If we were home and married, I would have killed a chicken and prepared hot broth, and not just for him, but for the both of us. It seemed whatever plagued Gianni's health had also afflicted me.

"You haven't been reporting to your cleaning position," Dr. Solomon said now. He had surprised me with a bedside visit. One of the nurses must have alerted him that in addition to my refusal to leave my bed, I had developed cold symptoms. He pulled a chair beside my bed and lowered his tall frame onto it. Leaning his elbows on his knees, he asked, "And you've been complaining of a sore throat?"

"Yes, but it's not that bad," I said, trying to downplay my symptoms. I hadn't seen Dr. Solomon since that day in his office. I worried he would bring up the kiss or, worse, try to embrace me again. "I've been in mourning," I added. "My favorite aunt passed away."

"I'm so sorry to hear that." Dr. Solomon held my gaze as if he were trying to convince me that he cared. I looked away, hoping he'd realize I wasn't interested in his sympathy.

"But it is an issue that you're no longer working." This statement snapped my attention back to him. What repercussions were coming my way for refusing to work?

"Of course, you'll be excused if you're ill," he said, grasping the tongue depressor from his medical bag. Motioning it toward my mouth, he instructed, "Let's have a look."

I resisted the urge to gag as Dr. Solomon pressed the wooden stick onto my tongue. He shined a light into the back of my throat and tilted his head from side to side. "It is a little red." Removing the tongue depressor, he added, "Perhaps the beginning of an infection."

I closed my mouth and tried to clear the unpleasant wooden flavor. A gust of wind rattled the window. Dr. Solomon turned toward the noise. "That rain isn't going to let up, is it?"

I remained quiet. I didn't want to engage in pleasantries with him. I was in no mood to talk about the weather or make any other small talk. And I feared giving him the impression that I enjoyed his company.

Removing the stethoscope from around his neck, Dr. Solomon instructed me to lean forward. He lifted my nightgown and held the round end against the bare skin of my back. I flinched from the icy chill of the metal.

"Take a deep breath… Hmm, interesting. And again." He moved the disk to a different location on my back. I filled my lungs one more time with a generous amount of cool air.

As soon as Dr. Solomon removed the stethoscope, I adjusted my clothing to address the draft on my lower back and the sensation of being exposed.

Dr. Solomon picked up his clipboard full of paperwork. "So, let's see here. You've been with us for three months. You should have been released, yet you're still here. Would you like to explain why that is, or shall I?"

What could I say? I'd received no letters from my brother or my aunt in Germantown for over a month. And Gianni had tried and failed to speak with my brother in person. While Gianni had made beautiful promises, I had nothing to show for it.

"Oh, yes, that's right. Still no inquiry in my notes from a family member." Dr. Solomon paused and raised one of his eyebrows. "Or anyone else of significance." Leaning within inches of my face, he asked in a low voice, "Nothing has changed since we last spoke. Has it?"

My breath caught in my throat, making me cough. I turned away as I fought to regain my composure. Visions of how our last conversation ended flashed through my mind. The window shook from yet another gust.

Dr. Solomon leaned back in his chair and studied me with what I could only describe as pity, combined with a dose of smugness. Pressing his hands together at the fingertips and holding them in front of his face, he said, "I've come to care deeply for you. How could I have released you in good faith when I didn't know if you'd have a place to live?"

After a brief pause, he added, "But now that you're ill, well, that does alter things..." He trailed off, as if lost in thought.

I sat fully upright. What was he about to say? I couldn't have expected what came next.

"As soon as this weather clears, I'm recommending you be sent to Philadelphia. This cough of yours is a serious setback. Your lungs sound troubling. You may need an operation."

"An operation? I barely have a cough. It just started."

"It's rather routine for tuberculosis patients," Dr. Solomon told me, pointing his pen like he was holding a scalpel. "We remove the infected tissue in the lung, thus eliminating much of the risk for a relapse."

I pressed my palm against my forehead as if to hold in the panic flooding me. "When will this happen?"

"Well, you're not going anywhere today, obviously. I can assure you that much." He stood. "In a few days, there'll be arrangements made for you."

Though I had many questions, the shock of being sent back to Philadelphia for an unnecessary operation caused me to stammer. I was at a loss for the right words in English. My situation had become more dire than I ever could have imagined.

Dr. Solomon walked to the door, his limp seeming more pronounced than when he first entered. Holding the handle, he turned toward me and added, "Don't let this worry you. You said you had nowhere to go. Now you have a reason to remain hospitalized." He grinned and smoothed back a lock of hair that had fallen across his forehead. "You deserve a better life. Have you given much thought to becoming a nurse? Maybe while you're recovering, you'll take time to consider it. There's so much I can do for you. You'll see. In time, you'll see."

All the blood drained from my face. Dr. Solomon held my gaze for a long beat before exiting. I kept my eyes trained on the door. Was I having a relapse? I didn't feel nearly as ill as I had this past summer. Did I really need an operation?

I had the sinking feeling that I was about to become even more entrapped in the hospital system. If Dr. Solomon had his way, I really would never leave, first as a patient, then as a nurse.

The only benefit of returning to Philadelphia was that I'd be closer to Gianni and within walking distance of my aunt. I pressed my hands together and squeezed my eyes tightly closed as I prayed that all my worries would soon be resolved. I envisioned not needing an operation and being released from the hospital. I pictured my aunt offering me a room, and my cousins, no longer considering me contagious, welcoming me with open arms. And I indulged in the dream that Gianni would prepare a home for us and take me as his bride. I had suffered so much over these past months. Surely the time was coming when I would see my reward.

Two days later, the weather cleared, and I was awoken by Nurse Edna at an impossibly early hour, telling me to pack all my belongings. As the sun rose over the hillside, I boarded a train bound for Philadelphia. My heart ached the entire trip, especially as I passed the Ardmore Station, knowing I was so close to Gianni but still a world apart from him. The train rounded a bend into Philadelphia, and a touch of relief at returning to the city eased the knot of worry in my chest.

Still, being admitted to the same hospital where I'd spent my summer in agony wasn't how I'd ever wished to return.

CHAPTER TWENTY-EIGHT

LA MIA VITA È INCASINATA!
(MY LIFE IS A MESS!)

December 11, 1921
Rush Hospital for Consumption and Allied Diseases
Philadelphia, Pennsylvania

I spent the entire week filled with angst over the possibility that I would undergo surgery. My heart beat in my chest like a crazed drummer as I entered the doctor's office. Dr. Masterson motioned for me to take a seat on a wooden chair facing him across his desk. He'd been the one to suggest I go to the sanitorium in Malvern. How would he feel about seeing me in his office again after only a few months? I lowered to the edge of the seat with my hands clasped on my lap to prevent them from shaking.

"First, let's start with the good news." His deep voice seemed to fill every inch of his small office. "I have determined that the proposed operation is unnecessary."

I exhaled. I hadn't realized I had been holding my breath until that moment. While I welcomed this good news with overwhelming relief, I had little time to enjoy it.

"I'm sure you're aware we have another pressing issue to address," Dr. Masterson said, knitting his fingers together and leaning forward, his sizable forearms resting on his desk. "I conferred with Dr. Solomon, and together we've come up with a special arrangement for your living situation. Or lack thereof, unless I'm mistaken."

My mind buzzed with scattered thoughts. "What kind of arrangement?"

"There's a hospital in Illinois willing to take you. They'll provide you with training to work there as a nurse." Dr. Masterson smiled beneficently, confident that he had solved all my problems.

"Illinois?" My grasp of American geography was still rather nebulous.

"Yes, near Chicago. It's a full day's train ride west. I'm sure you'll find it to your liking," Dr. Masterson explained as if it was already decided. "It's a fine facility."

Blood thundered in my ears. I responded by vigorously shaking my head no. Fighting against being intimidated by the doctor's deep voice and large size, I somehow summoned the courage to speak. "I can't. That's too far away."

"Well, I'm afraid you have no other options if you plan to stay in the hospital system. Certainly, you're in good health and can be released from here at any time." Dr. Masterson leaned back into his chair, which creaked as his hands gripped the armrests.

My head continued to shake.

The doctor either remained completely unaware or willfully ignored my agitated state. "You'll be transferred back to Malvern, where you'll have the Christmas holiday to make your decision. I suggest you inform your family. In the meantime, I'll start the paperwork for your transfer to Illinois."

"And when will I leave?" I asked, rising.

"I would say you should expect to be gone before the New Year." He reached for his pen and made a note.

Though I wanted to burst into tears, I kept a calm exterior as I stood with my shoulders square and my chin slightly raised. Only my balled fists might have given away my inner turmoil.

Dr. Masterson continued in a gentler voice. "I know it doesn't seem like it, but you are among the lucky ones. Not everyone leaves this hospital in such good health. I have treated many patients with your condition. Many of them never recover. And then, there are those that leave here in a hearse. Consider yourself extraordinarily fortunate."

But a day later, I sat on the uncomfortable bed in the small hospital room, feeling anything but fortunate.

"I might as well leave here in a hearse," I told Gianni after explaining the arrangements that were being made for me. I also showed him the letter I received from Aunt Isabella this morning. My cousin Gina had been placed on bedrest for the remainder of her pregnancy. Aunt Isabella didn't think it was wise to offer me a place to stay at her home. I wasn't surprised. After I hadn't heard from her in weeks, I knew my chances were slim. Still, it hurt that she'd given up on helping me. Unfortunately, there was nothing I could write to change her mind.

"Why haven't you written to your brother?" Gianni asked.

I picked up the new box of writing papers he'd brought and threw it at him, yelling, "What good will it do?"

Gianni jumped to dodge the airborne box, which crashed to the floor, splaying papers in all directions. "He told me he would help you. He said he'd offer you your room. All you have to do is ask him."

"He's lying to your face!" I said, my voice rising with every word. "He's a coward. There's no way Nicola is letting me set one foot inside their door. Once she has her say, you'll see how quickly that room he's offering no longer exists."

"I haven't found a house for us. What would you like me to do?" Gianni asked, matching my high volume. "Ask Mary, my landlady, to let you stay in my room with me? Do you really think that's going to happen?" He ran his hands through his hair, stopping at the nape of his neck. More quietly, he added, "Please, Rosie. Your brother is all we have right now. The doctors will agree to release you to him."

I called Gianni every awful name I knew in Italian. Then, I ordered him to leave, which he did with little hesitation.

I instantly regretted the gaping silence and solitude that followed. I felt like a child who'd just thrown a terrible tantrum. With no one to confide in, I prayed to my mother in heaven to help me. Then I prayed to Aunt Teresa's spirit to give me some guidance.

Finally, though it pained me to do so, I decided to write to my brother. I would swallow my pride and beg Tomasso to take me in once again. I would endure Nicola's looks of disdain if this path would lead to a life with Gianni. Whatever it took, going back to the factory, handing over every paycheck, Gianni was worth every bit of it.

***

Friday afternoon, two days before I was to return to Malvern, a knock sounded on my hospital room door. Slowly it opened, revealing my brother's face. Despite my hurt feelings, my heart warmed to see my own brother.

"Tomasso!" I greeted him with a hug.

"Hello, Rosie," he said with a smile.

I searched his face for a clue about what he was about to tell me. He looked worn out, thinner than the last time I'd seen him. Nicola was probably too busy gossiping around the neighborhood to cook a proper meal for him.

"How have you been? Is Nicola taking good care of you?" I asked, sitting down on my neatly made bed.

"I'm doing well." Tomasso slid a chair forward and took a seat. "My back has been bothering me, and I have a cold that won't go away."

"And the children?"

"They're all growing and keeping me busy. Nicola thinks she's expecting again."

"Oh," I said, surprise stealing my words. Finally I added, "Congratulations."

Tomasso shrugged in response.

Since I had put off the inevitable long enough, I moved on to the question hanging over us. "You received my letter?"

He nodded, crossing his leg over his knee. "I did."

"And?" I prompted, losing patience with his short answers.

"And," he said, setting down his leg, seemingly struggling to get comfortable in the chair, "I don't really have answer for you. I mean, I could offer you the attic room, but..." He wouldn't look me in the eye as he spoke. "It's been bad since you left. I lost my job. We barely saved enough to pay the rent on the house."

"But surely there are other jobs out there." I leaned forward, asking, "Have you looked?"

"Of course I looked," Tomasso said, shaking his head. "It's not like I haven't tried, but there aren't any to go around. If we're going to provide for you, you're going to need to work."

"I'm well enough to go back to work." I sat up straighter. I shouldn't have been shocked by Tomasso's poor attitude. After all, I'd never believed that he'd welcome me back into his home. Still, a part of me held onto hope. "I cleaned for the hospital in

Malvern. I'm healthy and strong now. I'll work in the shoe factory again."

"There's no jobs. Not even factory work." His elbows perched on his knees as his head drooped onto his chest. "And, well, Nicola is worried that we won't have a room for the new baby."

I stiffened. Maybe things really were as bad as my brother described, or maybe that was Nicola's convenient version of the truth.

"Tomasso," I pleaded, "if I don't have a home, they're going to send me to a hospital far away from here."

Keeping his head hung low, he said, "These are difficult times for all of us. Maybe if things turn around, I'll be able help you someday."

The flicker of hope that had been burning inside me extinguished in a curl of smoke. "But I need your help now!"

All these months, I'd resisted coming to my brother. Truly, I had no interest in ever returning to his home. But apparently, turning to my own brother had never been a viable option. Everything he'd told Gianni had been a lie, perhaps to appease Gianni for the moment so he wouldn't continue to bother my brother. When I humbled myself and begged for his help, Tomasso had nothing but empty hands and supposedly empty pockets. I couldn't believe his situation was as bad as he described, but there was nothing else to say.

Tomasso left soon after, the lull in our conversation too awkward for him to handle. He reminded me of the skittish chickens I used to tend in Torchiara. Even Piccolino had had more courage and dignity than him.

On his way out, he hesitated as if he was about to apologize. Instead, he said, "I wish you luck."

I wanted to tell him all I ever would have was bad luck from this day forward, and it would be his fault. However, I pursed my lips together as the door closed behind him. My hand balled into a fist as I fought the urge to punch something or someone. What would Gianni say once he learned my brother lied to him?

I raised my gaze to my window. Night had come already at this early hour, and the darkened glass reflected my pain-stricken face. Never in my life had I felt more hopeless, more frustrated, or more alone.

December 16, 1921
Rush Hospital for Consumption and Allied Diseases
Philadelphia, Pennsylvania

My Dear Gianni,
I am still in this damned and hopeless place. I feel my heart bleeding. I cannot help myself. I am miserable. My life is messed up. I am going through hell! How unhappy I am! Why do I have to suffer? Why do I not see you anymore?

No, my dear, this is impossible! I cannot live without you. I really don't know what to do. I am forced to embark on this journey to Illinois. I cannot do anything about it. I have no one who will help. My love, today my brother visited me. We spoke for about an hour. Nothing he said pleased me. He could not give me a positive answer regarding a place to go when I leave here. He told me he might have a place for me, but he lost his job and does not have money. He is unable to pay rent for me. Enough!

My love, for me there's no way out. Right now, fate is forcing me away from you, who is so dear. Within a few days, I will be very far from you. I am going back to Malvern this week. They will make me spend Christmas there. Afterward, I will go where the doctor will send me. Only the Lord knows if I will ever be near you again.

My love, the necessity of leaving is killing me. I assure you, the affection I feel for you will drag me to a lunatic asylum. I should not speak to you this way, but at this point, I cannot hold back.

Please, my love, have compassion for me and this excruciating heart of mine. I understand you can't do anything for me. How unfortunate that you haven't been able to receive me at your house. But at least give me some help, some comfort. See if you could do something to prevent me from going far away.

My love, I know these words upset you, but since I have no one to turn to, you are my only hope. If you can't do anything for me, do not tell me today because I'm beside myself. I see myself alone. I feel dazed. I have a thousand thoughts going through my head, but none of them is suitable for me. There is no hope. Not even the devil has a place for me. My heart aches. I do nothing but cry.

So, before I depart, I would like to be frank with you. My words will be sincere. I will hide nothing. My love, I believe I've been in love with you for a long time. And now, I don't know what fate has in store for me. I will be so far away from you. My dear, all of our hopes have vanished. I believed our future was of joy and happiness and not of emptiness. I truly feel dead! I don't know if we will see each other again. So, my love, I hope you find a way to forget me. Let not your sweet soul suffer as it has in the past for me. You go about your way. Enjoy yourself as much as you can. Do not neglect yourself by thinking of me. I don't want you to be this way. This is the lover's life—unlucky!

My love, I am not going on. I only want to see you one more time before I leave. Be at the train station on Sunday at two-thirty in the afternoon. They are sending me to Malvern. In the meantime, I send you a thousand painful thoughts from this heart of mine and many kisses.

Your Very Affectionate,
Rosa
P.S. Goodbye! Pardon my bad handwriting. I wrote this letter in bed!

PART III

TERZA PARTE

CHAPTER TWENTY-NINE

SE TU VAI VIA
(IF YOU GO AWAY)

December 18, 1921
Ardmore, Pennsylvania

My Dear Rosie,

With great distress, I am replying to your letter. Your going far away displeases me tremendously. And having suffered with you such a long time, I find you very hard to simply forget. Especially now, when the harvest of our sufferings is near, but you desire to cut asunder our relationship. I'm aware of the state you find yourself in. But what fault is it of mine? I would like to help you more, but your brother disheartens me. He is the reason I have been holding back.

The only thing I want to hear from you is if the doctor is ready to send you home or does he want you to stay at the hospital longer? This is why I've asked you for his address. I want to speak to him on your behalf. I don't want you to stay in the hospital. If the doctor is saying you can come home, why is he not releasing you? I cannot take it upon myself to have you released from the hospital. One never knows what the future has in store.

My love, your letter has truly pierced my heart. I never expected such a letter. If you go away, you may never write to me again. I, on the other hand, will be on my last breath. I hope you do not have doubts about my love for you. I have always loved you, and I will love you forever. It doesn't matter where they send you. As long as you remain faithful and write to me, I will wait with open arms. Truly, our love is the most unfortunate love humanity has ever seen. But I am always hopeful that the good Lord will find a way to let us meet again. Fate has been unkind to us. But with the Lord's help and time, the moment shall come when I will be able to offer you happiness and a better love throughout our entire life.

My love, today I was at the train station. At two-thirty in the afternoon, the time you told me you were going to be there. I was disappointed when I did not see you.

But let's not get upset about anything. Holidays come to make us happy. And I hope even away from your family and your dear love, you do your best to have a Merry Christmas. Forget all your pains and enjoy yourself. Receive my dearest greetings and very loving kisses.

Forever Yours,
John

December 21, 1921
Rush Hospital Country Branch
Malvern, Pennsylvania

Adored Gianni,

Today, I received your letter. In short, you tell me you're displeased with the way I spoke to you. I have told you before, my dear, do not get upset when I tell you such things. After I said them, I felt bad. You also say I have ended things with you. This will never happen. There is no way I am ever going to forget you. Besides, I never told you I don't want to see you. You are mistaken. You have suffered greatly for me, and you can never forget it. I feel the same way about that. I could never sacrifice myself for you and then abandon you. I would go crazy with remorse. So, my love, I am not going to say anything else. Worry not about me. I love you now more than before. I fall asleep with your name on my lips. Your name is fixed in my mind. I no longer think about anything else.

My love, you tell me my brother is the reason you have hesitated to do more for me. I want you to know that he has no power over me. I am an adult. He cannot oppose me. So, if you truly love me, do not let anything bother you. The only thing I want is for you to write me often. And please don't make me worry about you.

When you come to visit next Sunday, I would like to speak at length with you face to face. In the meantime, I send you many greetings and a thousand kisses.

Yours Always,
Rosa

CHAPTER THIRTY

AUGURI DI NATALE
(CHRISTMAS GREETINGS)

December 23, 1921
Rush Hospital Country Branch
Malvern, Pennsylvania

Gianni,
    I wish our love would shine like the Christmas Star throughout our entire life!
    Rosa and Gianni for a thousand years!
    Very Best Wishes and Merry Christmas! I hope by the New Year we will be together.

Regards and Kisses from
your Rosa!

December 25, 1921
Rush Hospital Country Branch
Malvern, Pennsylvania

Christmas at Malvern had come in many forms. Still, other than the addition of decorations and a few records playing Christmas music, it seemed as if it were any other Sunday. From the extra activity of visitors to the nurses walking in and out of rooms unannounced as they made their rounds, it all felt sickeningly familiar. And, like the few Sundays Gianni hadn't been able to visit, this day was passing in the same depressing and mundane manner.

I had held onto the hope that Gianni might surprise me right up until I didn't see him emerge from one of the taxis. He was most likely spending the day at his Aunt Carmela's. He would be surrounded by his family and the delicious aromas emanating from his aunt's kitchen. They would be celebrating her return to good health, and there would be loud conversation, lots of eating, plenty of drinking, and happy music. I wished I could be there with him. Making everything worse, I hadn't heard from him in a week. Did he miss me, even though the last time we saw each other hadn't ended well?

If only I had received a recent letter or a Christmas card from him, I would have been reassured that he was indeed making plans for our future and that he had contacted Dr. Solomon. Surely Gianni must have written. Due to the holiday, the mail service had been more delayed than I had ever experienced. The timing couldn't be worse for me. I could be sent to Illinois any day now. I couldn't live with the thought that my last words to Gianni were harsh and unloving. When I'd ordered him to leave my room that day, I hadn't meant for him to be gone forever.

If only I had seen him at the train station before I left Philadelphia. So much could have been discussed. I could have apologized for my angry outburst, even if my unwillingness to contact my brother had turned out to be well-founded. My departure from Philadelphia had been pushed back three hours. Still, I'd thought Gianni might have waited. When he wasn't there, I could do nothing but leave. He and I were clearly being pulled apart by an unfortunate whim of fate. Heartache had followed our relationship from nearly the beginning. Why should the end be any different? It had been a beautiful love affair cut short, like a rosebud plucked before it could fully blossom.

I walked the hallways of this hospital that had begrudgingly come to feel like the home I'd never wanted, glad to be out of my newly assigned room. Upon arriving last Sunday, I'd noticed a woman with distinctly disheveled brown hair sitting with her back to me. I tried my best to go unnoticed, but it didn't take long for Elizabetta to turn toward me.

"You again," she said with that unsettling smile of hers.

My stomach dropped. I swallowed my fear as I tried to present a calm demeanor.

"Don't worry. I don't bite," Elizabetta said, seeming almost friendly until she added, "much."

Would I need to sleep each night clutching my letter opener for protection? I tried to ignore her mocking laughter, but every muscle in my body tensed. Surprisingly, so far Elizabetta had left me alone this week. However, every second I was in her presence, I remained on guard. I wasn't going to allow myself to be lulled into a false sense of security.

I had remained on guard when I met with Dr. Solomon as well. I had hoped my healthy state would prevent me from needing a checkup. However, Dr. Solomon had specifically requested to see me.

"Rosie!" he'd exclaimed as I'd entered his office on Friday morning. "So good to see you again. Here, take a seat. We have much to discuss."

Smoothing the back of my dress, I complied. Coming around his desk, Dr. Solomon perched on the edge of it so that he and I were in close proximity. "Your time here has ended," he said in a gentle voice, his hair falling across his forehead in that way that made me want to cut it off. "What do you want to do?"

"I want to go home. But I..."

"Have nowhere to go," Dr. Solomon finished, saying what I couldn't bring myself to. He smiled, pleased. "Then it's settled. You'll be sent to the hospital that Dr. Masterson, I believe, mentioned to you. It's a day's journey from here. But once you're there, you'll be given work for the next six months."

"When will I leave?" I asked, panic rising from deep in my chest. My heart beat *no, no, no*. "I need to speak to my fiancé." Gianni hadn't formally proposed marriage, but I wanted Dr. Solomon to take my relationship seriously.

Shifting his tall, trim frame off the edge of his desk, Dr. Solomon asked, "You have plans to be married? When?"

"We do, but I'm not sure when." I dropped my gaze to my lap.

"I see." Dr. Solomon lowered to a bent knee beside me. Cupping his hands around mine, he explained in a low voice, "Well, then, I'm afraid there's no other choice for you. I have plans myself to transfer to our Illinois facility. I do hear it's quite a fine hospital, right outside the city limits of Chicago. I could show you around the city when you're not working. I'm sure you'll come to love it there."

I opened my mouth to argue, but I had no words to plead my case. I had no answers. I had no home.

Dr. Solomon held my gaze for several uncomfortable seconds. Would he try to kiss me again? Fearing he might, I pulled my hands from his overly tender grasp and turned my head into my shoulder.

"Well, I must get going," he said in a more professional manner, rising. "As one of the few doctors not celebrating the upcoming holiday, my services are in great demand." Grabbing his clipboard off his desk, he walked me to his office door. "See you soon," he whispered, winking at me as if we shared a secret, then strode down the hallway, barely favoring his right leg, with almost a bounce in his step.

I reached for the cross around my neck. Though nothing had happened that could be considered improper, everything about our conversation still felt as if it had been a betrayal to Gianni.

As I entered the lobby on Sunday, I sought out every distraction possible to avoid returning to my room. Evergreen wreaths adorned the windows, and there was a large decorated spruce tree. I stopped to examine the variety of colorful ornaments hooked to its branches. Christmas in America took some adjustment. In Italy, there wasn't a chubby old man in a red suit delivering presents. There was Befana, an ugly old witch who flew through the air on a broomstick. And presents weren't received until the Epiphany on January 6th.

By then, I could be far from here.

Perhaps because I found myself in a similar situation, a memory flashed into my mind of the first time I'd been in the hospital in Philadelphia, facing my fears of being sent far away. The compassionate yet feisty Maria had given me strength then, and her words seemed to apply even more now. "Sometimes a girl has to look out for her own best interest," she had told me. "I can tell you're a strong woman like me."

I *was* a strong woman, I reminded myself. I had survived the death of my mother at a young age, an unloving stepmother, the week-long journey across the Atlantic, the tedious hours of factory work, my brother's vindictive wife, an infection that had taken me to the brink of death, and months trapped in this place. My heart would be broken into a thousand pieces if I no longer had Gianni in my life, but somehow, I would find a way to bear the pain. Although I'd never love anyone as passionately and as fully as I loved him.

The stately grandfather clock on the opposite side of the lobby chimed the top of the hour. With each ring, a little more of our precious time slipped away. If Gianni and I were to have any hope at a future, a beautiful ever after with a home filled with the laughter of our children, then he needed to act quickly. Because as the clock ticked off the seconds to the year's end, the two of us were running out of time.

Chapter Thirty-One

L'ultima Lettera
(The Last Letter)

December 26, 1921
Rush Hospital Country Branch
Malvern, Pennsylvania

My Adored Gianni,
I am quickly replying to your dear letter. You can't imagine how happy I am knowing you are in good health. I want you to know I am also in good health. My love, I was very worried I hadn't received any news from you for several days. But today at the second mail delivery, I received a dear letter from you and a postcard. So, this evening, I feel much better.

My love, in your letter, you said you received a letter from me sent from Philadelphia. I don't know how this can be. Maybe the lady who wrote the return address on the envelope made a mistake. I didn't want her to write the address, but she insisted. Maybe she purposely wrote it wrong. She is very jealous of me since I have you and she has no one. Enough! This is nothing.

My love, I want you to know, Sunday I was desperately alone, just like a dog. I cried the whole day. You tell me you can no longer live without me. But if you knew what is in my heart, you would truly say, "I am crazy for you." I can no longer rest.

One Sunday a week is not enough to make me happy. I would like to see you every hour to embrace you in my arms.

 My love, I met with the doctor. He told me the time for me to be here has passed. He asked me what I want to do. In short, I cannot explain everything to you in a letter. When you come to visit me, I will fill you in on the rest. I told the doctor I need to speak to you. So, my love, tell me what to do. Please do not get upset with me. I do not have a home to go to. If I did, it would not be such a big issue for us.

 My love, I can no longer write, for my time is limited. Please come Sunday. I will speak to you at length. Do not worry. We will find a way to be together. Meanwhile, I send you the dearest greetings and a thousand dear kisses.

Your Very Affectionate,
Rosina

CHAPTER THIRTY-TWO

COSA STAI FACENDO COPODANNO?
(WHAT ARE YOU DOING NEW YEAR'S EVE?)

December 31, 1921
Rush Hospital Country Branch
Malvern, Pennsylvania

I stood at the hospital's front desk, grasping the narrow candlestick base of the telephone in my left hand while pressing the cup of the receiver against my ear with my right. A faraway voice asked for the location and the number of where I would like to call. Peering at a small piece of paper laid out on the desk in front of me, I leaned my mouth toward the base and read the information to the operator. I gripped the telephone's smooth base tighter as I listened to a long sequence of clicks and snaps.

I much preferred the ease of letter writing over taking a chance the wrong person would answer on the other end of the telephone. However, I needed to relay an urgent message to Gianni, and by the time my letter arrived, it would be too late. The mail hadn't been reliable this past week anyway. In addition to the Christmas correspondences overburdening the postal service, Elizabetta's new job of working in the mail room definitely hadn't helped matters. Even if I had no proof, I was certain Elizabetta, looking to take out her anger and her jealousy on me, had changed the address on my letter last week. Why else would Gianni be confused over whether I was in Philadelphia?

The nurse behind the front desk tilted her head impatiently, as if I had tied up the hospital's phone line for too long. I squeezed my eyes shut, praying to hear Gianni's voice inside the bell-shaped receiver.

A woman's voice answered instead.

"Hello, this is Mary speaking," the woman said.

Mary? Then I remembered. Gianni's landlady!

"Hello? Anyone there?" she asked.

Fearing she might disconnect the call, I spoke quickly and loudly. "Mary, I need you to get an urgent message to Gianni. I mean, Giovanni DiFerdinando."

"Who is this?" she asked.

"It's Rosina, Gianni's girlfriend," I said, glancing toward the nurse behind the front desk, who was motioning for me to hurry up.

"Hi, hon, how are you? Oh, Giovanni speaks so highly of you. I said bring her around so I can meet her. And he said you're in a—"

"Mary," I said, cutting her off. "Tell Gianni that I'm about to be sent away. To the hospital in Illinois. I'm leaving in two hours on a train bound for Harrisburg, Pennsylvania. I won't be here tomorrow when he was planning to visit."

"Oh my! That's terrible news," Mary said. "Such a pity. He's at the club. I don't know when he'll be back. It's New Year's Eve, you know."

"I know." Tears gathered at the corners of my eyes. "Please tell him I'm sorry."

"I'll—" A crack of static erased the rest of her words.

Another voice came on the line. "You've been disconnected. Would you like me to try again?"

The nurse behind the desk stood with her hands out, ready to take back her precious telephone. "No," I said, replacing the receiver onto the hook as sadness overcame me.

A half hour later, I walked into the front lobby carrying all my belongings in two handle bags and wearing a scarf, a woolen hat, and my warmest jacket over one of my better dresses reserved for traveling. Inside, such warm layers felt stifling. I wanted to tear it all off and return to my room, to wait and hope I could see Gianni tomorrow after all, even if it meant another night with Elizabetta.

"I don't understand, why wasn't I given more notice?" I asked Nurse Edna, who waited by the front windows to accompany me to the train station. She had a scarf wrapped around her head so snuggly I only could make out her dark, beady eyes.

She kept her focus straight ahead on the driveway outside the window. "From what I understand, you've been informed of this move since well before Christmas. I don't understand how you seem so shocked."

I couldn't take the heat another second. Ripping at the buttons on my coat and tugging at the scarf around my neck, I couldn't hide my agitation. "I need to see my boyfriend one more time before I leave. We really are planning to get married, and if I'm so far away..." I trailed off, not wanting to say what I feared and knew to be true: the distance would be the end of us.

Nurse Edna glanced at me before returning to her surveillance at the window. "Tell me this," she said, crossing her arms. "If this young man, your boyfriend, is so intent on marrying you, why hasn't he had you released? There's been plenty of time. So where is this boyfriend of yours?"

I pulled off my hat and my scarf with one swift motion. Between the heat of the lobby's wood stove and my boiling anger, I'd have crawled out of my own skin if I could have.

Nurse Edna let out a small laugh. "I'd put that back on if I were you. Your taxi has just arrived, and it's *deathly* cold out there."

Not waiting for me to take her advice, she swung the front door open wider than necessary. An icy breeze rushed in and nearly took my breath away. Rather than let Nurse Edna gather any perverse joy over my discomfort, I grasped my two bags and walked into the bitter winter day uncovered.

Inside the taxi, I replaced my hat and scarf, refusing to make eye contact with Nurse Edna or her condescension. Vowing not to say another word to this bitter woman, I gazed out at the dull gray afternoon. Raindrops splattered against the window, obscuring my last view of the hospital. The pouring rain replaced the tears I wouldn't let fall.

If Gianni's landlady failed to get him my message, he would arrive here tomorrow, not knowing I was hundreds of miles away. With no choice other than to surrender my fate to a higher power, I recited the Hail Mary over and over in my head. Only a miracle could save our love.

CHAPTER THIRTY-THREE

TRENI IN DIREZIONE OVEST
(WESTBOUND TRAINS)

December 31, 1921
Malvern Train Station
Malvern, Pennsylvania

The Malvern Train Station was housed in a rectangular brick building with simple wooden arches that extended the roof over a narrow boarding platform. The first time I'd ever arrived at this station, the world had still clung to its summer greenery and the air had been warm and humid. I had been in a positive mindset that day, thinking this hospital in the country would be a welcome change from the crowded city. This afternoon, as I prepared to leave for yet another unknown hospital, I had little hope for anything good.

Nurse Edna walked toward me, holding my boarding ticket. I resisted the urge to snatch it out of her hands and rip it to shreds. Fortunately, she couldn't read my mind as she informed me in a bland monotone voice, "Due to the inclement weather, your train has been delayed. I suggest you find something to occupy yourself with while we wait."

The delay lifted my spirits. Perhaps the weather would get so bad, they'd cancel all services. I'd gladly sleep at this musty train station if it meant I wasn't sent away.

Taking a seat on a long bench inside the station's waiting area, I wondered how it had come to this. Nurse Edna's earlier words haunted my thoughts. Yes, I had known about the hospital's and, more to the point, Dr. Solomon's plans to relocate me. I had informed Gianni in enough time. Still, when Nurse Edna announced that I would be leaving today, it had come as a complete shock. I had begged to be allowed to stay one more day so that I could visit with Gianni and discuss what to do. Nurse Edna explained that Dr. Solomon had insisted. I wasn't left with any option other than to pack my bags. Travel plans and accommodations had been arranged, and whether I was prepared to leave or not, today was the day. A new patient would be arriving to take my bed at Malvern. Dr. Solomon would meet me in Harrisburg, where we would complete the trip to Illinois together.

Sighing deeply, I blinked away the tears blurring my vision. I used to look forward to Sundays. In Illinois, every day of the week would surely blend into one miserable existence.

After exhaling loudly several times to calm my emotions, I allowed myself to imagine Gianni's landlady somehow getting him my urgent message. I pictured him dashing out of the Italian Club and sprinting down the block. Perhaps it was raining in Ardmore as it was here. Large raindrops would splatter against Gianni's face as his lungs threatened to burst from the exertion of running as fast as he could. He would have one thought on his mind: seeing his Rosina one last time before she was taken away.

Perhaps he'd dodge a couple walking hand in hand, lose his balance, and stumble off the curb. The ground would rise rapidly to his chest as a horn blared. He would smell the pungent exhaust as the vehicle's front fender screeched to a stop inches from his head. Rather than apologize as he usually would, Gianni would return to his feet and will his fatigued legs to keep moving all the way to the Ardmore Station. But wouldn't the train station be packed to capacity with crowds of well-dressed people off to New Year's Eve celebrations? He would wonder if he was too late. Perhaps the ticket clerk would inform him about the same delays I was experiencing here at Malvern. Gianni would plead with the man, explaining that it was an emergency.

It all seemed so impossible. Instead of finishing the story running through my imagination and risking an unhappy ending, I redirected my attention to the small station house. I walked over to where there were pamphlets and trinkets for sale. Nurse Edna sat hunched forward, reading a book. The station operator, a short, balding man, made eye contact with me. I gave him a slight smile to be polite.

"Looks like a nasty storm out there," he said, trying to strike up a conversation.

"How bad do you think it will get? Bad enough to cancel service?" I asked, hope clear in my voice. Out of the corner of my eye, I noticed Nurse Edna's posture stiffen.

"That'll take a blizzard," the station operator said. "But you hear that on the window?"

I listened closely and noticed for the first time a tiny pinging.

"That's the rain freezing up into little ice pellets. Nasty stuff to walk in, but nothing our trains can't handle." Pride filled the station operator's voice.

Disheartened, I turned away. For the better part of an hour, I went over every inch of the Malvern Station. I studied every last item and detail to exhaustion. From time to time, Nurse Edna sent me sideways glances as if I were about to lose my mind. Truly, she wasn't far off. I couldn't stand not being able to tell Gianni goodbye, even if only by phone. Again tears threatened to spill down my cheeks. Once I had some privacy to grieve all that I'd lost, there'd be no stopping them.

"Well, looky here," the stationmaster said, distracting me from my battle with my emotions. "The three-fifteen is due to arrive just over an hour late."

"Finally," Nurse Edna said, adjusting her scarf and turning toward me. "Hopefully you'll make your connection in Harrisburg, or you're in for a long night."

Sighing, I walked to where my hat and coat were draped over a chair. All was lost. Gianni might be standing at the Ardmore Station, out of luck and out of time as well. If he was there, would he give up? Or would he find a way to board the next Westbound train?

I shook my head. Gianni most likely sat at the Italian Club, celebrating the New Year with no idea that I was leaving. The story I'd concocted in my head was just that: a fantasy to pass the torturous wait as I faced the inevitable.

After properly bundling up for the cold, I followed Nurse Edna through the door and out to the train platform. The whiteness of the ground was unexpected. The rain must have changed to snow during the last hour and a half while I'd paced inside the station. The thin coating crunched beneath my boots. Taking care not to lose my balance, I nearly walked into the back of Nurse Edna, who had stopped to allow several passengers to disembark the newly arrived train.

Stepping to the side, I took one last look at my surroundings. The snow had transformed the station house and the countryside into a completely new world. The sun broke through the clouds at the horizon, illuminating the sky in a rosy hue. A sensation of peace, despite the long, lonely journey ahead, descended upon me like the gently falling flurries. For some reason, I believed everything was going to be okay. Though my mind objected, I kept my eyes on the sun as it persisted despite the clouds and the approach of night.

The sound of rapid footsteps pulled my attention away. A man rushed past me. He seemed frantic, almost losing his balance on the slick surface as he switched his attention from left to right.

"Let's go," Nurse Edna told me in a gruff, impatient voice.

I defied her instruction and remained in place. I couldn't take my eyes off the man who had paused his frantic gestures to watch the sunset. When the man turned in the opposite direction, I thought I was dreaming. I had given up all hope. And yet, standing before me was the most handsome face I'd ever seen.

CHAPTER THIRTY-FOUR

UNA CHIAVE
(A KEY)

December 31, 1921
Malvern Train Station
Malvern, Pennsylvania

"Gianni?" I whispered, my voice cracking with emotion. The man who had seemed to be a stranger mere seconds before now stared at me with an awestruck expression.

"Rosie?"

He slipped and slid toward me, and I reached my arms out to help steady him.

"I thought I'd missed you," he said, out of breath.

"I thought you didn't get my message in time." Even with his face inches from mine, I still couldn't believe he was here.

"I did. I got it." Gianni's grip tightened on my arms. "My landlady, Mary. She found me and told me. I'm here."

From behind me, Nurse Edna cleared her throat. "It's time to board. Tell your boyfriend goodbye."

I looked toward her and the train with its open doors. A family with two young children climbed the steps into the passenger car. Turning back to Gianni, I spoke quickly, the urgency making me rush my words. "They're sending me away. Right now. This is my train."

"You can't go." Gianni's eyes widened as he said it.

I dropped my gaze as I told him through emerging tears, "I have no choice."

Nurse Edna strode toward us and said in a voice dripping with irritation, "The train is boarding. It's time to go."

"No," Gianni said in a firm voice, releasing my arms and addressing the nurse. "She's not going anywhere."

"Oh, really?" She stepped between us and in front of Gianni. Her demeanor reminded me of one of the strict nuns I'd had as a schoolteacher in Torchiara. The nun had once twisted one of my misbehaving classmate's ears to the point it brought him to his knees. I worried Nurse Edna might do the same to Gianni.

She pointed her crooked finger at him. "You're too late, and there's nothing you can do." Then she latched onto my elbow and pulled me toward the open door of the train.

"Please," Gianni said, blocking her progress. "I spoke with Rosie's doctor. I thought it was all settled."

Nurse Edna swatted at the air toward Gianni as if she were shooing away a pesky bug. "You're wasting our time. Unless you have a reason for being here, you need to get out of our way, or I'll call the authorities."

"I do." Gianni reached into his pocket and produced a key. I gasped as he explained, "I have a house for Rosina to live. We're going to get married. Please, have some compassion."

From the open door of the train, the conductor made his last call for boarding. Nurse Edna stared at Gianni and then at the key in his hand before finally resting her gaze on me. For a glimmer of a moment, I detected a touch of warmth in her eyes. But then her expression clouded over and returned to its usual harshness. Turning her attention toward Gianni, she said in her most aggressive voice, "This better not be a lie, or I'll have you held liable. You understand?"

Gianni nodded.

Nurse Edna waved off the conductor. "I'll secure us all a cab back to the hospital," she said, not bothering to hide her disdain. She shuffled away along the boarding platform.

Turning to Gianni, I examined the key he'd produced as if by magic. "Is this for real?" I asked, also out of breath as my heart raced. "You have a house for us?"

Gianni laughed, shaking the key, causing it to jingle against the ring. "It's small, but it'll do."

I didn't fight the tears as I shook my head in disbelief.

"Rosie, listen to me," Gianni said in a tender voice, pulling me close. "I'm sorry I took so long. But I'm here now. And if you'll have me, I want to marry you. It would make me so happy to love you for the rest of my life. I told your doctor that. I was coming tomorrow to have you released. I wanted to surprise you. I couldn't stand that I might lose you."

The brakes of the train released with a whoosh. It was almost too much to comprehend. Gianni stood in front of me, his eyes searching mine for an answer. He reminded me of the first time we met at his aunt's party. How alone I had felt that night, knowing only Antoinetta. Until I'd met him.

The train engine groaned to life, followed by the squeal of the wheels pushing forward on the track. I thought about that day at the amusement park, how the fear I'd felt on the roller coaster had been eased moments later by our first kiss on the boat ride. As the gears clanked, pushing the train into motion, I remembered all the times Gianni had been there at my hospital bedside when so many others failed to visit. And now, when all hope had seemed lost, he was here with a key that would open the door to all my dreams coming true.

"Rosie," Gianni said. "I always write this to you, but when I'm with you, I can't seem to find the courage to say it."

I looked into his kind eyes. "What is it?"

"I love you."

"Oh Gianni, I love you, too," I whispered, pulling him in for a kiss.

A gust of air swirled around us as the train picked up speed, leaving the station. Gianni wrapped his arms around me and deepened the kiss. Nothing in the world seemed to matter, only the warmth of his lips on mine and the exhilaration of not being forced onto the departing train.

Finally, as if it were happening in a beautiful dream, we parted just enough for Gianni to say the words I most wanted to hear. Considering all that I had gone through, these three words meant even more to me than "I love you." They were all I had wanted to hear since this nightmare had begun.

Smiling, Gianni told me, "Let's go home."

CHAPTER THIRTY-FIVE

ROSE PER ROSINA
(ROSES FOR ROSINA)

January 1, 1922
Philadelphia, Pennsylvania

We were married shortly after under sunny blue skies, with only wisps of clouds floating on a cold breeze.

I had in my possession "something old," the cross pendant from my father in Italy and "something new," my beautiful dress and veil. While I didn't have "something borrowed," I did have "something blue," a piece of blue fabric from the dress Aunt Teresa had stitched for my doll when I was a girl.

After the ceremony, as we waited to have our picture taken, we watched and admired another newly married couple posing for their photograph.

"They both look so happy," I whispered to Gianni.

"Just like us," he whispered in return, giving me a peck on the lips.

Happy wasn't a strong enough word for the way I felt. I still couldn't believe all that had changed in a day's time. Now we had no restrictions on our time together, free to come and go as we pleased. And best of all, we could finally be fully and completely alone to express our love.

"Next," the photographer called to us as he worked the mechanisms on the camera to load the film.

We exchanged congratulations with the other couple as they walked off. Since I was taller than Gianni, especially in my heeled shoes, I took a seat on a chair the photographer had positioned in front of the camera. Gianni took his place behind me.

The photographer bent behind the camera tripod and looked through the lens. Lifting his head over the camera, he asked, "No flowers?"

I showed him my empty hands. "It doesn't matter."

"Whatever," he said, bending down toward the camera again.

Gianni stepped out from behind the chair. "Hang on a second. I'll be right back."

I sat alone for an awkward minute until he returned, holding an enormous bouquet. "Roses for Rosina," he said, handing them to me.

I gave him a surprised, confused look.

"Your 'something borrowed,'" he explained, "from the bride we were watching earlier."

"Oh, how nice of her." I spotted the other bride by the doorway. "Thank you!" I called to her. I positioned the gorgeous snow-white roses across my lap and smiled at the camera.

At the pop of the flash, my mind went back to June, when Gianni had sent me flowers after I had been newly admitted to the hospital. They were the first flowers a man had ever given me. I'd told him on that day, "May the next flowers you give me be on our wedding day." Little did I know then that my request would be granted.

Later that evening, Gianni handed me the same key he'd brought with him to the train station.

As we stood at the front door of a small yet charming home, I placed the key into the lock, and with a snap, the door opened. Gianni scooped me off my feet. I shrieked with delight as he carried me inside and on to the rest of our life together.

Epilogue

Da Allora in Poi
(Ever After)

We rented that small house in Ardmore for a few years before saving up enough to buy the home of our dreams a few blocks up the street. I finally had a place I could truly call my home. Situated on a corner property, the house came with a yard large enough to plant a plentiful garden. I grew tomatoes, corn, string beans, figs, peaches, apples, and cabbage. When I had the ingredients, I would make homemade pasta.

When the Great Depression hit, that garden helped feed our large family. With such demand on the kitchen in the main part of the house, I set up a smaller kitchen in the basement. There I jarred fruits and vegetables and set up shelves to store them. Soups made with beans and anything in season or preserved from the garden sustained our six growing children. Our seventh child, a daughter, was born as the Depression came to an end.

Eventually, times improved, and we decided to use the extra space in our cellar to make wine, which we sold throughout our Italian neighborhood in Ardmore. Eight barrels lined the far wall opposite the cellar steps, five of which held reds, the other three whites. It was so good that some mornings I filled my coffee mug with a bit of our wine. Often, I waved and wished good morning to our neighbor with the mug of wine in my hand, delighting that she had no idea of my indulgence!

While I'd been busy taking care of our home and tending to our babies, Gianni spent the early years of our marriage becoming a successful shoemaker, eventually opening his own business. And by the spring of 1929, he'd saved enough to make one of his longtime dreams come true when he purchased a Paige-Detroit Motor Car. For its time, the car had all the modern features, including a cigarette lighter. Years later, our sons took such a fascination in the lighter that they ended up breaking it.

Gianni eventually became president of the Italian American Club he had often frequented as a young man. He held leadership positions in several similar clubs in the area as well. His stature in the community earned him the nickname, "The King." Our son John became "The Little King."

By World War II, our oldest son, Pat, was of age to enlist. I feared for him. Gianni, recalling his own experiences, tried his best to keep Pat out of the war. He secured Pat a job, making it possible for him not to be drafted. However, Pat, feeling guilty about being unable to do his part for his country, visited the draft office where his friend worked and enlisted in the Navy. I was heartsick. When Gianni learned what his son had done, he was the most upset I had ever seen him. Pat went on to be a part of the D-Day Omaha Beach Invasion on June 6, 1944. Thank the Lord, he survived.

A year later, our second son, John, enlisted in the Marines once he graduated high school. He was followed soon after by our third son, Richard, or Richey as everyone called him. John went on to be part of the brigade that raised the American flag at Iwo Jima. Although he was there to witness and be a part of the iconic moment, he wasn't one of the six men in the famous photograph.

After his time in the service, John went on to work in the Philadelphia Shipyard. He wasn't there long when a man fell on him from where he'd been working up above. John survived this incident, but he was shaken that the man who'd fallen had succumbed to his injuries. He left the shipyard and took a position working for a Gulf Oil station on City Line Avenue. He took great pride in doing his very best in servicing each and every car that entered his station. One such car happened to belong to the president of Gulf Oil. He was so impressed with John's initiative, he offered John a job at the home office for Gulf Oil, managing the creation of service stations throughout the country. John went on to have a successful career. So much so that he purchased rental properties and retired early to manage them. In his retirement, John became a master orator, teaching Carnegie classes on "How to Win Friends and Influence People."

As for our four daughters, the oldest was named after me, Rose, as was the Italian tradition. The next three girls I named by searching the headlines for mentions of a female celebrity in the edition of the *Philadelphia Inquirer* printed on the dates of their births. Whichever glamorous actress happened to be featured became the name of our newest baby girl, leaving us with Lillian after Lillian Gish, Norma after Norma Shearer, and Diana after Diana Durbin. Four beautiful names for my four beautiful daughters.

All seven of our children led successful lives and had families of their own, producing twenty-three grandchildren. My dreams all came true. I loved cooking our weekly Sunday dinners when everyone would gather around the table. After we had cleaned up the dishes, some of my grandchildren would join me on my front porch, where I'd share with them stories about my pet hen Piccolino and how I almost got caught playing with my only doll by my evil stepmother. By then, *Cinderella* was playing in the theaters, and so I called myself an "Italian Cinderella."

Over the years, I did manage to return to Italy. It was wonderful to return to the place of my childhood and to see many of my family members, most especially Filomena. She marveled so much at my American clothing that I offered to trade with her. Upon my arrival home in Philadelphia, no one recognized me, as I looked like an Italian villager!

With Gianni's passing when he was only in his sixties, most likely from complications resulting from the mustard gas he'd been exposed to in World War I, our beautiful time together came to an end.

I lived on to the age of eighty. It was my hope that our story would live on and on for future generations. So, I made sure to store some of the most important pieces from my life in a particular box. I explained to my children that no matter what happened to the house, which they would surely sell, they must never get rid of this box. And so, I placed in it the doll from Aunt Teresa, the cross from my father, a variety of photographs of Gianni and me from before we were married, and a photo album filled with the letters Gianni and I had written to each other while I had been hospitalized. Those letters had been the bond that held us together. In those words and in all that had happened between the lines was the most important story of my life: the story of our love.

About the Author

Audry Fryer is an author and professional freelance writer from Pennsylvania. Formerly a teacher, Audry wrote her first novel while her toddler son and twin babies napped. As her children have grown into teenagers, she has continued to expand her writing career. Audry lives with her family and a pug named Pickles in a quiet corner of Southeastern PA. To learn more about Audry, please visit her website at www.audryfryer.com

ACKNOWLEDGEMENTS

On behalf of the author, Audry Fryer, and the story's creators, Linda Kotowicz, Susan Schobert, and Laurie Shanaman, we would like to acknowledge and offer our deep-felt gratitude to everyone who has provided support and played an essential role in creating this novel.

First, we would like to give an enormous, heartfelt thank you to our families and friends. From simply listening to our highs and lows in bringing this book to publication to being an early reader, your love and support throughout this entire process meant the world to us!

A special thank you to Biagio Dorso for the loving care and extraordinary attention to detail in the translation of the letters. Your ability to decipher the unique Italian dialects of Rosina and Gianni gave us this beautiful gift - their story.

Thank you to Anya Kagan of Touchstone Editing for providing a keen eye for editorial detail and spot-on story suggestions that elevated this novel to its best version. We couldn't have transformed a collection of letters into a cohesive story without your help and expertise.

Thank you to accomplished author and friend Lark Brennan, who inspired us to continue with our dream of publishing. Your assistance and recommendations were priceless.

Thank you to our dear friend Linda Presutti. Very early in the process, when Laurie told her about the newly discovered letters and the story they told, Linda immediately suggested to name the book "Until Next Sunday" and the title really connected with us, and so it stuck!.

Thank you to Lindsey Teske, Of Ink and Pearls Publishing, for all your help in bringing this novel into the world. Thank you for your patience and persistence in formatting Until Next Sunday to look phenomenal on both the printed and virtual pages. And we appreciate your efforts in helping us market the book so that readers far and wide can enjoy this powerful love story.

Finally, and most of all, Linda, Susan, and Laurie, would like to send their endless love and gratitude to their grandparents, Rosina and Gianni, for preserving these letters so perfectly so that they could be found so many years later. Thank you for giving us this beautiful example of how love can overcome hardships and obstacles and not only survive but thrive for many generations to come. We cherished our Sunday gatherings, the Sunday feast you'd prepare, the stories Grandmom would tell us. But until now, we never knew how truly special Sunday really was to you!

BOOK CLUB DISCUSSION QUESTIONS

1. In your opinion, what is the significance of the title, Until Next Sunday? Do you like this as a title choice? Do you feel this title supports one of the themes in the book?

2. Do you agree with Rosina's decision to leave Italy for America? Over the course of the story, do you think Rosina regrets or remains steadfast in her decision to start a new life in America?

3. How would you describe Rosina? How does her character grow and develop throughout the events of the story?

4. Why do you think Rosina encounters a similar situation in America with her brother's wife as with her step-mother in Italy? Do you feel Rosina is a victim or a contributor to each of the strained relationships?

5. What's your first impression of Gianni? Why do you feel Rosina is attracted to him? Also, as the story progresses, does your impression of Gianni change and in what way?

6. Until Next Sunday falls under the genre of historical romance. How well do you feel the story stays true to other books you've read in this genre? Does it remain true to the tropes of historical fiction?

7. Do you like the inclusion of the letters in the story? Why or why not? Do you have a favorite line from one of the letters? How does this book compare to other books that include love or other types of letters?

8. Did you believe Rosina when she wrote "It's over," in a letter to Gianni? Do you think Rosina was justified in her anger or being overly dramatic?

9. Do you agree with the circumstances leading up to Rosina being moved to the sanatorium in Malvern? Do you feel Rosina could have found a way to avoid going there or was it her best option at the time?

10. After experiencing a pandemic and quarantine in your lifetime, how does that help or hinder your perspective on Rosina's condition of possibly contracting a contagious disease and, as a result, her limitations on receiving visitors when she was hospitalized?

11. Do you feel Rosina's brother's and sister-in-law's refusal to allow her to return home after she was suspected of contracting tuberculosis was a legitimate concern or a convenient excuse?

12. What are your thoughts of the facility in Malvern? Which character that Rosina meets there do you like the best and which character(s) best fit the description of villain?

13. What are your thoughts on Rosina's interactions with Dr. Solomon? What are your impressions of him and how does his character impact the story?

14. The story is set in 1921. Is this a time period that you would like to visit or live in? Why or why not? Also, how well is the time period portrayed?

15. What are some of the overall themes of the story? Are these themes well-developed or more nuanced?

16. Immigration is a major theme in the story and remains newsworthy today. Did reading about Rosina's and Gianni's immigration stories alter your perspective in any way about our modern day immigration policies or issues?

17. Do you like or dislike how the love story evolves throughout the book? Do you like the end result of Rosina and Gianni's love story? Is it what you were expecting or were you surprised?

18. Why do you think it takes Gianni so long into the story to act on Rosina's behalf? Do you feel Rosina is too reliant on Gianni to improve her lack of a living situation? Considering women's role in society in 1921, do you think Rosina could have taken more responsibility for her personal welfare?

19. How would Rosina's life have changed if she did take the train to Chicago at the end of the story? What would have happened to Rosina's and Gianni's relationship?

20. If (and possibly when) Until Next Sunday becomes a movie or series, who would you cast for the roles of Rosina and Gianni? Who would you cast for other characters in the book?

21. What rating would you give Until Next Sunday out of five stars? What did you like the best about how the story unfolded? What would you change? Would you recommend this book? To whom?

Made in the USA
Coppell, TX
19 April 2022

76792621R00163